I0656790

Louise Carnahan

Little Doctor Victoria

A Southern Story for Boys and Girls

Louise Carnahan

Little Doctor Victoria
A Southern Story for Boys and Girls

ISBN/EAN: 9783337002381

Printed in Europe, USA, Canada, Australia, Japan

Cover: Foto ©Andreas Hilbeck / pixelio.de

More available books at **www.hansebooks.com**

LITTLE

DOCTOR

VICTORIA

A SOUTHERN STORY FOR BOYS AND GIRLS.

BY

LOUISE CARNAHAN

Author of "Polly's Lion"

Entered according to an Act of Congress in the year 1899,
by Carnahan Publishing Company, in the office of the
Librarian of Congress

Mammy Hilaria
and
Little Doctor Victoria

PREFACE.

To Parents, Guardians and Teachers:

I hope that this little book may give pleasure and some instruction to many young people. I do not expect the story to please those whose taste has been vitiated by sensational novels.

I have tried to write a pleasing and wholesome story for innocent boys and girls. I do not think that a disclosure of the nether side of this world is good for young people. I would rather fortify the young soul against evil by filling it with a love for the true and the good and the beautiful. The motto of my life has been "Onward and upward."

If I have seemed to over-emphasize the moral power of the human will, it has not been because I am unmindful of the value of Divine grace; but because I believe that moral heredity as a factor in the production of character has been exaggerated of late. I am unsophisticated enough to confess that I am an optimist. It seems to me that the extreme statements of the doctrine of moral heredity so prevalent to-day involve this logical chain-- Pessimism, Atheism, Despair, Suicide; against which teaching my heart and mind and soul revolt.

LOUISE CARNAHAN.

CHAPTER I.

Gray Cliff, the old Virginia home of the Kenyons, stood on the high bluff overlooking the James River and a large extent of the surrounding country. The house was a handsome building of stone, with rounded towers and many gables. Numerous doors and windows gave the mansion a friendly, hospitable aspect that was fully justified by the character of the generous inmates. The extensive grounds were laid out in formal order, and planted with trees, shrubbery, and flowers of every bright and glowing color. Beyond the enclosure of a stone wall which surrounded the house, orchards, meadows, and grainfields extended far back to a forest of giant trees; with a back-ground of high rugged rocks piled up against the sky. In front of the house a rose garden sloped toward the entrance, where heavy iron gates swung open.

The family of Gray Cliff consisted of the father, Colonel Richard Kenyon, and his two sons, Victor and Howard. Victor, the elder, was a physician of promising ability, and full of enthusiastic love for his profession. He was of fine physique, tall, strong and handsome, and as fair as a Saxon of old. Howard, the younger, had selected the ministry as his profession. He was a contrast to his brother; slight of figure, dark of complexion and possessing the charming vivacious manner of his South Carolina mother. He had quiet, domestic tastes, and was well satisfied with his simple country parish, and the faithful love of his good people.

Colonel Kenyon had at one time filled the office of Senator from his state, and was known by his neighbors as "The Senator." His wife had been dead many years, and his only daughter, Jane, was married, and now living in New York City.

The house was virtually presided over by "Aunt" Hilaria, the old black "Mammy" of the family. She had really fine executive ability, and exercised a despotic sway over the other servants. As the servants of an old Virginia family always considered themselves a part, and a very important part, of the household, we will do them the honor of mentioning the principal ones by name.

"Aunt" Hilaria's family held the most responsible positions in the household. Ben, her eldest son, was the coachman, Judy, his wife, the cook, and Gipterene, her youngest child, the little maid of all work. There were several grand-children, the most conspicuous of whom was Paris, Ben's eldest son, and the favorite grand-child of Aunt Hilaria, or "Granny," as he called her.

Like many old southern Mammies, Aunt Hilaria worshiped her master's children, but "Marse Vic," the eldest born, was her supreme idol, and the devotion was shared by Paris, who followed his master like a faithful dog.

The plantation adjoining Gray Cliff, was owned by Judge Thomas Carter, who lived in quiet, bachelor seclusion, with a house full of well-fed, well-clothed negroes, to whom "Marse Tom" was a righteous Judge and good master, though feared by every young darky on all the surrounding plantations, as he was the Justice of the Peace. Paris was the only one who ever managed to slip through his judicial fingers.

A thick hedge divided the plantations, and this hedge

was the cause of many disputes, particularly on the Judges part, about the possession of certain eggs found in it.

One morning in September, Paris, who was an early bird, was seen poking his woolly head in and out of the hedge, looking for turkey eggs. With a low exclamation of triumph, "Hi! hi!" he darted under the thick bushes to the opposite side of the barrier. He had discovered a nest of speckled treasures. Having placed them carefully in his brimless hat, he was crawling back witht his doubtful possessions, when he was startled by the threatening voice of Judge Carter, who was inclined to be an early bird himself.

"You black rascal! put back those eggs; don't you know they belong to me?"

"Why, Marse Tom, I's foun, dese aigs on our side ob de haige, dey 'longs to us sho."

Paris was quick to detect the suppressed amusement in the Judge's usually grave face, and taking advantage of this leniency, he hurried away with his treasure. His young master, Victor, who happened to be looking from his bed-room window, saw Paris stealing through the shrubbery with something under his arm, and called, "Paris, come to me!"

"Yes, sah, I's comin'."

But before obeying, he dropped on his knees and deposited the eggs under a convenient bush, which was all quite apparent to his master's eyes.

When he presented himself in the room, he noticed that his master wore a new suit of gray cloth, and with the adroitness peculiar to his race, he tried to evade the coming interview.

"Marse Vic, yo' sho' hab got a fine suit ob close," and

taking the skirt of the coat in his small black hands, he affected to examine it with great interest.

"Paris," said his master, "where are those eggs you had in your hat?"

Paris looked up with bland innocence, scratched his woolly head, and said, "d....dey under de rose bush. Yo' want to see dem aigs, Marse Vic?"

The master walked leisurely down to the front gallery, and the young rogue soon appeared holding the hat so that his ragged sleeve would partially conceal the eggs. He watched his master's face with amusing anxiety.

"Paris, you got those eggs on the other side of the hedge, they belong to Judge Carter. Go at once and carry them back to the nest; then go to Judge Carter and tell him I sent you to return his property, and to ask pardon for stealing the eggs; do you understand, stealing them?"

Paris would have insisted that the eggs belonged to the family if any one else had accused him, but he always recognized Marse Vic's penetration, and never attempted to deny the charge; and with a "Yes, sah!" he took the eggs back to the nest, where he found the Judge still strolling along.

"Marse Vic say yo' may hab des ole aigs, dey not fraish no how."

He glanced at the Judge, who kept a steady eye on the culprit, then suddenly casting his eyes down, Paris began to bore his naked toes into the soft turf,—conscience was at work! He raised his head, with a shy look, and said, "Marse Tom, I's done tole yo' a lie; dis what Marse Vic say, 'Go back and ax de Judge to 'scuse yo' fo' stealin' de aigs.'"

The Judge smilingly pardoned the boy, and told him

he might this time carry the eggs as a present to his "Granny," and the next time he caught him stealing, he would—and he significantly shook his cane at the retreating boy.

Paris looked back, and called out, "Marse Tom, am we quits?"

The pleasant smile and nod from the Judge were assurance enough that he was fully pardoned, and he went on his way as happy as a lark.

Dr. Kenyon stood in the gallery of his old home in deep meditation; he held in his hand a basket and a pair of garden shears, but seemed to forget that he intended to use them. He looked about him with lingering interest, as if to take in every detail of his surroundings. At last, he descended the broad steps and entered the garden; cutting the fresh half-blown roses, he clipped the thorns from the stems and filled the basket, moving almost unconsciously among his treasures.

Paris, who was never very far from his young master, now made his appearance, and approached the gray figure with a very demure expression on his roguish shining face.

"Marse Vic, is yo' gwine to le'me go wid yo' to ole Kentuck?"

The master gave him the basket in silence, and Paris followed him with earnest, pleading eyes; then, to force his attention, he said, "Yo' sho is sick dis mornin', Marse Vic, kase yo' is lookin' way off, and not mindin' dem roses at all."

Dr. Kenyon could not resist a smile at his little servant's appeal.

"Paris, don't you think it is enough to make me sad to leave my home and all you, my people, and go away amongst strangers?"

"But yo' kin carry me wid yo', an' I's kin be comp'ny fo' yo'. Please lemme go, Marse Vic."

Paris had suggested a new idea to his master, but without seeming to notice the boy's anxiety, he took a delicate note from his breast pocket, and laying it on the fresh roses in the basket, said, "Paris, carry this to Col. Dorcey's, and leave it for Miss Mildred."

Paris took the basket, and swinging himself out of the gate, he raised the basket to the crown of his head; at the same time casting a look over his shoulder to catch some encouragement in his master's face.

The negro is very keen to detect a change in the countenances of those they serve.

Dr. Kenyon was about to leave the old family homestead, and settle in Kentucky. After a sojourn of several months in that state, visiting an old college friend, he had decided to remove there. This friend, Mr. Tyler, possessed extensive lands along the border of the beautiful Ohio River. Some fine lands adjoining were for sale, and the young Doctor was persuaded to cast his lot with his friend, who was also a Virginian.

Dr. Kenyon immediately began improvements, with a view to building on a charming site overlooking the River. His estate reached to the suburbs of one of Kentucky's largest cities, affording him the opportunity of practicing his profession, as well as of enjoying country life.

He returned home to settle up his affairs. His mother had left him considerable property, including in the inheritance, Mammy and her family. He had not thought of taking any of the servants with him until the house was ready for occupancy, having made an arrangement to board with his friend until then; but Paris had suggested a new idea.

There was a little house of five rooms on the plantation, formerly occupied by the overseer. This could be put in order and made comfortable, and Mammy could keep house for him.

Victor loved home and domestic life, and since his return from abroad, some time before, he had taken much of the responsibility of his father's plantation upon himself. Col. Kenyon being elected Senator about that time, spent several years in Washington. Unlike his sons, politics had great fascination for the old Colonel.

The charm of his old home seemed to have new attractions for the young Doctor this lovely morning. He lingered in the garden until Paris returned with the message—a tiny note from the sweet young girl who had promised to be his bride.

Months must elapse before he could have his home ready, and return to claim her promise to go with him to his new abode. His thoughts were on those things, and he had quite forgotten his little servant, who still stood respectfully waiting for a chance to say something that was on his mind.

Suddenly his master looked down, "What is it, Paris?"

"Why, Marse Vic, Miss Millie say yo' mus' sholy carry Granny an' me wif yo' w'en yo' go, kase yo' will need us to take keer ob yo'."

"I will think about it, Paris, you may go now."

The boy bounded away highly pleased with his hope. For his master to "think about it" was almost as good as a request granted.

Dr. Kenyon now visited all the cabins to say good-bye to the old servants who were not able to come to the "great house." Many of them were confined to their beds with the usual infirmities of the aged negro—rheumatism, and "misery in the back." The old withered hands, were kindly pressed by the strong, white ones of the young master. Many a blessing was given by these simple, faithful people. Each one received an encouraging word, and a gold coin to "remember him by."

He next visited the stables and barn-yard to take a farewell look at his dumb pets. Of the splendid horses in the stables, he had selected at his father's request two fine thorough-bred trotters to carry to his new home. The old Colonel would not admit that even Kentucky, boasting the finest horses in the country, could produce any equal to the stables at Gray Cliff. Ben had just harnessed this handsome pair named Guy and Dan to the new carriage, to show off its beauty. This pair of horses were Paris' admiration. He looked at them now in silence, then turned to his master, "Marse Vic, dem' chesnut hoss's is sho sma't nuf to talk, ef dey had de right sort o' mouf."

Marse Vic smiled as he patted Dan's glossy back.

A little picaninny, in a red slip, now made his appearance in the barn-yard. A large turkey gobbler, with proud wings scraping the ground, espied this bit of color in his domains, and attempted a closer inspection of little Hayden's presence; but Hayden beat a hasty retreat through the brier hedge that skirted one side of the yard. His lusty screams soon betrayed something worse than fright. Dr. Kenyon sent Paris to his aid, who soon came carrying him on his back. A thorn had pierced the little black foot. As Paris laid him on the ground before his master, Hayden held up the wounded foot with tearful submission for the doctor's knife. The master knelt at the boy's side and tenderly removed a great thorn from the small heel. This done, Hayden rolled over on his back.

"O, Marse Vic., will 'ou sen' fo' de wheel-bar' fo' Paris to tote me home?"

Of course, Paris was dispatched for this conveyance, and Hayden was borne to the cabin, with the happy consciousness of being an object of commiseration to all who saw him.

Later in the afternoon, Paris, with the eagerness of bearing news, rushed into his master's study.

"Marse Vic, Miss Mary is sho comin' up de road in her ka'age, an' Unc' Jo' he drivin' de wagon, all pile up wid trunks, and all Miss Mary's servants ridin' on de top. Dey sho movin'; am dey gwine to lib wid us?"

Miss Mary had, indeed, come to take up her abode at Gray Cliff, and with her had come numerous house-servants; for the sweet old lady would sooner have left her precious trunks, packed with fine linen, rich laces, and silver ware, than one of these people, her old familar attendants. Each one had a place in her household that could not be filled by even her brother's servants.

This arrangement had long been desired by her brother and nephews, but she would never, until now, consent to leave her own home, the dear scenes of her happy childhood. No one but her favorite nephew, Victor, could have persuaded her to make this change. He pleaded the loneliness of his father and brother when he should leave them.

Her own residence was only a mile distant from Gray Cliff, but Victor, even as a child, had always been troubled about Aunt Mary's living alone. He always paid her a visit in the evening "to see that she was safe."

As he grew older, this sense of protection over her increased; and now his desire was fully gratified, he had all his dear ones together—though Miss Mary Kenyon had consented with some reservations. They wished her to lease the old home, but this she would not do. No, she would never allow strangers to tread the floors sacred to her parents' steps.

Aunt Mary was a thoroughly aristocratic Virginia lady, with all the provincial pride and exclusiveness of her class.   She was coming now to give her brother's home that grace and warmth that only a refined and gentle woman can bestow.

Colonel Kenyon, Victor, and Howard all went out to give her a cordial welcome to Gray Cliff.

At supper that evening the affectionate old lady and the three gentlemen sat long, discussing plans for Victor's journey and future welfare.

When the brother and sister had retired to their rooms, Victor went slowly to his study.

Paris,.who had been waiting in the hall to see his master leave the dining room, hastened after him with a big split basket of chips on his head. He had kindled a little fire on the hearth in the room, for the nights were chilly, and the basket of chips was only an excuse for following his master in order to discover what chance he had of accompanying him to Kentucky.

He knelt before the fire piling on the chips, and all the time the great prominent eyes followed the gray figure. At last he broke out, with a sob in his voice,"Marse Vic, po' ole Granny is so mis'ble, she is a sittin' in de corner by de chimbly a cryin' kase yo' gwine to lebe her ahind yo'. Dad say Granny will sho kick de bucket dis time."

Getting no response, he set up a piteous wail. At this his master was aroused from his own reflections, and remembered Paris' appeal for himself and Granny.   He looked at his watch in a hurried way, then at the boy on the hearth.

"Tell Mammy to come to me at once."

Paris ran with swift feet to Mammy's cabin.

"Granny! Granny! Marse Vic say come long quick," and to hasten her, he caught her hand and pulled her to her feet.

Poor Mammy had been in the depths of despair.

"What Marse Vic want me fo'?"

"Jis yo' come quick, kase he's gwine away soon to see Miss Millie, an' yo'll miss him sho."

Old Mammy wiped her eyes on her apron, and hurried off to her master's study, which she entered with a low courtesy.

"Marse Vic, dis boy say yo' want me—I's done pack all yo' fings ready fo de trunks, all in tip-top style."

And at the thought of these preparations, the old woman's tears flowed afresh.

Her master turned with a pleasing smile, "Mammy, can you get ready for a journey by to-morrow evening? I have decided to take you with me to Kentucky. I intended to speak of it sooner, Mammy, but I have had so many things to attend to to-day."

Mammy propped her hands on her ample hips, and laughed joyously through the tears.

"Laws, honey, I's done pack all de close I's got, an' was jus waitin' fo' yo' to ax me. I's spected yo' would ax me all de time till dis ebenin' an' I done giv it clar up."

"You know, Mammy, that I have intended to have you and your family with me, but thought it was better to wait awhile; however, there is a little house on the plantation that I can occupy while they build my new home, and you may keep house for me—but I thought you loved the old place, Mammy; why are you in such a hurry to leave it?"

Mammy turned a perplexed face to her master,—something had troubled the old woman that no one knew anything about. It came out now.

"Kase, Marse Vic, I's don't want dat 'ere Hannah to boss me, an' she is gwine to do it sho, w'en yo' lebes."

Hannah was an old servant of the Kenyon's; and many years before, when Mammy's young mistress came as a bride to Gray Cliff, she brought Hilaria as her maid. As time passed she became Mammy to her mistress' children, and gradually gained authority over the other servants, which Hannah secretly resented because she was not a "Kenyon servant." After Mrs. Kenyon's death, Mammy continued her power in the household through her young master, Dr. Kenyon. But now "Marse Vic" was about to go away, and Miss Mary Kenyon was at the head of the house; consequently, the Kenyon servants would come into power again. Mammy, who was a shrewd woman, saw her scepter departing, and wisely wanted to withdraw with honor.

Dr. Kenyon looked at Mammy a moment, as if trying to comprehend the state of things, then threw back his head and broke into such a merry laugh as startled his father and Aunt Mary in their quiet rooms above. In all his intercourse with his servants, he had never suspected this dormant jealousy.

Poor Mammy was much confused by her master's amusement, but he hastened to relieve her embarrassment by telling her that he really needed her assistance in planning the kitchen, pantries, etc., in his new house, and would not think of leaving her behind.

Mammy's face was now radiant with delight at the prospect of managing a new kitchen, built after her own plans.

Paris, who was looking on, began to think that it was

time that his name was mentioned, and to fear that in pleading Granny's cause he had defeated his own. His master noticed the lugubrious expression, and turning to him said: "Go, Paris, and help Mammy get your things ready."

The delight that spread over the shining, black face was comical, and Mammy was equally glad. As she said, it was "good-luck fo' a chile to go wid one on a journey."

She had not forgotten Paris in her secret preparations, but had smuggled his best "Sunday close" into her old trunk in case of emergency; so she assured her master that she could get Paris ready, saying,

"His Sunday close am all clean, an' I kin soon wash out his ebery day close, kase dey will do him to trabble in. Nobody is gwine to notice dat nigger nohow."

This was perfectly satisfactory to Paris, who expressed his delight in numerous absurd tricks,—thrusting his head into the split basket, and crawling round behind his Granny to "scar' her."

Mammy thanked her master, and Paris hurried her away, as he had hurried her in, to tell the joyful news to the other servants, giving vent to his happiness by turning handsprings from the house to the cabin.

Before bed-time Paris' "ebery day close" were flapping on the clothes-line, and Mammy spent half the night ironing and packing the wardrobe.

Paris, in the meantime, had made his way to Col. Dorcey's to tell his triumph to Miss Millie. He found 'Mandy, Miss Millie's maid, in the kitchen, who wanted to know what he had to say to her young mistress.

"What yo' want wid Miss Millie? She nebber ax fo' yo'."

Paris was equal to the saucy maid.

"Min' yo' bisness, yo' go ax Miss Millie if I's kin see her jes' a minute."

Mandy finally went to get the desired permission, and returning, said to Paris,

"Yo'll fin' Miss Millie in de dinin'-room."

Paris tip-toed through the great hall to the dining-room door and stood waiting till a sweet voice said, "Come in, Paris."

He was quick to interpret the expectant look on her face, as he was often entrusted with very precious notes to this charming young girl; and his words now answered the unconscious look:

"Marse Vic didn't sen' me, Miss Millie. I's jes come on my own hook. Marse Vic gwine to carry me an' Granny wif him. He is, fo' sho. Aint yo' glad, Miss Millie?"

"Yes, Paris, I am, indeed, glad you are both going with your master."

Then, with the privilege of his class, he said,

"Miss Millie, didn't yo' ax Marse Vic to lemme go wif him, kase he sort o' smile when he read yo' note; an' den in de evenen he sen' me fo' Granny?"

"O, yes, I said I wanted you and Mammy to go with him."

"I's much 'bleeged to yo', Miss Millie, an' I's gwine to take good care o' Marse Vic."

He evidently ascribed his good fortune to the doctor's lovely sweetheart.

Making his best bow, he was leaving the room when the young lady said,

"Come over to-morrow, Paris, I shall have something for you."

This filled him with new delight.

The sad leave-taking of Dr. Kenyon and his family

was over, and he was seated in the great carriage ready
to drive to the station to take the five o'clock train.
Mammy was already on the box with the driver and
Paris was perched on the rumble behind, wearing a pair
of new gloves, the parting gift of Miss Dorcey. Gipterene,
or Gip as they called her, made her appearance with
wailings loud, if not pathetic, to refined ears. Here were
her mother and Paris going on this wonderful journey,
while she was left behind.

Dr. Kenyon, always considerate of his servants, called
Gip to the carriage door and gave her a shining piece of
gold, telling her to buy herself a new frock to wear at his
wedding.

Gip smiled through her tears, not so much for the
the gold piece as for the confidence her young master
had given her; for, next to Mammy, she was the first of
the servants who had heard this interesting news from
the master's lips. To add to her pleasure, her master told
her to get up on the rumble beside Paris, as he wished
her to go as far as Col. Dorcey's.

When they reached the gate, he gave her a tiny note
for his lady-love, in which he had commended the sor-
rowing Gip to her kind sympathy,—saying, as he gave
Gip the note,

"Miss Mildred will be kind to you. Be a good girl
and do what Hannah tells you, and you shall not be
separated from your mother very long."

Miss Millie and Gip stood watching the carriage until
it passed out of sight; then the lady turned to the little
black maid with words of comfort; but the tears in the
brown eyes of the mistress were not called forth
by sympathy for Gip. She, too, wept for one of the
travelers.

Gip, seeing the tears, caught up the white robe of the lady and reverently kissed it.

Millie read the note as she walked up the avenue to the house, and calling Gip, told her how soon the months would pass, when her master would come again and take her with him. She had in her mind to say, "take us," but she withheld the confidence.

Miss Millie had noticed that Gip was not tidy in her dress. The buttons were off the back of the cotton frock she wore, and the apron strings in knots. She took her to her own room, and gave her a little work basket, supplied with needles, thread, and tape, and soon taught her to use them herself. Gip readily promised to keep her clothes in neat order.

Gip now untied the corner of her red cotton handkerchief and displayed the five dollar gold piece that her master had given her.

"Marse Vic done gib me dis to buy a new frock; no pusson can buy frock stuff but Mammy and she don lef' me."

Miss Millie was particularly interested in reforming Gip's manners, who, not having a mistress at home, had not been brought up as carefully as little maids generally were. She knew that Dr. Kenyon expected to supply their future home with servants from his own household, and had intended taking her own maid; but 'Mandy had proved herself very quarrelsome and disagreeable with the Kenyon servants, so Miss Millie had resolved on leaving her behind, and instead to train Gip for the position, as she would then not have to contend with the usual jealousy between servants of different households.

Miss Millie promised Gip that she would select the frock for her, and that Aidy, her own seamstress, should make it for her.

CHAPTER II

Beechwood, the Kentucky home of Dr. Kenyon, was beautifully situated on a hill overlooking the Ohio River, commanding a view of three cities.

Dr. Kenyon had allowed himself many months to prepare a home suitable for his bride, and not a day had passed but he was glad that he had brought his old Mammy with him, instead of leaving her until his return, as she had given him many wise suggestions in regard to domestic conveniences in the planning of his house. It was a proud day for Mammy when her master took her with him across the river to the big city, where he went to select furniture for the new house.

Beechwood was a forest of fine old beech trees, and the new house which faced the river was erected in a clearing where some of the largest trees were left for a pleasant shade.

The building was in the style sometimes called "Colonial," and was undoubtedly very handsome and imposing as it stood surrounded by stately trees. The time for its completion had come, and Dr. Kenyon looked upon his new home with pride and delight.

The furniture was all in place, the last carpet laid, the lace curtains hung, and even the dainty linen for table and beds carefully done up by Mammy's own hands, and laid away with a tiny sprig of lavender in each fold. Everything was at length ready for Dr. Kenyon's return to his old Virginia home.

It was the last night before his journey, and the Doc-

tor was making his usual rounds of inspection before re-
tiring. Sitting in the moon-light on a bench at the
kitchen door were Mammy and Paris. They were true to
their instincts, and always held themselves aloof from
the "strange niggers," as they called the Kentucky servants who were hired about the place.

They were having a private talk, and did not see
their master, who suddenly coming upon them was
standing at a little distance in the shade. They were
discussing the wedding, with its attendant feastings,
back in "Ole Virginy," and there was a sadness in poor
Mammy's voice as she recounted to Paris the good
things there would be on that happy occasion—of the
turkeys and chickens, and young pigs—the latter, in her
opinion, the best of all; and when she came to Aunt
Charity's frosted cakes, jellies and creams—"Honey, dey
jes' make my mouf watah. Dey sure will hab a lubly
time, and nobody will think ob ole Mammy."

Dr. Kenyon returned without being seen, to his room.
He wrote two letters, one to his father and one to Aunt
Mary, saying that he would bring Mammy and Paris
back with him; telling them of Mammy's complaint, and
begging that she be allowed her old position in the
household during her stay at home; that it would gratify
the old woman to see him married, and he wanted to
give her the pleasure.

The next morning as Mammy brought him his coffee
at breakfast, he facetiously asked her if it would be very
inconvenient for her to accompany him back home.
Mammy was, this time, genuinely surprised. She had
made no secret preparations for this journey.

"Why! Marse Vic, is yo' sure nuf gwine to carry me
back wif yo'?"

"Yes, Mammy, I think we should all miss you at the

wedding, so get ready. The train will not leave until this evening and you will have time."

Only Mammy's good training prevented her rushing from the breakfast room while her master was at the table, to begin her preparatons; instead, she bustled around the room. "Laws, honey, I's nearly crazy wif dis news." Then seeing Paris, who was standing behind his master's chair with a very untimely grin on his face, "But—Marse Vic is yo' gwine to lebe Paris 'hind us?"

"O, no! Paris knows he is to accompany me; that is all arranged."

This was too much for Mammy's jealous nature. Even the unexpected joy of going herself could not compensate her for the fact that Paris had been chosen before her, and that he knew he was going when she had been pouring out her heart to him the night before.

The master explained that it was necessary for only Paris to accompany him; but Paris, having told of her desire to see the wedding, he had concluded to let her go.

Spring had again put on her daintiest robes of tender green, and all nature seemed to rejoice with Dr. Kenyon when he set out on his errand to carry away the maiden who awaited his coming.

Mr. Tyler, the doctor's friend and nearest neighbor, had ben informed of all the arrangements for the return of the happy party, and was full of interest and pleasant anticipation. Mr. Tyler, his wife, and Percy, their only child, had come the evening before to bid the doctor good-bye, and to allow Percy to present his gift for the bride. His mother had taught him a pretty little speech for the occasion, which he delivered very charmingly without an error. He was a beautiful child, with dark rich complexion, curling brown hair, and great solemn gray eyes. No one had the power to bring such merri-

ment to these solemn eyes as our Paris. His cunning
tricks never failed to call forth a merry laugh from the
little one; and the "quality chile," as Mammy called him,
was a source of rare delight to the fun-loving black boy.
He was not allowed to carry the child beyond the great
iron gates of the Park, but Paris would "tote" Percy
on his back down the avenue to this limit. Many a jolly
ride he had! Paris would say, "Now, yo' 'tend I's yo'
hoss, and jes' whop me much as yo' want; but w'en dis
hoss gits to kickin' yo' mus' hole on tight, kase dis is
a mighty f'actious hoss, an' mebby he'll fro yo'." Little
Percy's parents had a brilliant future planned for their
only son; but as yet the highest ambition of the boy was
to be "toted" on Paris' back.

Our travelers arrived in due time at Gray Cliff, and
received a cordial reception. The Doctor's old home
was a scene of happy confusion, and the Dorcey household one of delightful preparations. Miss Millie had
not been idle. The wonderful trousseau had occupied
months of steady sewing on the part of her seamstress,
quiet Aidy; to say nothing of the many trips to Richmond, and even to New York, to see dressmakers and
milliners, and to select exquisite fabrics of satin and lace.

Of course the dear mother had to accompany her
when the linens were to be selected. No one but an ex-
perienced housekeeper would make these important pur ·
chases. The rich damask table linen, and the fine, heavy
bed linen, must all be tested by her dainty hands.

A great improvement had taken place in Gip. She
had spent much of her time at the Dorcey mansion, and
Miss Millie had trained her to be a skillful and excellent
lady's maid. Miss Mary Kenyon had attended to Gip's
moral and physical training, and eight months had
wrought wonders in the appearance of the slovenly

weeping Gip we left with Miss Millie taking her first
sewing lesson.

Gip now hurried over to Poplar Grove to carry the
news to the servants that "Marse Vic," Mammy and
Paris had come, and to show the presents Mammy had
brought her. The pretty red frock, with white cotton
lace frilled around the neck, had almost turned Gip's
head with joy. She could not rest until she had carried
the treasure over to display to Mandy's admiring eyes;
but poor Gip was doomed to disappointment in the effect her happiness would produce on the envious
'Mandy. She sneered at the red calico dress, felt the
quality of the lace frill, and said she would not wear cotton lace. Amanda had accompanied her young Mistress to New York on her shopping tours, and had
learned to make nice distinctions. She had also been
accustomed to doing up her Mistress' laces; yet, she retained all the negro's taste for gaudy dress, and was
really envious of Gip's good fortune.

Leaving Gip standing in the door-way, Amanda went
back to the ironing of her own white swiss dress which
she was to wear at the wedding, as morally damp as
the muslin ruffles she now began clapping in her hands
to prepare for the heating irons. At this moment, she
heard her Mistress' bell, and hastened up stairs to the
call.

With all Gip's improvement, a spirit of mischief
showed itself at times; and now was her temptation.
'Mandy had insulted her—scorned the beautiful dress
that Mammy brought all the way from Kentucky. Resentment was hot within. She looked round the kitchen
through indignant tears. Seeing a pan of dirty water
she seized it, ran to the ironing-board, and thoroughly
sprinkled the pure white dress. At that moment she

heard 'Mandy coming, and made a wild rush for the hedge that would screen her from view until she reached the road. On she fled! The red garment streaming out behind her seemed to act upon the enraged 'Mandy like a signal in the arena of a bull-fight. She was gaining on her enemy.

Gip looked over her shoulder, remembering that she would have to cross a stream in the meadow, in the short route she had taken. This stream was spanned only by a precarious log. She renewed her speed, gained the crossing, but in her terror she lost her balance and fell shrieking into the stream. She heard 'Mandy's triumphant words, "I's got yo' now, sho!"

The water was not deep, but poor Gip was too terror-stricken to struggle, and lay in the shallow stream, shouting "Bro' Ben, bro' Ben, bro' Ben! 'Mandy gwine to kill me, come quick."

Her rescuers were already in sight, having heard her first scream. Brother Ben, Mammy, Paris, and the dogs, were all rushing to the spot, arriving just in time to save Gip from the infuriated 'Mandy. She was soon in Mammy's arms, while Ben crossed the stream to interview the pursuer who had withdrawn a little from the scene of action.

Failing in vengeance, poor 'Mandy's tears began to flow, and she told Ben what Gip had done to her clean white dress. Ben was gallant enough to tell her he was very sorry, and to beg her not to cry. But he thought Gip had been sufficiently punished by her fall into the stream, especially as the cause of the trouble, the red dress had suffered the same misfortune. It was wet, and heavy with sand clinging to its folds.

Mammy was not so readily conciliated, and continued dire threats against 'Mandy.

The wedding day, the 30th of April, came bright and joyous, glorious with sunshine, early blossoms and singing birds. Hundreds of people, white and black, rejoiced with the young Doctor of "Gray Cliff," and the sweet, youthful bride-elect of Poplar Grove.

Long before the hour for the ceremony, the servants of both households were attired in their best garments, Mammy had proudly seated all her young people on a bench at her old cabin door, with many injunctions not to move, for fear of "mussin'" the stiffly starched skirts, or disarranging the various colored ribbons that adorned each solemn figure.

Very soon they were relieved of this oppressive strain by the appearance of George, the footman from Poplar Grove. He came over to show his neighbors his new livery; he was very vain of the dark blue coat with brass buttons, the tall hat with velvet band and shining buckle. He had even brought his white gloves, but these he would not desecrate by trying on, before the grand occasion for which they were intended, "to open de bride's ka-age do'." He strutted back and forth before the admiring crowd; his coat buttoned up to the chin, displaying his slim waist, and his hat set jauntily on the side of his head. He was a "likely yellow boy," as such were termed, and knew his good points.

The children's laughter brought Mammy out. She surveyed "dandy George" from head to feet, then said, "Dem libery is nuffin new. I's seed yo' gran-dad war jis sich close as dem—jis new cloth, dat is all."

Paris was ready to go back with George, for of course there was more to be seen at "The Grove" than at "The Cliff" on this occasion. There was to be the scene of the feast—the wedding breakfast—after the ceremony; and

Paris hoped to get a glimpse of the table in the dining-room. After seeing the preparations he went out on the lawn to await the coming of the bride and groom, and in the meantime got into a dispute with Lem, a boy of his own age; but was interrupted by the appearance of Uncle Jeff, driving the prancing horses in the handsome old family carriage up to the door of the "great house."

Mischievous Paris whispered to Lem, "I's a gwine to git eben wid yo'."

Uncle Jeff discovered that he had left his driving gloves in the stable, and sent Lem for them. He was a slow, dull boy, and before he was fairly started Paris darted off to the stables, secured the gloves, and hid himself behind a tree until Lem was in the stable; then shutting and locking the door, he made off to the house, leaving Lem fastened up. He received thanks from the pompous Jeff, and was in time to see the carriages arrive from Gray Cliff.

The groom, with his best man occupied the first one, then came the great family carriage with his father and Aunt Mary. The bride now appeared, walking between her father and mother, the happy 'Mandy bearing the train of white brocaded silk, and the long veil of lace. This day was 'Mandy's triumph; the glory of serving her young mistress on this grand occasion compensated her for being left behind when her mistress went to her new home. She wore the same white dress Gip had marred, now pure and fresh, with a pink sash tied about her waist, and a wreath of artificial roses crownng her dusky head.

Gip was not behind in paying tribute to her new mistress. She had gathered a basket of fresh flowers and carried them to the church, and as the bridal party drove up, she strewed them along the path to the church door. Miss Millie noticed this pretty tribute from the little maid, and rewarded her with a lovely smile.

The Rev. Howard Kenyon was to perform the ceremony, and the Bishop being present on his annual visitation was to pronounce the blessing. They were already in the chancel. The organ pealed forth a grand wedding march, and the beautiful bride, leaning on the arm of her father moved up the aisle.

The happy groom had entered the church from the vestry room, and stood, with his best man, at the chancel rail awaiting the bride.

The solemn marriage ceremony proceeded, the earnest responses were given, and the last words spoken that made Victor and Mildred man and wife. Again sounded the joyous strains of the organ as the procession moved out, the bride now leaning on the arm of her husband, the father and mother following.

There is often an element of the ludicrous attending a solemn occasion, and it was not absent now. The Doctor's big dog had followed the carriages to the church and sat demurely on the portico until the bridal party appeared. When he saw Miss Millie, who was accustomed to notice him, he sprang towards her; but Paris seeing the danger, caught the dog by the collar and drew him aside. It was a dilemma with Paris for a moment. He knew if he let go his hold on the dog, he would instantly make his way to the chancel rail, and he could not make up his mind to lose sight of the ceremony within; so, with ready wit, he drew the dog inside, forced him to the floor and sat down on him, resting his elbows on his knees with characteristic coolness. This caused a titter among the black people in the gallery, but for once

Paris was serious, and took not the slightest notice of this amusement at his expense.

But Paris had yet to answer for his cruelty to poor Lem, who was still shut up in the stable. When George who was Lem's brother, returned from the church, he found him in sad distress, and resolved to make Paris suffer for his fun.

Paris was not as culpable as it seemed. He really did not intend to leave the boy there,—he expected to release him as the company was about to start; but the excitement had driven the circumstance from his mind.

George waited his chance, and it soon came. He found Paris chasing the turkeys with a carriage whip, and taking it from his hand, gave him a severe thrashing; which the boy took with his usual stolidity. He always boasted that whipping could not make him cry.

The wedding party with their guests had returned from the church, and were assembled in the spacious parlors to receive the congratulations of their friends.

In the meantime, the dining-room was left to the inspection of the black people. Uncle Jeff, by right of his age, had the privilege of conducting the company in to view the decorations.. All the greenhouses, as well as the gardens, for miles around, had contributed flowers and vines for beautifying the house. At the head of the gorgeous display of silver, glass and china, were placed two tall backed chairs adorned with bows of white satin ribbon and streamers reaching to the polished floor. As Uncle Jeff escorted the company of colored guests, as well as the family servants, he waved his hand with pompous dignity toward the seats intended for the bride and groom, and said, "My young Mistress and her gemmen take de place ob honor yo' see."

While assisting the butler in serving, Jeff had taken

in every detail of etiquette at a wedding breakfast, and was ready to observe all the formalities in the servant's hall.

When their feast was announced he approached our old Mammy from Gray Cliff, and giving her his arm, led the way to the table, saying, "yo' shall hab de seat at my right han', kase yo' is de Mammy ob de groom. Yo' was de fus one to see him open his eyes on dis worl' ob sin and mis'ry, an' it am 'spectable fo' yo' to sit at de head ob de table on dis solemn 'casion."

Negroes are singularly susceptible to the influence of imposing ceremony; and whether it be an occasion of joy or sorrow, pageantry always impresses them profoundly.

Mammy took the seat, laughing in appreciation of the honor, and said to Charity, Jeff's wife, "Yo' mus'n't feel jealous ob old granny, kase Jeff is ony actin' foolish like." Mammy had been brought up to respect the rights of man and wife.

Jeff was the master of the toasts at the servant's feast. The first, to "De lubly bride, an' de handsome groom," "May dey lib long an' prosper in de lan' where de L'od lead dem, to Ole Kaintuck." Then turning to Mammy, "An' may Mammy neber want a good fat possum to grease de taters wif."

Paris, now thinking himself slighted in the distribution of blessings, called out, "Unc' Jeff, yo' done fo'got me. I's gwine to dat promis' lan' too."

This speech of Paris' roused such a jolly laugh that the strain of formality was broken, the cups of cider were raised aloft and drunk standing; then the practical part of the feast began in earnest, seasoned with many jokes at one aothers expense.

The bridal party was to leave for New York at five

o'clock that day where Dr. Kenyon intended to spend a short time with his sister, Mrs. Richmond.

The servants from both plantations were assembled along the avenue at Poplar Grove to see the travelers off. The younger portion had collected a number of old shoes to throw after the retreating carriages to insure "good luck" to the happy pair.

The Gray Cliff carriage was to carry the bride and groom, while others followed to give a parting greeting at the train The sweet bride, in her pretty traveling dress of dark blue cloth, came out leaning on her husband's arm. The dear father and mother, standing in the door-way, holding each others hands, looked after their child with unconscious sadness in their faces. Though satisfied with the choice their daughter had made, they could not part with her without pain. Finally amidst showers of rice, and throwing of old shoes, the carriage started.

The week after the wedding, Mammy, with all her family, Ben, his wife, Judy, Paris, Gip, Dolly, Chloe and Hayden, started on their journey to Kentucky, in order to have all things ready for the arrival of their Master and Mistress.

Ben had charge of the live stock. Besides the Chestnut trotters there was "Hero," the Doctor's favorite riding horse; Black Beauty, a beauty indeed, that Ben had trained with the side-saddle for "de young Mistis;" the Doctor's favorite dog, "Gerome," and lastly, a coop of pet chickens.

Mammy and Ben jointly ruled the travelers, though many hot discussions took place in regard to seats and disposing of baggage, before the party was settled.

Poor Ben's patience was well nigh exhausted by the time the train started. He was always very respectful to his mother, but on this occasion, he was excusable in saying under his breath, "Mammy is suttinly like a ole settin' hen, she am so hard to please wif a nes'; but w'en she git sot down dar she sticks."

CHAPTER III.

Beechwood is now the scene of a pleasant bustle, for the young Master and Mistress are expected home.

Our old Mammy and her family have been three weeks settled at Beechwood. Mammy and Paris had the pleasure of showing the rest of the family all the beauties and curiosities of the place. Now all were on tip-toe of expectation—Master and Mistress would surely bring each one some gift from the great city where they had been sojourning since their marriage.

Everything was in readiness for their reception; nothing could be added to the preparation within the house; for the hundredth time Mammy had gone through the spacious rooms with her peacock feather duster, just to put in the time, for no speck of dust was to be found on furniture or floor.

Mammy could not control her own excitement, much less that of the younger servants. For an hour Ben and Paris had been polishing the surface of the new carriage, and had the chestnut pair harnessed long before the hour for leaving. The carriage was to be used for the first time, and Mammy, Judy and Gip, all came out to see it leave the stables. All must smooth the beautiful pearl-gray cushions, corded with pink; and Mammy even allowed Gip to "try de cushions" by bouncing herself up and down on the easy springs.

Ben and Paris sat on the box, rigid with self-import-ance, as the carriage waited on the ferry-boat to be taken across the river to the station. They enjoyed the sensation made by their fine turn-out on the black people standing round.

They had reached the station long before the train was due, but at last the shrill whistle was heard, and the engine arrived. Ben looked after the prancing horses, for they were not accustomed to all this confusion; and he had his hands full to hold them in; but Paris had the privilege of standing where he could catch the first glimpse of his Master at the car window.

Dr. Kenyon, too, was on the lookout for some of his people, and the familiar voice of Paris—"Howdy! Marse Vic," was very cheering to his ears; "Dad got de ka-age ober yonda wa'tin' fo' yo'."

As soon as the car stopped Paris bounded in to secure the satchels, before the great monster would rush on again, and carry them off.

Joy and welcome shone on the little bright, black face as he met his Master and Mistress. He was the first object from home to meet their eyes, and Paris received more notice than was altogether good for him.

Ben could now approach with the horses. He was always quiet and well-mannered, and his salutation was as usual, decorous. "I's mighty glad to see yo' Marse Vic an' Miss Millie. I's hope yo' 'joyed yo' trip." "We did indeed" said the master shaking Ben's hand cordially, while the mistress asked kindly for Ben's family.

The husband and wife breathed a sigh of relief and comfort as they took their seats in the carriage, and saw the horses turn homeward. "Beech-wood" could be seen from the Ohio side of the river, and as the Doctor pointed out the large white house, surrounded by tall forest trees, standing on the distant Kentucky hill, his wife followed the direction of his

hand with eager interest. It was to her the first view
of her future home. And soon they were at the large
white gates, wide open, where all the servants from
Mammy down to Hayden stood waiting to receive them.
Mammy was the first to offer her welcoming hand
"Howdy! Marse Vic, howdy, Miss Millie;" then seizing
her master's hand, great tears of joy standing in the faithful old eyes, "Bress yo' soul, honey, I's pow'ful glad to
see yo' and my young Mistis."

Gip ran round to the other door of the carriage where
she could get close to her dear "Miss Millie." She stood
on the steps and expressed more in looks than words,
her devotion to her mistress.

Judy put in her hand over Mammy's shoulder, saying,
I's not gwine to wait fo' Mammy, she stan' dar till de
cows come home."

Poor Dolly! who was always behind, could only get
near enough to bow her woolly head, saying, "I's was de
fus to see yo' comin' any how, an' tole de res'." Chloe
danced about saying, "I tole Granny dat Miss Millie
would hab dat gray frock on kaze it am warm weathah."

Little Hayden now limped up. As usual, something
was the matter with his foot; it was the big toe this time,
tied up with a liberal display of bandage, while he made
his slow way on his heel. The Master told Judy to lift
him into the carriage, where he settled down at their
feet in supreme satisfaction.

The park road wound round a hill in picturesque
curves. As they approached the house more cultiva-
tion appeared; wide borders of sod, green and fresh,
filled in with shrubbery, lined the avenue. The air was
laden with the fragrance of violets, hyacinths and lilacs.
All this floral wealth had been planted out the autumn

before, and was a genuine surprise and pleasure to the young wife.

The house was surrounded by wide galleries, furnished with iron settees, having plenty of cushions with pale blue and pink chintz covers, and soft rugs in front of each seat; giving a restful home-like appearance of welcome.

As Mildred ascended the steps, she turned to her husband: "O! Victor, you did not tell me of half the beauty of our lovely home. Everything is so beautiful! How wise and considerate it was of you to send the servants on before us; they seem to unite the dear old home with this, our charming new one."

Mammy led the way to their rooms, and then went her way to superintend the serving of the dinner.

In the dining-room, they found a wealth of exquisite flowers, sent over by their friends, the Tylers, who had gathered from their own green-house the rarest blooms. Of course the dinner was pronounced "delicious." It was the result of Mammy's and Judy's skill combined.

The day after their arrival, the Doctor and his bride received a visit from their neighbors, Mr. and Mrs. Tyler, and little Percy. After the introduction of the bride, and the usual congratulations passed, Mrs. Tyler said "Mrs. Kenyon,"—the name startled poor Miss Millie, it was yet so new to her—"I should have waited a day or two before paying this visit, but Percy's desire to see you could not be restrained; let me present our little boy, who is already an enthusiastic admirer of yours."

Percy was advancing with his little hand outstretched in formal greeting, when Miss Millie, with charming grace, leaned forward and opened her arms to the pretty child. Percy sprang into the arms and pressed his rosy lips to her soft cheek. It was love at first sight on the part of both. Mrs. Kenyon placed him on a seat at her side, where he could hold her hand, to which he still clung.

During a pause in the conversation, little Percy, who was now just four years old, said, "Mrs. Kenyon, are there any more like you?"

They all laughed at the boy's solemn inquiry, and Mrs. Kenyon said, "Percy, do you mean, have I any sisters like me?"

"Yes, that is what I mean."

"No, my child, I have no sisters, and no brother, unless you will be my little brother."

The boy looked puzzled a moment, "O yes, I will be your brother, but I want a bride just like you. Will you find one for me?"

The child had heard his parents talking about the doctor's "bride," and concluded it would be a very desirable possession, if he could find one like his new friend.

Mrs. Kenyon, laughingly, promised to find a bride for the admiring Percy.

He looked at her with grave eyes, and said, "Can you find one with eyes that laugh as yours do now?"

His mother thought this too personal, and the precocious boy was allowed to go with Gip to visit the barnyard and other objects of childish interest.

Percy's parents were evidently as much pleased with the lovely young mistress of Beechwood as was their promising son.

At parting, Percy asked permission to come every day to see the lady, saying, "I want to see you when no one else is here; then you will let me talk to you."

Mrs. Kenyon assured him he would be always welcome, and they would have many nice little talks.

June and July were happy, busy months at Beechwood. There were the usual visits to receive and return; then followed dinings and other entertainments, given in honor of the Doctor and his wife. The "Virginia Belle," became a great favorite in society, and the three cities within visiting distance of Beechwood vied with each other in paying attention to the young mistress of that hospitable home. But Mrs. Kenyon and her husband recognized a higher sphere of life than mere fashionable pleasures—their position involved duties which they would not neglect for any social allurements. Both as planter and physician, Dr. Kenyon had many dependents; and his increasing practice brought him in contact with, to him, a new class of people—the hardworking poor—and he determinded to do all he could to improve their condition. Mrs. Kenyon sympathized with her husband in his plan, and furnished many of her own for the improvement of the people of her household. She loved her husband's profession, and took a real interest in his patients. Their life now began in earnest. Sometimes Mrs. Kenyon would accompany her husband on his round of visits into the cities, for he practiced in both towns. Many sufferers remembered the sweet lady who brought them delicacies and wines, and always a bunch of flowers from green-house or garden to refresh them.

This providing for the sick and suffering outside their own family was as new to Mammy as to the young Mistress; but they worked and consulted together to prepare the daintiest dishes, and to fashion garments for the comfort of some poor old woman or little child that the Doctor had mentioned to his wife. She did not confine her attentions to the poor; her friends everywhere learned to look for the sweet sympathetic face in the hour of sickness and sorrow.

Among the first opportunitites of her ministering to

others was presented by her little friend Percy. One night, after the family at Beechwood had all retired, the Doctor was roused by Charley, a black boy from the Tyler place, sent in haste for the Doctor, with the message that Percy had been suddenly taken with a severe attack of croup. The Doctor was soon at the little sufferer's side, but perceived at once that the child's malady was increased by a restless desire for something. The Doctor was not long in discovering that the little one was begging his parents to send for Mrs. Kenyon. They had tried to dissuade him from urging this request until morning; but as soon as the Doctor learned what was disturbing his little patient, he sent Paris back with the buggy to bring his wife to the child's bedside.

When Mrs. Kenyon entered Percy's room he reached out his little arms with a pleading gesture, "I knew you would come. I wanted you so much. Will you tell me where I shall go if I die of croup like Andy did?" Andy was the child of the cook, who had died during the Doctor's absence. His death had made a strong impression upon the mind of this sensitive child.

Mrs. Kenyon laid the feverish little head back on the pillow, and tried to comfort him; but he insisted—"I know you can tell me."

Mrs. Kenyon took his tiny hand between her own soft cool ones, and looking into the child's earnest face, said, "Into the dear Saviour's arms, little one."

Fixing his wide-open eyes on hers, he asked, "Is He a friend of little children?"

"Yes, indeed, darling; a dear friend who told the people once, 'To let the little children come unto him.'"

He had been gasping for breath while talking, but now the medicine was having its soothing effect; he was breathing with comparative ease. He soon fell asleep, still clasping his friend's hand in his own.

This was the beginning of many appeals from poor little Percy to know and be taught things that it ought to have been the pleasure and duty of his parents to teach him. He begged to go to church with his friends, and so fell into the habit of joining the Kenyons every Sunday morning, to accompany them to church.

CHAPTER IV.

Summer, Autumn, and Winter passed with the happy inmates of Beechwood in pleasant usefulness and serene enjoyment of their charming home.

When Spring came again bringing violets, hyacinths and lilacs, with their sweet fragrance, it brought also another flower, the most precious that ever graced a home. This treasure made its advent in the early hours of morning, and Beechwood was all aglow with light, and rejoicing over the welcome arrival of "little Missy" from baby-land.

This was Mammy's special occasion for rejoicing— her hour of importance and dignity in the family. It was her privilege to announce to the household the advent of this wonderful baby. She was particularly proud of the fact that, in her opinion, "Missy favored the Kenyons."

"She is sho like Marse Vic," she said, "The same bu'ful blue eyes, de gol'en ha'r an' de proud Kenyon nose."

Never did a little one receive a more cordial welcome. A precious gift the happy parents considered their little daughter; and friends and servants, alike rejoiced with them, as if indeed the little one was a gift from Heaven.

Day had not yet dawned when the happy father sought his silent study; perhaps to offer thanks for this new, sweet responsibility committed to his care. Walking to a window overlooking the eastern sky, in order to catch the first ray of morning light heralding his child's first birthday, he beheld an unexpected sight. A brilliant comet met his gaze; its splendid curving tail reached

far above the horizon, while the blazing nucleus shed a
light that cast shadows of objects on the earth. Dr.
Kenyon beheld the beautiful stranger with a touch of
awe, recalling the legendary story that comets foretell
a life of great renown to those born under their magic
sway. It was a passing thought, for no superstition
found a lurking place in the sound understanding of Dr.
Kenyon.

While he still watched the glowing visitant, Mammy
entered the room, and seeing the wonderful stranger
over her Master's shoulder, she cried out in amazement,
"Fo' de Laud's sake, Marse Vic, is dat a comet?"

"Yes, Mammy, come and see it."

But Mammy had thrown herself down on the floor,
and covered her head with her apron. There she sat, and
rocked herself back and forth, crooning to herself as if
chanting an incantation. The Doctor went to her, and
taking her by the arm, said, "Mammy, what is the meaning of this? I fear you are tired out; come, get up, and
go to your room and get some rest."

But Mammy only uncovered her head, and pointed at
the object of terror. "Marse Vic, my po' little Missy is
sho bo'n fo' bad luck; dat is de debbel's lante'n; he's
swingin' it up dar to see de po' chile, an' he will sho rule
her life, and make her hab a ter'ble bad temper."

"Mammy, you must stop this nonsense," said Dr.
Kenyon, "I cannot let you talk this way—you are
crazy."

"No, Marse Vic, ole Mammy all right in de haid."

Dr. Kenyon bade her get up and seat herself in a chair,
and then said, "Mammy, you must not talk in this foolish way. You can give me no good reason for thinking
that this comet will bring misfortune to my precious
child,—I never knew you so silly;" for Mammy still

rocked herself as she sat looking at the heavenly body that had for her such mortal terror.

"Tell, me," said the Doctor, "what you know about this absurd superstition."

"I's hern tell all my life 'bouten de bad luck dat dem comets bring on de po' little chil'n. My own Granny tole me 'bouten de night dat Rogal Orion was bo'n in South Calliney. One ob dem comets jes sling hisself up in de sky dat same night, an' sho's yo' bo'n, dat boy growed up an' killed his brudder; an' de spurit ob dat brudder jes hole on to po' Rogal till he done commit sureside."

Dr. Kenyon listened patiently, but with silent amusement, to Mammy's story, and then said, "Now Mammy, will you not admit that I know more about such things than all the crazy darkies you have heard talk about it?"

"Yes," said Mammy, with a weird cadence in her voice, "I know dat yo' is sma't, and skillified as a docto,r an' all dat white folks know, but Marse Vic, yo' not got de spurit to fin' out what de cullud folks know widout any learnin'. I's tell yo' young Master, it am de truff—an' we git it from no books. Away back in Afriky de people tell der chillen, an' de chillen tell der chillen, an' nobody but dem as has de spurit can onderstan' de language."

"Aunt Hilaria," (the doctor sometimes called her by her name when he was vexed with her), "that is all mere nonsense; it is just as absurd as carrying a rabbit's foot in your pocket for good luck, and I have, myself, heard you laugh at that."

"Yes, honey, dat's so; but I's laugh at de young white misses fo' carrying de rabbit's foot a hangin' on de fan, kase dey don' git it de wrong way. De cullud boys catch de rabbits fo' de ladies, an' dey jest get any kind. But de right way is to go to de grave-yard, in de dark ob de moon, at midnight, and catch de rabbit a runnin' ober de graves, den take de lef' hind foot. Dat am sho good luck."

Dr. Kenyon could not restrain a laugh at Mammy's account of the "right way" to obtain the coveted talisman; but, speaking seriously, he said, "Well, Mammy, I see it is useless to try to convince you what nonsense all this is; but one thing I will insist upon, you must not teach such absurd things to my child."

"Laud! honey, I's teached it to yo' all yo' life, an' what harm has it done yo'?"

There was sound logic in Mammy's argument; what southern child was ever injured by the dear old "Mammy's" absurd, fantastic, often gruesome, tales told at the nursery fireside, with the child cuddled in her protecting arms?

But Dr. Kenyon was not only a practical man, but he was a man of science, and had made up his mind that his child should not, even in childhood, be influenced by the weird superstitions of the black servants, and after charging Mammy again not to repeat the superstition of the comet to his daughter, he dismissed her.

Presently, Mammy returned carrying in her arms a soft white bundle, her kind old face pressed against a tiny head. The Doctor took the bundle in his arms, and examining the small pink face, said, "Mammy, she will be like me; I wish she had inherited her mother's beauty."

But Mammy, quick to defend her own nursling, said, "I's mighty glad little Missy is gwine to look like my own ole baby."

In the morning, a reception was held for little Missy, at which Mammy presided. This was to present her to all the colored people of the household. Baby was arrayed in one of her prettiest robes, with a rich lace cap on the small head. Mammy sat in state, with the baby on a pillow on her lap, while the servants filed in and gathered round her chair.

Of course, Mammy had been informed of the baby's name, that she might present her formally to the people. "Victoria" seemed a grand name, as Mammy announced it, but she had a name of her own selection in reserve.

Gip was asked to serve cake and black-berry cordial to the guests, and when Mammy raised her glass to her lips, she said, "Let us drink to the health ob Little Doctor, kase she is sho like her papa."

This toast was responded to with enthusiasm. The name met with more approval than the beautiful one derived from her father's name, Victor. Even Chloe and Hayden seemed to appreciate the appropriateness of this name. And so our "Little Doctor" was first introduced to the household servants.

Dolly asked to see the tiny feet, and Hayden must count the pink toes; but just then Mammy discovered that Hayden carried a chicken bone in his hand, and giving him a sharp slap on the ear, exclaimed, "Git away, yo' young nigger, wid yo' greasy han's from dis white chile."

Hayden backed away from Granny with tears in his eyes saying, "Dis chicken laig am good fo' a baby gal." He had brought it as an offering to Little Doctor, and Granny had given him a blow for his good-will.

Paris carried a note from Dr. Kenyon to the Tyler family announcing the arrival of little "Victoria"; but when Mrs. Tyler mentioned the name before Paris, he said, "Granny say her name 'Little Doctor.'"

"Ah, well! I dare say Granny has given her a very suitable name," said Mr. Tyler.

Percy Tyler was greatly interested in the advent of a baby at the home of his friends, and was impatient to see the new-comer. At length the day came when he was to pay his first visit; and, dressed in dark blue velvet, his brown curls falling over a large lace collar, with his tiny card in one hand, and clinging to his mother's hand with the other, he was ushered into the presence of the dainty little lady, who was on her very best behavior for the occasion. She even condescended to open her lovely blue eyes, and stretch out her fingers for Percy's admiration, who, after regarding the baby for awhile, said in his usual solemn way, "Mammy, do you think Victoria will love me when she grows up?"

Mammy would only venture to say, "'Honey, jes yo' wait an' ax her when she comes to years ob 'scretion."

The answer did not satisfy the little boy, and he turned his eyes to meet his mother's smile. Mrs. Tyler was often called upon to explain to her inquiring child the mysterious sayings of old Mammy; and she now told him he must wait until the baby knew him, and then he might ask her the interesting question.

The next important event in our "Little Doctor's" life was her baptism, which took place about six weeks after her birth. Aunty Jane and Uncle Howard paid a visit to Beechwood to be present on this occasion, as they had been chosen to be her sponsors. The ceremony took place at the church, the rector officiating, and was followed by an elegant dinner-party at Beechwood.

This ceremony in the church was another occasion for Mammy's importance—she was to carry the baby to the font; and among other things her own costume was not to be overlooked. Her old finery was inspected, and her

choice finally fell upon a big flowered lawn, yellow pre-
dominating; a large leghorn bonnet, the front towering
above two bunches of wool that graced each side of her
head; a black lace shawl, the gift of her Mistress and
valued above all her possessions, which was picturesque-
ly draped about her ample shoulders; while a peacock
feather fan, attached to a ribbon at her belt, finished her
costume.

She was very proud of her charge. This was her first
attendance at a church baptism, and Mammy fully expected to give the baby into the rector's arms. She had
already settled in her mind how she would manage to
spread out the folds of the beautiful embroidered robe
before the baby was presented to the admiring congregation. Mammy, like all her race, had an eye for effect
as well as color. But nothing ever turns out just as we
expect, and she was disappointed when Dr. Kenyon took
the child and gave her to its sponsor, Aunty Jane. But
poor Mammy's chagrin reached a climax when she saw
the clergyman hold the little one close in one arm, the
dainty lace frills of the robe twisted about the little feet
with no regard for appearances. "A mussin' up all dem
fine frills, an' showin' nuffin 'ceptin' jes one end ob de
sash," was what Mammy said to Gip, as she waited with
the baby in the carriage for the rest of the party to leave
the church.

Percy had asked as a great favor that he might stand
at the font beside the baby. He held Mrs. Kenyon's
hand to the close of the ceremony, and was allowed to
drive home with the family; for he was included in the
invitation to the dinner-party given in honor of this
happy event.

Poor old superstitious Mammy had not forgotten her
early dread of the comet's influence; and as her little

charge grew older, and began to show the natural
temper of babyhood, Mammy secretly ascribed it all to
the baneful comet. She had accustomed the little one
to her cold bath, as she was strong enough to bear it;
and Little Doctor, with her vigorous constitution, enjoyed her play in the water every morning. One morning she resisted all Mammy's arts to coax her out of the
tub, and when she lifted her out by gentle force, she
threw herself into a tempest of rage. With screams and
kicks, she struggled in Mammy's hands, and finally with
a sudden jerk, she plunged back into the water. Mammy,
who was frightened out of her wits, expected to see "de
debble" carry her off bodily, and looked with comical
alarm at the pretty smiling creature as she lay in the tub
perfectly satisfied with her performance.

Gip shared with Mammy the care of the baby, and
could often charm her into good humor when even
Mammy failed. She had a quiet, gentle way that soothed
the impulsive child. She was the one to discover the
first pearly tooth, much to Mammy's disappointment;
but she was loyal enough to show it to Mammy, that she
might be the one to carry Little Doctor to her mother,
and announce the treasure found.

These same tiny pearls gave poor Gip many a proof of
their fine edge. On one occasion, Gip was holding Little Doctor in her arms while she was eating a
peach, the child struggled to reach it, and Gip
gave her the peach, turning the whole side of the fruit
to the little open mouth; but baby, who did not recognize
such nice distinctions, wanted the side that Gip had bit-
ten. This being refused, the tiny hands clutched Gip's
wool and tugged fiercely. A negro's head is not her
most sensitive point, and Gip only laughed at this weak
vengeance; but Little Doctor was quick to perceive her

mistake, and seized poor Gip's too prominent ear between her sharp teeth. Now, indeed, she made her vengeance felt. Gip's screams of pain soon brought her
Mistress to the spot, but already the tempest had ·sub-
sided, and Little Doctor was tenderly caressing the
bleeding ear.

Good faithful Gip quickly put her hand over the
wound to screen her charge from punishment; but Mrs.
Kenyon removed the hand, examined the ear, then taking the baby hand she gave it a sharp slap. Tears started
to the lovely eyes, but it was not anger now. She put
her arms round Gip's neck, smoothed the dusky check
with the little hand, still smarting from her punishment,
and said, "Poor Gippy! I so sorwee."

It was when Little Doctor was about three years old,
that Percy came under her wrath. With all his devotion
to his little playmate, he had a boy's natural love of
teasing, and his common amusement was throwing up
and catching her dolls, which never failed to rouse an
indignant protest from the child. On this occasion the
subject of this athletic treatment was a handsomely
dressed new doll. Victoria stormed and pleaded in turns;
but Percy assured her that the doll should not fall, and
resisted all her efforts to catch it. Suddenly she rushed
from the hall, where they were playing, into the dining-
room, and seeing a pitcher of cream on the table, she
caught it up, hurried back to the hall, and, before Percy
was aware that she had left the spot, she poured the contents over his pretty new suit of blue cloth. Percy dropped the doll, and stood looking at the cream dripping
off his clothing.

Poor impulsive Little Doctor was almost instantly
penitent. She came to him, took up the corner of her
tiny white apron, and began to wipe his sleeve, saying

in a motherly tone of reproof, "You 'voked me to punis' you,"

Mammy came to the rescue, removed the liquid from Percy's clothes, and then went down on her knees to clean the rug. Victoria stood with her hands clasped behind her looking on; then, kneeling down beside the old woman, she took the turbaned head between her little white hands, and turning the disturbed old face towards her own, said, "Mammy, I think you better punis' me, 'cause my Mother is away, and I mus' be punis'ed."

"No, honey, Mammy will neber do dat. 'Taint fo' me to chastise my po' little lamb; but I's gwine to pray fo' my baby dat de ole bad-man won't git her in his powah.

The scene in the hall shortened Percy's visit, and he went home—more thoughtful than usual. The resentment towards his little playmate had already vanished; he knew he was to blame more than the little girl. He was not an impulsive child, but he could sympathize with his younger companion in the vexation he had caused her; and on his way home he was thinking what he could do to show Victoria that he bore her no ill-will. Suddenly his face brightened, and he started, as he sat beside old Joe, who was driving him home. A relative, sometime before, had sent him a pair of beautiful Newfoundland dogs, gentle and well trained. Percy was very fond of his dogs, and prized them very highly, but in his generosity he had resolved on parting with one of them.

That same evening, Jo came over leading "Wiley," the prettiest one, by a cord, and carrying a tiny note. Mrs. Kenyon read the note to her little daughter, and explained that the pretty dog was her very own, that her little friend had sent it to her with his love, and begged forgiveness for having ill-treated her doll, "Mimi."

Victoria was much touched by Percy's generosity.

She admired her doggie very much; and when she found that her little friend had sent her the prettiest one, she appreciated the gift still more highly; but a cloud settled over the bright happy face, as she leaned on her mother's shoulder and whispered, "Mother, did Percy 'member that I was rude to him?"

"No, dear," said her mother, "I think our little Percy too kind to remember that naughty act of my little girl; and now, what shall I say in answer to this pretty note?"

"Tell Percy I'm so glad he sent me 'Wiley,' 'cause he is the prettiest one, and I'm so sorry I was rude to him."

Paris took charge of Wiley, after unfastening the cord from the brass collar; but soon found he had his hands full in holding the dog after Uncle Jo left; though in a few days Wiley settled down in his new home, very well contented, especially with the fun-loving Paris, who soon taught him many cunning tricks.

CHAPTER V.

"Mrs. Kenyon, please let Victoria go to dancing school this afternoon. We are going to have a grand march and a pretty Scottish dance, when we all wear plaid scarfs."

It was Percy who spoke. Though he was now a boy of nine years, he had never lost the tender interest he had felt for the baby Victoria. He had been attending the dancing school for some time, and had often asked for Victoria to accompany him.

"Yes, Percy," said Mrs. Kenyon, "I will take her to-day. I think Victoria is old enough to begin her lessons now, and you may ask your mother to let you go in the carriage with Victoria. How would you children like that?"

"O, that will be splendid," said Percy and Little Doctor together.

The children were all assembled in the hall ready for the grand march, when our party arrived, and Percy and Victoria took their places in the procession.

A mischievous looking boy just behind them annoyed our little girl by keeping his feet moving before the march. She was unaccustomed to other children, and was perhaps too exacting. The boy noticed her annoyance, and when the march began, he purposely stepped on the heel of Victoria's slipper. The slipper pulled off, and the procession came to a stop. Percy saw the act, and turned to the boy, but before he could speak, Little Doctor took up the slipper and gave the offender a swift slap

in the face. His shriek of pain brought the teacher to
the spot, and Victoria shrank closer to Percy, who held
her hand tight in his own, and looked quite able to defend his partner.

The teacher inquired the cause of the trouble, and
when Percy explained, he said, "Served him right, little
lady," and turning to the boy, "Ned, you may step aside
until the after the march."

Percy carried the shoe to where Mrs. Kenyon sat, and
Mammy put it on again; then they joined the merry
throng. At the close of the first dance, Ned Burton, the
offending youth, came to where Victoria sat beside her
mother. "The teacher told me I should ask your pardon; but I think Miss Victoria, that you should ask my
pardon for striking me in the face. I never saw a girl
do that way before."

Victoria was silent, but Mrs. Kenyon answered, "Do
you not see that you gave the first offense? Yet, if
you offer the apology from your own sense of politeness,
I am sure Victoria will pardon you, and acknowledge
her regret that she lost her temper and was rude to
you."

Ned looked down at his shining pumps, and then with
a frank smile, "Well, I am sorry that I was rude. Now
shall we be friends?" He held out his hand to Victoria,
who placed her own in it with a timid grace unlike the
little fury who had assaulted the boy a few minutes before.

Dr. Kenyon was in the habit of taking Victoria with
him in his phaeton when he went to visit a patient where
there was no contagious disease. She enjoyed the privilege very much, especially when she was allowed to
carry the basket of dainties to some poor sick person, or
to the little children who always crowded the humble

abodes of the poor people, where her father gave his attendance without charge.

One morning the family carriage was at the door at Beechwood; and Victoria, thinking she was going to drive, ran to the pantry and filled a little basket with things of her choosing. She hurried round from the back of the house just in time to see the carriage drive off with her parents inside. They each threw a kiss to their little girl, but she noticed nothing but the fact that they had gone without her, and running down the avenue, she cried after them, "Please wait for me, I want to go, I want to go too." But they were in a hurry, and did not stop.

She looked through her tears at the retreating carriage, and then turned to her dog, Wiley, who had followed her, and said, "Willey, let's you and I wun off, that's what we'll do." Wiley wagged his tail in hearty consent; and the two, the little child and the big dog, set out together. The long white road went straight to the city, and the child and dog plodded along in the dust. Victoria had unconsciously held on to her basket, but she soon tired of it, and gave it to Wiley to carry in his mouth.

Little Doctor was not dressed for a walk; her arms and neck were bare, the pretty head only covered by the golden curls; and the little feet in slippers. She passed cottages nestling along the wayside, with bits of gardens round them; no one noticed the child, and on she went, stopping here and there to pluck a fresh morning-glory, or a sprig of golden-rod.

When opposite an old rickety house, a great dog ran out and made an assault on Wiley, who was not slow to drop the basket and return the assault with vigor. The yelping of the dog brought out the mistress of the house, a Mrs. Fox. She had a milking bucket in her hand, which she used with telling effect on poor Wiley's head.

She separated the dogs, and when the dust of the affray had cleared a little, she saw the small white figure standing in the road, speechless with terror. The woman was still excited, and said with a hard, high-pitched voice, "Bless my soul! Child, what's you doin' there, a-standin' lookin' on instid o' stoppin' your dog a-eatin' up mine?"

The child made no reply; Mrs. Fox said; "Sissy, what's your name, and where do you live?"

Just then a boy and a girl came from behind the house; and seeing the child, the boy cried out, "O, Ma, I know who that little girl is; she belongs to them rich folks what lives at Beechwood. I kin take her home, Ma."

The girl now came up and examined the little ones clothes, "Say, Sissy, what's your name?"

Victoria was more responsive to the gentle voice of the girl, and said, "My name is Little Doctor." They all laughed at this; and Mrs. Fox remarked, "Whatever did they call the child sich a name as that for?"

The boy was anxious to take the child home, hoping for a reward; and the two chldren had just started with Victoria, one on each side, when they met Paris coming on horseback, riding furiously. "What yo' go run'd off fo' little Missy? We jes found it out, and Granny is scart so she jes gaspin' fo' bref."

Mrs. Fox lifted the child to the saddle before Paris, who set off without a word to the disappointed Foxes.

Ducy Fox, the little girl, about nine years old, had taken more than a passing interest in the charming little stranger; and the next morning found her at the great iron gates of Beechwood, looking through with timid

curiosity. Victoria, who was walking with Mammy, saw
the girl, and hastened to the gate. "Are you the girl
who spoke kindly to me on that big road where the dogs
were fighting?"

"Yes, I spoke to you. And we were going to bring
you home when that nigger come." "That was Paris,"
said Victoria, not liking the opprobrious word that the
common white people generally used.

"Well, aint you afraid of that big woman who speaks
so—loud?"

"No, that is my Ma," said the girl with downcast
eyes. Little Doctor, who delighted in giving, turned to
Mammy, who had followed her charge to the gate.
"Mammy, you go and get something nice for this little
girl, some cake and some jam," and added, "and a little
piece of ham,"—she was not allowed but a small bit of
ham herself, so she asked it as a special favor.

Mammy went for the food, while the little one gathered her arms full of flowers to give the stranger. When
Mammy brought back a basket filled with provisions
poor Ducy was so eager to investigate its contents, she
could not be prevailed upon to stay longer, much to Little Doctor's disappointment. This was the beginning
of an acquaintance between the child of the mansion and
the child of the squalid cabin.

The incident on the "big road" was really the beginning of better days for all the Foxes. Dr. Kenyon
found some work about the place by which he could
employ the boy, Sam Fox, and enable him to earn clothing for himself, of which he was in sad need. Mrs. Kenyon provided comfortable clothing for Ducy; and when
the winter term of school began, all the children were
sent to the nearest District School, Mrs. Fox remark-

ing, "You'uns is the first rich folks that ever helped me bring up my young'uns."

As Christmas drew near, all the family at Beechwood werecheerfully busy preparing for the celebration of that day. It had been decided that a Christmas tree would be the most enjoyable entertainment for the children of the neighborhood, the Foxes included of course. In the new plan of providing Christmas cheer for the poor children in the neighborhood, the old-time custom of giving presents to the household servants was not forgotten.

Ben had secured a beautiful, symmetrical cedar tree, which was set up in the hall and loaded with a greater variety of fruit than ever a tree was known to bear.

According to the old Virginia custom, the servants all came to the "great house" at break of day, first to cry "Chrstmas gift!" to all they "caught," as they said; and next, to wish all their master's family a "Merry Christmas!"

Already the hall was lighted and a cheerful fire burning in the dining-room, when the pathetic voices of the negros were heard singing their Christmas carol, as they came in a small procession from their quarters to the house.

Dr. Kenyon took the gifts from the tree, while Little Doctor distributed them. The child was always in her element when she was giving to others. Her bright smiling face betrayed the delight she felt in this, the first Christmas tree of which she was Lady Bountiful.

Mammy was the first called, and her old eyes sparkled with pleasure as she received, in a capacious apron, her bundle of gifts. She had not seen its contents yet, but there was a beautiful fancy shawl that Mammy had been wanting very much, bought by Little Doctor herself, and patted and kissed as she thought how it would please Mammy; then a pair of carpet slippers and a big box of candy.

Ben, Judy, Gip, Paris, Dolly, Chloe and Hayden all came in for a generous share of wearing apparel, with candy and toys for the little ones, and plenty of tobacco and snuff for the older ones, both men and women. Paris was jubilant over the possession of a fine large jews-harp; and with his natural gift for music, he was not long catching all the popular airs of the day.

After breakfast, the children of the neighborhood came to receive their gifts. The Foxes, from the mother down to little Maude, all came, admired the tree, and carried away more than they had ever expected to possess of this world's goods.

CHAPTER VI

The day Little Doctor was five years old was one of unusual trials to poor Mammy. She was always distressed at any exhibition of temper in the child; and, as she declared, "De chile jes seems 'sess'd wid mischief dis day."

Ducy Fox had given Victoria a pretty kitten. She loved the gentle creature dearly; chiefly because it bore her capricious treatment with perfect docility, even allowing Little Doctor to dress her in cap and gown and put her to bed, dosing her with "cat-nip tea" made of rose leaves.

Mammy, who had been watching her charge for some time as she played with her kitten, the white skirts flitting in and out of the shrubbery, suddenly saw the child dash off towards the kitchen, holding the kitten by the neck at arm's length. Mammy followed as fast as her old legs would carry her, but before she could reach her, Victoria had plunged the kitten into a tub of water. Mammy was in time to save the gasping, dripping kitten from the watery grave.

"Chile, what fo' yo' want to drown yo' po' little cat? Dat am so wicked."

"No," said Little Doctor, still angry and excited, "Suzette is wicked, she scratched my arm;" and she showed a long scratch on the delicate wrist.

"Honey, I'll be boun' yo' was a-maulin' her, and she was only tryin' to save herse'f."

"No, Mammy; I was just looking down Suzette's

throat to see if she has a gizzard like the chickens, and she was so wicked she scratched me." Shaking her wise little head, and looking towards the tub, "I think the water will take the temper out of her, but I wish I had given her some oil instead, I think it would do her more good."

She took her dainty little handkerchief and wiped the kitten's face, saying to Mammy, "Please wipe the rest of her with your apron."

Mammy had no idea of putting her white apron to such a use, and called Hayden to bring a towel. He soon came holding the corner of a towel, while the rest of it dragged on the ground. Mammy made believe she was breaking a switch from a tree, and he dashed back for one he knew would please "Granny."

When he came, she said, "Now, yo' git down dar mighty quick, and wipe dat cat dry as fire."

He glanced up at Granny, saying, "She got eight mo' lives ter take—dey got nine to 'gin wif, sho as I is yo' gran'son."

Her father had given her a small bottle of olive oil, with which she was fond of dosing the young darkies on the place. Hayden always took the medicine; but Paris after the first dose, managed to slip the bottle away, and fill it with molasses instead of oil. As Little Doctor never took her own prescriptions, she did not discover the deception, and Paris was a willing patient. Even Mammy was subjected to this treatment. She would gravely feel her pulse—"Mammy, you have a high fever, you must take two quinine pills," and then she would open a little pill-box with bread crumbs rolled into pills, and Mammy would swallow them with a make-believe wry face.

The birthday, with its pleasures and pains, had come

nearly to a close. Victoria was having her last romp with Wiley on the lawn. Paris stood by prompting the dog to do his best tricks for Little Doctor's amusement, while the other black children joined in the fun with clapping of hands and shouts of laughter.

No one noticed that a gentleman on horseback was approaching, until he called to Paris to take his horse. Victoria's attention was still occupied with the dog, and she did not notice the gentleman until he playfully caught her in his arms, and raising her off her feet, said laughingly, "I have brought Little Doctor a birthday gift, but she must give me a kiss for it."

Old Mammy had always observed a charge from her mistress, when Victoria was a baby, that no gentleman but those of her own family were to be allowed to kiss the child. Mammy had impressed the idea on the little one herself; and now twisting herself suddenly out of his arms, she demanded, "Are you my uncle?"

Dr. Harris was a junior partner of Dr. Kenyon in his city office. As Victoria knew him perfectly well, this rebuff was rather mortifying; and, not to be conquered by a little miss of five summers, he again caught her up gently, and kissed the rosy cheek. But he paid for his temerity, for at the same instant, a sounding blow on the ear, from the too ready hand, made him quickly release the offended little maid.

Paris was now rolling on the ground in convulsed laughter. The doctor muttered something as he passed the mischievous young darkey, and retreated towards the house with as much dignity as he could assume; but he had to meet another enemy. Wiley, seeing the struggle, thought it a part of the sport, and slipping up behind the doctor, he caught him by the leg and held on, notwithstanding a vigorous kick, until Paris came and pulled the dog off. The gentleman hesitated a moment, and then walked on to the house.

Victoria, child though she was, had a keen sense of propriety, and at once felt the indignity she had caused the gentleman. She went to seek her father, and tell him her trouble. Dr. Kenyon listened with ill-concealed amusement at the child's account of the Doctor's salutation and her prompt resentment; but he explained to his little daughter that the doctor meant it kindly, and did not know that it would give offense; so, he thought she should go to the library where he was sitting, and apologize for the annoyance she had caused him.

Little Doctor hesitated a moment, then said, "Father, I wish you would go with me, 'cause Dr. Harris is so very—vexed."

The father took her hand, and the two went together to meet the offended visitor.

The matter was soon explained, and the doctor graciously accepted the apology, saying, "Miss Victoria, it was my fault; it was rude in me to attempt to kiss a little lady against her will, and I ask your pardon. Will you forgive me, and let us be friends?" and he held out his hand with extreme courtesy.

Victoria placed her own offending one in his, with a sweet smile and her characteristic bow.

As Dr. Harris was taking his leave, an hour later, he presented our faulty little heroine with a beautiful silver-mounted riding-whip.

With a hearty shake of the hand, Dr. Kenyon said, "Harris, it is fortunate for you that you did not present the whip before you stole the kiss," and the Doctor withdrew with a merry laugh.

Our Little Doctor had many thoughts in her small wise head that no one knew anything about. That

night, as Mammy was putting her to bed, she was unusually quiet; and as she kneeled at the side of her
downy bed to say her evening prayer, Mammy wondered
at the soft little sigh that escaped her lips.

When Mammy lifted her into the dainty nest, and
arranged the frills and smoothed the folds of the pretty
night robe, she awaited the usual "Thank you, Mammy,
kiss me good-night." Instead she turned her eyes up
to the sky-blue canopy of her bed, and whispered,
"Mammy, do the angels love wicked children?"

"Well, honey, I knows dey loves chillens gin'ally, but
I thinks dey mus' hide der faces wid der wings when a little chile am very wicked."

"But what does a child do, when she has been very
wicked? What do you do, Mammy?" she suddenly
asked, as if the old woman's experience was more to the
point.

"Why, la! honey, I's jes gits down on my ole marrow-
bones, and prays to de good Laud to make de ole man
go 'way fum me. Dat's de way I does."

"Please, Mammy, take me up, I must say other
prayers. I only said, 'Now I lay me,' I did not ask the
good Lord to forgive me."

Again the golden curls were bowed, and the hands
folded together; but this time the old turbaned head was
bowed beside the golden one. When she had finished,
she smoothed Mammy's cheek saying, "Excuse me,
Mammy, for keeping you up so late, but you see I had
to ask forgiveness 'bout Dr. Harris," and, lowering her
voice, " 'cause he said a bad word to Paris when he
laughed at the doctor."

"But hit sems to me, honey, dat he is de one to ax
fo' givnes fo' sayin' dat wicked word," said Mammy, with
more logic than conscience.

"But you see, Mammy, I caused it; Paris laughed when I boxed the doctor's ear. He did not know that I heard what he said, and I did not tell father, 'cause the doctor thought he said it to himself.".

She nestled down to sleep, well satisfied that she was forgiven for the sin Dr. Harris had committed.

One morning as Victoria, with Dolly, was gathering violets under the hedge, she heard wheels on the graveled drive, and peeping through the foliage, she saw a gentleman and little boy in the phaeton, driving rapidly towards the house. The boy was crying piteously, which at once roused Little Doctor's sympathy, and holding the violets in the corner of her apron, she followed them to the house.

She found them in her father's office; and Dr. Kenyon introduced his little daughter to Mr. Ward and his son, Hartley. The boy's hand rested on the doctor's knee, and a case of instruments was on the table at his side. Little Doctor came quite near to the patient, with the curious interest she always showed in any surgical operation. A large splinter had pierced the palm of the child's hand, and his father feared it might cause lockjaw.

"Now, my little man," said Dr. Kenyon, "be brave, and we shall have it out in a second."

Little Doctor turned her eyes to the boy's pale face and quivering lips; and, at once, with womanly tact, set herself to entertaining the little patient. She told him of her dog's amusing tricks, of her cat's pretty pranks, and, in a burst of confidence, even related her attempt to drown Suzette because she had scratched her; but seeing a faint look of pity in the boy's eyes, she turned up the little sleeve, and said, with pouting lips, "See! what the vicious thing did."

The splinter was out almost before Hartley knew it, and he looked on with interest at Little Doctor unwinding a strip of linen from a roll of bandages, which she handed her father just as he raised his eyes to take it.

Mr. Ward laid his hand on the bright curly head, and said, "Why my dear, you are a real little doctor."

The child looked up quickly; "Little Doctor is my name, you know, Mr. Ward.

"Ah, is that so! You certainly merit the name, my little one."

"My mother calls me Victoria, but I like Little Doctor the best. Mammy gave me that name because I look like my father."

Victoria now hastened out, and in a few minutes returned with Dolly carrying the coffee urn on a waiter with a plate of dainty waffles and maple syrup. Breakfast was over at Beechwood, but the thoughtful child soon prompted the cook to prepare the refreshments for her guests in the office.

She spread a snowy napkin on the study table, where Dolly placed the waiter; and our little hostess proceeded to serve the coffee, while Dolly stood behind her chair. Mr. Ward and Hartley enjoyed the coffee very much, for they had left home before breakfast.

When they left the office, Victoria gave Hartley the violets she had gathered, telling him, "I love violets next to Wiley;" as they drove off, Mr. Ward and his son thought they had never seen so charming a little girl.

CHAPTER VII

Little Doctor had long wanted a case of medicines of her very own; but her father had not thought it wise to place drugs in such youthful hands; though he noted with satisfaction how cautious she was in the use of the innocent little remedies and small knife and tweezers he allowed her to handle.

All the black children went to Little Doctor with almost as much confidence as they did to "Marse Vic" himself; from a splinter to a stubbed toe, they carried all their slight wounds to her. And now she was about to have a real medicine case; but it was yet a profound secret, as it was to be a surprise on her seventh birthday.

Just after breakfast, on the happy day, her father told her he wished her to accompany him to the big city to help him in shopping. This was always a rare treat for our little girl, and she bounded away in joyful anticipation to get ready for the trip. She particularly enjoyed sitting in the carriage on the ferry-boat, watching the water rushing by; but this time her mind was too much occupied with the object of her visit to the city to heed other attractions.

They drove to Ashton street and stopped at a large dingy-looking building. Victoria was surprised at the appearance of the building, for she had in her mind the brilliant show-windows on Emery street. She followed her father up the steps of a hallway, into what seemed like a work-room. A smiling little, withered old man came forward and spoke to her father, and turning to her said, "Is this the 'Little Doctor?'"

Dr. Kenyon introduced Victoria, who began to wonder what it all meant; but a glad light soon shone in her eyes when she saw Mr. Smith take from a drawer a beautiful brown Russian leather case, and proceed to open it before her father. In its pink satin lining lay some shining instruments.

Victoria could control her curosity no longer; "O, father! who is it for?"

"It is for my Little Doctor, if she likes it."

"O, father, is it really mine! I am so glad, I can scarcely believe it. See! the dear little knife and the beautiful scissors," eagerly examining the contents.

Little Doctor readily excused the dingy stair-way, when she knew she had been in the work-shop of a very superior case-maker, where her father always dealt.

They next went to a famous drug store, where the entrance was fine enough to satisfy the beauty-loving little girl. There they spent an hour fitting out the new case with the necessary drugs—a tiny bottle of ammonia, another of camphor, another of glycerine; and then Little Doctor told the clerk to be sure and put·in a bottle of turpentine, as she needed that more than anything. Of course some olive-oil and a bottle of rose-water, the latter for her own use.

When the case was filled, and Victoria had clasped it with her own hands and tucked it away in the carriage at the door, they turned their steps to another brilliant show-window. This was a jewelry store; but they only stopped long enough for Ben to go in and bring out a parcel in his hand. Her father put it into his pocket, saying it was her mother's purchase. Victoria was willing to wait awhile, for she knew it was something for herself.

On their way home, Little Doctor held her precious case clasped in her hands, while she told her father what remedies she had used on Wiley's foot when he caught it in the coon-trap that Paris had carelessly left too near Wiley's haunts.

When she reached home, she rushed to her mother's room to tell her of the medical case—just as if Mrs. Kenyon did not know all about it. After it had been duly examined and admired, Mrs. Kenyon said, "Now, I have something to show my little daughter," and opening the parcel that Ben brought from the jeweler's, she put a pretty case into the little hand. Victoria unclasped it with ready fingers, and found a tiny gold watch of exquisite workmanship, with a long dainty chain attached, nestling on a cushon of white satin.

"O, mother, what a lovely watch!" exclaimed Victoria, and she threw her arms round her mother's neck, kissing her ardently. "It was just the one thing more I wanted to make me perfectly happy. I must show it to Mammy," and she rushed off to the kitchen where Mammy was in the midst of her family. All gathered round to see the new watch; then Victoria took the precious gift and hung the chain round Mammy's neck, tucking the watch in her belt, and standing off to see the effect. Of course, then, each one must try it on, with as much pride as if it were her very own, unconscious that each mouth displayed sets of white ivory far more precious than the bit of gold and jewels. Mammy looked on with admiration at the effect, though she said "Yo'uns no mo' fitten to war a gold watch den a peag."

Little Doctor soon had an opportunity of putting her medical-box into practical use. Hayden was her first patient. He was jumping from a wood-pile, and struck a piece of board with a nail driven through it, the nail entering the sole of his foot. His frantic shrieks soon brought Mammy, who pulled the nail out by aid of the board attached to it; she then sent Dolly for Little Doctor.

Victoria took the new case and a small roll of bandages, and telling Dolly to bring a foot-tub of hot water, she hurried away to her patient. The first thing, she ordered the foot to be put into the hot water to cleanse it and sooth the pain. Then she saturated a bit of cotton with turpentine, and bound it on the wound, managing the bandage "Jes as well as Marse Vic," as Mammy declared. "She is suttinly a bo'n doctor, like her pa, on'y Marse Vic nevah had sich a blazen temper as my po' little lamb;" and Mammy continued, with a solemn shake of her turbaned head, "an' dat all come fum dat ole comet, hit's gwine to git my young Missy in some trouble 'fo' she die."

Old superstitious Mammy, with all her good sound sense, and the warnings that her master had given her against discussing this absurd notion, could not refrain, now and then, from bringing up the subject, even in the presence of the child.

Victoria had overheard her mutterings, and understood more than Mammy was aware. "Mammy, what do you mean? I heard you say that once before—about the comet. Do you think a comet could hurt me?"

"No, honey; no, hit's jes some o' ole Mammy's foolishniss."

But the child was not satisfied with the explanation, and went directly to her father. She found him reading in his study, and going close to him, she laid her head on his arm, and raising her eyes to his face with a look of grave perplexity, "Father, how can a comet make one naughty? Mammy says the comet makes me have a naughty temper.

Dr. Kenyon's anger was thoroughly aroused. He had always been very indulgent with the negroes' harmless superstitions; he had heard them all his life, and they had made no more impression on his mind than Mammy's weird old cradle-songs; but he thought this a serious matter. He took the child on his knee and explained in simple words the nature of a comet, and how foolish it was of Mammy to imagine that the comet could have any influence over us.

Dr. Kenyon might have told the little one that there was an ancient legend that ascribed a very different influence to the comet, that of foretelling great distinction to one so fortunate as to be born under its sway; but he would not have his child's mind filled with any legends, or "sayings," until she was old enough to understand that they were no better than fables.

He now sent Victoria to her mother, and rang the bell for Paris. When he put his woolly head in at the door, his master told him to send Mammy to him.

Mammy came in with a very demure face, for she knew she had done wrong in expressing her old traditional notions before the child. Her master gave her the most severe reproof she had ever heard from his lips. At the close of the lecture, poor old Mammy went down on her knees and vowed, " 'Fo' Laud" she would never mention the subject again to any one.

When Victoria returned to her father, he sent her to the music room for his violin, and as he tuned it, he said, "What shall I play for my little girl?"

She thought for a moment, then gleefully answered, "O, I should like 'Fisher's Hornpipe,' Percy has been

teaching me that pretty dance," and the small hands
went into position and she stood ready to begin.

It was Doctor Kenyon's custom to entertain his child
when he knew any sadness or trouble had distressed her,
as he knew the power of music on her sensitive nature.

Dr. Kenyon's birthday was also the birthday of his
country—the Fourth of July. Victoria was preparing
a surprise for her father in the way of a gift. It was a
piece of her own handiwork—a tiny pin-cushion of pale
blue satin, embroidered with pink daisies. She had just
acquired this accomplishment, and the first completed
work was done on the cushion for her "dear father."

She finished it the evening before the Fourth and
placed it in a pretty little box with a landscape on the
lid. When she went to bed, she had Mammy put it under her pillow that she might see it the first thing in the
morning, and carry it to her father before he left his
room. But morning brought a disappointment; Dr.
Kenyon had been called away in the night and had not
returned.

Luncheon hour came, and she had not yet seen her
father. Her mother told her she had a note from her
father saying he was so busy in his city office that he
would not be home until dinner time.

The little girl bore her disappointment very sweetly,
and was patient and lovely all day, and was now rewarded by hearing the wheels of his phaeton on the gravel at
the door. Dr. Kenyon hurried into his study; he had
just been called again to a patient who was alarmingly
ill.

Victoria followed her father, with the precious little
cushion in its box. He was at his desk preparing some
powders in tiny papers; but put his arm round his
daughter and kissed her affectionately.

Standing with her hands behind her, "Father," she said, "guess what I have for you!"

He smiled at her, but went on folding the powders in the bits of paper, saying, "I think it is a flower for my button-hole."

"No, guess again."

Her father was very weary and preoccupied; she saw this, and laying the box before him, she stood waiting for him to take off the cover, her face beaming with delight. Unfortunately, he did not understand, and supposing the box was the gift, he took it up and admired the picture on the lid, kissed his thanks, and laid the box on the table.

This was too much for poor Little Doctor to bear. Some children will say, "Why did she not open the box?" But our heroine was a proud little girl, and very impulsive, as you all must know by this time. She thought a slight had been offered the treasure inside, and catching up the box she tore off the lid, seized the dainty cushion, and rushed from the room. Her father looked after her in surprise, though he had not yet seen the intended gift. He was too hurried to inquire into the matter, and left the house again at once.

Judy, in the kitchen, was startled at seeing little "Missy" all dressed in a lovely white embroidered mull, with pink sash and pink slippers, dash into the quarters and throw something into a pan of gravy that was on the table.

"Why, honey, what' is yo' doin', yo'll git yo' close all spiled sho?"

But "honey" was already gone, only the white skirts and a pink streak of sash were seen, as the little one fled around the corner. On she sped through the orchard, into the meadows, and on, to the blackberry hedge that

skirted the woods. Anger, humilated pride, and wounded feelings, all contending in the swelling heart.

Here she threw herself down exhausted. The blackberry bushes concealed her from sight, and she sat crying softly, the little bosom heaving with emotion. She
was too tired to think; and after awhile the golden head
drooped against the bushes. She had fallen to sleep.

A bird fluttering among the leaves over her head awoke
her. It was an anxious mother-bird looking at her nest
of young ones, which she thought perilously near the intruder.

Victoria opened her eyes wide with pleased
curiosity, and saw the nest so near that the nestlings
could have pecked at the rosy lips, which smiled at their
eager cries for their mother. She softly drew aside, that
she might not alarm them, but kept them still in view.

Very soon she recalled the cause of her being alone in
this lonely spot. A great sigh came from the weary
heart as she looked around. The anger was all gone;
she began to think she had been very naughty; she recalled her father's dear sad face as he looked at her in
surprise when she fled from his presence. Then it
came to her mind that maybe he did not know the cushion was inside the box; and all at once, it seemed very
clear that she had made a mistake. She longed to throw
herself into his arms, and tell him how sorry she was.

She got up and looked around, as if to hurry home; but
it was all strange to her, she did not know which way
she had come. A gay butterfly alighted on the puff of
her sleeve, and she watched it without moving; when it
flew away, she followed its flight with eager eyes.

"O, pretty butterfly! if you could only tell my dear
father where his little girl is, and that she is so unhappy!"

She saw some soft green moss a little further under the bushes, and creeping closer lay her flushed cheek on the cool green pillow, and soon was in the sound sleep of tired childhood.

Company had been invited for dinner; and when Percy, who was one of the guests, came, he inquired for Victoria. Mammy was called, but she knew nothing of her; she had been busy assisting the ladies in removing their bonnets as they entered, and thought her little charge was in the parlor. She now went in search of her.

Gip and Dolly had not seen her, but Judy told of the scene in the kitchen, and how she had fled towards the orchard. The servants did not dare tell their mistress that they had allowed the child to wander away; and she was entertaining her guests in happy ignorance.

Mammy, Gip, and Dolly set out to look for her. The dinner was delayed on Dr. Kenyon's account, so the absence of the servants was not noticed by their mistress. Wiley, the dog, followed them, seeming to understand their mission, and darted off ahead of the party, until he reached the blackberry hedge; there he stopped, smelling along the ground, then suddenly turning, he ran back to Mammy, looking up into her face and wagging his tail. Again he set off towards the hedge. This time Mammy followed, wailing as she went, "My po' lamb lost in de woods, an' night comin' on." The sun was yet two hours high, but Mammy always imagined the worst.

The dog disappeared for a moment, and then Mammy heard a piteous cry, "O, Mammy! Mammy! come to me, I'm lost."

The old woman ceased her wail, and hurrying to the spot whence the sound came, she called, "Wha is yo', my own little lost lamb? Mammy is huntin' fo' yo'."

Victoria crept out of the hedge, Wiley following her; Mammy rushed to her, and clasping the little figure in her arms, wept and laughed together. Gip and Dolly were called and they all set out homeward.

Before they reached the house, they met Dr. Kenyon. On his return from his visit to the patient, he missed his little daughter, and finding none of the servants in the house, he went to the kitchen, where Judy soon told him that Victoria was missing, and that Mammy had gone after her. As he was turning away, Judy thought of the pin-cushion, and running after him with it in her hand, she told him of the scene in the kitchen; how "Little Missy" had rushed in, throwing the pretty thing into a pan of gravy, and running off.

The Doctor took the poor little cushion, and a new light broke over his face. He recalled the empty box on the floor, after the child had left his study. As the facts became plain to him, he laughed in spite of his anxiety; but there was a pathetic catch in his voice. Putting the cushion in his pocket, he hurried away to meet the searchers returning with the stray lamb.

He took the child from Mammy's arms, and pressed the little form to his breast. Victoria clung to him, whispering, "Father, you didn't know the cushion was in the box, did you?"

"No, darling, I did not think of looking into the box; but then, we men are so stupid, you know. I have the little cushion now, and will never part with it."

In the meantime, the news that Victoria was missing had reached the parlor; but before Mrs. Kenyon was much alarmed, the Doctor made his appearance carrying her in his arms.

Mammy took her to her room to change her dress, and then went down and quietly asked if Little Doctor would be allowed to come to the table. She was granted permission, as Percy would have been very lonely without his little friend by his side.

No allusion was made to the anxiety she had caused, but Victoria knew that she had been very naughty and deserved to be punished. Percy did not find her as cheerful a companion as usual. When dinner was over, she caught her mother's hand and drew her aside, saying, "Please, dear mother, forgive me for being so naughty."

Her mother always pardoned her so very freely, that she was soon her bright self again, and she and Percy waved their beautiful new flags, and joined in our National airs to their heart's content. The last air sung was, "My Country 'tis of Thee, Sweet Land of Liberty." Our tired Little Doctor's eyes closed, the curly head dropped, and she softly slid from her chair to the carpet saying, "My Country—." Her father quickly picked her up amidst sympathetic voices, and carried her off to Mammy.

Little Doctor had inherited love of country. Both father and mother were patriotic, and her great grandparents on both sides had led in the fight for liberty. When very small, she used to say, with much delight, "I am going to the Fourth of July."

CHAPTER VIII.

The Kenyons had been making their annual visit to Virginia, when their return was somewhat hastened by the sudden decision to send Victoria to school. She had for some years been under the instruction of her mother, but Dr. and Mrs. Kenyon had long been considering the different systems of education, with a view to their daughter's instruction; and had now decided that the public school system afforded the best aid in carrying out their plans to fit their child for a useful life.

She was strong and vigorous in mind and body, with a decided inclination to put into practice whatever she learned. Her parents were much gratified at this trait of Victoria's; and in order to develop and discipline her character they considered it necessary to bring her in contact with the different classes of society, while she was young enough to sympathize with them; and to come in touch with their real life as children.

They had a powerful opposition from their relatives in Virginia, who cherished the old aristocratic idea that a girl's education should be conducted through boarding schools and private masters.

Dr. and Mrs. Kenyon were in perfect harmony in the subject, and the discussion of the matter while away had only strengthened their resolve to place Victoria in the public school of the city nearest Beechwood.

The first morning in October found our little heroine starting out for her training. She was a brave child; but was yet unacquainted with the rougher side of

children's lives. This Monday moring she was up very
early, full of interest and curiosity to begin her school
days.

Dolly, her own maid, was to accompany her—Victoria
would scarcely have known herself without Dolly. She
was seven years older than her young mistress and was
devotedly attached to her. Mrs. Kenyon had given
Dolly strict injunctions as to her care over Victoria, and
Dolly was as delighted, in her way, as Victoria herself.

All the servants—Mammy, Gip, Judy, Chloe, Paris, and
Hayden—assembled on the lawn to see "Marse an'
Mistis" take the "baby" of the house to school.

Mammy had prepared a delicious little luncheon and
stowed it into a small basket which Dolly carried on
her arm. The new books were put into the carriage, and
finally the family appeared, and all took their seats; Victoria between her father and mother, and Dolly on the
front seat in charge of the books and luncheon.

As the carriage drove off, Paris shouted, "Three
cheers for our Little Doctor going to school!" The
cheerful voices responded in a long hurrah!

The school-house was a large building of brick surrounded by an extensive play-ground; and as the
chestnut horses from Beechwood drew up before the
gate, the school children gathered round to see the
new-comer; and surely our little girl, in a fresh
gingham dress and a dainty white sun bonnet, was a
pretty enough sight to reward them. The violet blue
eyes looked eagerly from one to another, and at last a
nod and a smile greeted some familiar little face.

Mr. Ray, the Principal, met them at the door, and Dr.
Kenyon introduced his wife and daughter. A charming
young lady stood near, her brown eyes beaming with
pleasure on the bright little girl who was to be her pupil.

Mr. Ray introduced Miss Sloan, and she came forward and took the child's hand in hers, while she joined in the conversation in regard to Victoria's advancement. A great bell now sounded that made the new pupil start, at which Miss Sloan smiled and pressed the little hand.

Her parents kissed her good-bye, and her teacher led her into a great room, and gave her a nice new desk. Dolly was allowed a chair in the hall where she could see "Little Missy." Mrs. Kenyon had thoughtfully provided a picture book for Dolly, but the living picture inside the school-room was enough to entertain her for the present. Victoria was shown the places in the new books, and followed the classes in their recitations. But she was not required to recite this first day.

The noon recess came, and all who did not go home proceeded to prepare their luncheon spreading it out on their desks without much formality. Dolly, who did not fancy this democratic way of eating, stood with the basket in her hands undecided how to serve her young Mistress' luncheon. Miss Sloan seeing her hesitation said, "Come with me, Victoria," and led the way to a small room adjoining the recitation room. It was neatly furnished, and at a window a table was set with a snowy cloth, where the teacher's luncheon was served. She invited Victoria to join her at the table.

Dolly grinned with satisfaction at this conventional observance for her young Mistress. She set out the good things Mammy had prepared, and with ready, practiced hands served them both. Mammy had included a bottle of fresh milk, and Victoria was delighted that her teacher enjoyed it. Miss Sloan kindly told the child that she should expect her always to take luncheon with her.

Victoria went out to the play-ground and found the

cheerful, animated scene before her very amusing, and looked on with lively interest; but after awhile she began to feel lonely, as she was not asked to join the games, and but for Dolly's presence, she would have broken down and wept.

Presently, two girls left their companions, and approached Victoria. After examining her clothing, one said, "Why do you come to a free school? I should think your folks were rich enough to send you to a select school."

This impolite address may seem very strange to the public school children of this day, who are accustomed to all the refined privileges of first-class education; but in those days there was a foolish prejudice in favor of boarding-schools and private instruction; and the more ignorant class of people imagined that because the schools were supported by taxes they were therefore not fit for the rich. As we have seen, Dr. and Mrs. Kenyon were quite independent of that common notion, and had full confidence in the advantages of a popular education; but their daughter had never heard of this question of social distinction; and did not know how to reply to the girl's rude remark, who continued, "Say, why do you bring that nigger with you? I think it looks stuck up."

Dolly now thought it time to interfere, and stepping between her young mistress and the girl, who was taller than Dolly herself, she whispered, "Missy, yo' mus'n't min' what dat gal say, she no quality folks nohow."

Victoria turned without a word toward the school house; Dolly followed, casting a frown at the offenders which she intended as a severe reproof. The girls returned to their companions, laughing derisively at Dolly's resentment, and sending a parting insult after

Victoria, "Look at the black cloud behind you!"

Victoria went to a side entrance to escape the taunts of the thoughtless pupils; but there on the steps came upon another girl, and was about to retreat, fearing another attack. The girl was holding her head down and her hand to her face, while blood trickled through her fingers. Little Doctor's sympathy was quickly aroused, and going close to the girl, she knelt at her side, saying, "What is the matter? Can I do anything for you?"

"Don't you see my nose is bleeding?" the girl answered in a fretful tone; but Little Doctor took no notice of the manner, and simply said "I think I can stop the bleeding, if you will let me." The girl, looking up for the first time, said, "O you are the new girl! Yes, you may do anything you please—if you can only stop it before school takes in."

Victoria sent Dolly for a napkin, a piece of paper, and some water, and folding the napkin she wet it, and gently turning down the girl's collar she laid the cool folds on the back of her neck; then taking a bit of white tissue paper, she made a small plug and placed it in the bleeding nostril. The bleeding ceased almost immediately.

The patient looked at Victoria with surprise, saying, "Why, you are as good as a doctor! Where did you learn to do such things?"

"My father is a doctor," said Victoria, "and I hope to be one some day."

The girl, Sallie Sprigg, caught Little Doctor's hand, and pressed it cordially, "Well, you are the nicest and the smartest girl in this school, and I will always take your part. There are some pretty mean girls and rough boys here, but I am one of the big girls you see, and they don't trouble me; you will find it to your advantage to have me for a friend, little girl. Now, tell me your name,

before all those children come," she said, as a crowd of
girls were seen approaching.

"My name is Victoria Kenyon, but I am more used to
the name Little Doctor—that is what Mammy calls me."

"And that is what I am going to call you," said Sallie.
"So now good-bye, Little Doctor, with many thanks for
your skill," and with a smile, the "big girl" disappeared
through the door-way.

Our poor little one was very weary before the great
bell rang for four o'clock. She heard some of the girls
who sat near her whispering about her; and although
she did not understand what it all meant, she knew they
were not friendly words. Her longing eyes were often
turned to the door to see Dolly's dear face. It had never
looked so familiar and home-like, and it took all the
brave little girl's courage to keep back the tears when
she thought of home.

The welcome sound of the bell came at last, and the
children formed in procession to move down the great
stairway. Dolly stationed herself in a nook in the hall,
where she could see her little charge as the procession
passed along. At sight of the child, the round black face
broke into a smile that would have redeemed much
coarser features than faithful Dolly's. She rushed forward and took Victoria's hand, but the monitor rebuked
this informality. Dolly was not to be restrained now,
and with the saucy retort, "Yo' is not my mistis, an' I's
gwine to take keer of my little Missy," she marched at
Victoria's side.

The carriage from Beechwood stood at the gate, and
Dr. Kenyon was waiting for his darling. As soon as
Victoria saw him she rushed into his arms, and gave way
to the tears she had so bravely kept back. He lifted her
into the carriage, where her mother was waiting to com-

fort her. She knew it had been a hard day for her child, and she could not wait for the home-coming to have her little one in her arms.

The school children looked after the receding carriage, and one asked, "What is the matter with that little girl, did she get hurt?"

Yes, she was hurt, but they did not know that it was their thoughtless, unkind treatment that had wounded the tender heart of the "new girl."

Mammy, and her children and grand-children, were gathered at the gate to welcome Little Doctor home. It had been a dreary day for Mammy, too. She caught her "baby" in her loving arms, while Gip and Judy and Paris all gathered round looking at their young mistress as if they expected to see some great change wrought by this first day at school.

Hayden took a practical view of the situation. His solemn face showed none of the hilarity of the others. Coming forward, his fat hands folded on his back, and deliberately looking at the tear-stained face on Mammy's bosom, he asked, "Missy, did you get a whoppin' terday?"

They all laughed at Hayden's pertinent question; even Little Doctor herself, who answered, "No, Hayden, I was not punished at all, but I did not find it very—cheerful at school."

In spite of her first unhappy day at school, Victoria was of too courageous a nature to yield to the weakness that Mammy would have encouraged; so, with the tender but firm support of her parents, she bravely persevered, and before the week was ended she had become acquainted with many of the girls, and was feeling very much at home among them.

Mammy had learned through their familiar talks at

night that Little Doctor had not once given way to temper, which was a source of much comfort to the old woman. She had never had much respect for schools—a
governess was her idea of a proper instructor for a young
lady; but she began now to think that schools might be
of some use after all, as Missy was certainly improving
in point of temper. Mammy had yet to learn that human
nature does not change all at once, so Little Doctor's
first outbreak of temper at school was quite a shock to
too sanguine Mammy. It came at the close of the second week.

Friday afternoon, as Victoria was entering a door at
the head of a flight of outside steps in the rear of the
school-house, a large girl rushed past her, heedlessly
striking her with such force that she lost her balance and
fell to the floor. She was not really hurt, and would not
have resented an accident, had not the rude girl, as she
ran down the steps, called back to the victim of her carelessness, "Pick yourself up, Queen!"

Victoria made no delay in picking herself up and—
seeking vengeance. She looked back and saw the girl
seated at the bottom of the steps sharpening her slate
pencil on the stone. The first thing that caught her infuriated eyes was a bucket full of water on a table in the
hall. She seized it with both determined hands, carried
it to the door, and turned the contents on the unsuspect-
ing girl at the foot of the steps. She was completely
drenched. Dripping from head to foot, she scampered
up the steps with wrath in her eyes.

Dolly, who was never far from her mistress, placed
herself before Victoria, saying, "Run, honey, fas' ez yo'
can to de teacher, she looks like she gwine to kill yo'!"
But Victoria stood her ground, looking every inch the
"Queen" that the girl had called her. The wrath sudden-

ly died out of the girl's eyes as she looked into the face of the insulted child. She hesitated a moment, and then turned and walked away, the water dripping to the floor as she went; but before she had gone many steps Victoria was at her side.

"I am very sorry for what I have done, Jennie, I was so angry, I did not think it would make you so wretched. What can I do?

"I don't think you can do anything. I would not mind it much, but you have ruined my new dress; yet, I must be honest enough to tell you I deserved it, though I didn't intend to trip you up."

This generous admission on the part of Jennie Bell was like coals of fire on the head of poor impulsive Little Doctor. She caught up the skirt of the dress and tried to wring the water from its folds. "O, what shall I do!" she exclaimel in real distress; then, suddenly, "You must let me drive you home. The carriage is at the gate, I saw it just this moment."

The children were gathering round the scene, one of them had informed a teacher who came into the hall, and seeing Jennie's condition, told her she must go home at once and change her clothing. Jennie shivered slightly, which Little Doctor took for a sign of a chill, and hurried her out and into the carriage without delay. Dolly followed, bringing Victoria's cloak. At sight of it, she exclaimed, "O, Dolly, that is just what I want! Here Jennie, let me put this around you," and she folded it about the girl's shoulders. Dolly turned the white of her eyes up at her mistress, in evident disapproval of the pretty silk-lined wrap being put to that use.

Paris was on the box with his father and at the appearance of such an unusual occupant of the carriage, he tittered audibly. Ben, who was propriety personified, pinched Paris' arm to reduce him to order, but Paris persisted in whispering, loud enough to be heard inside, "She jes looks like she been swimmin' in de ribber."

When they reached Jennie's home Victoria told Paris to ring the door-bell, and she got out herself and went with Jennie to meet her mother, who was already on the steps with an anxious face. Victoria hurried to her, "Mrs. Bell, do not be alarmed, Jennie is not ill, she is only wet—I did it, and am so sorry." This was said with a sweet, pleading voice that few could resist.

Jennie passed her anxious mother without a word, who looked after her daughter a moment, and then turned to the child, with, "How did it happen, Miss?"

Victoria hesitated now, but Dolly was not so scrupulous, "Scuse me mistis, I's saw de whole row. Miss Jennie knocked my Missy down on de hard stone steps, den she say, 'pick yo' se'f up, queen," den Missy got up, an' lookin' 'roun' wid her eyes jes ablazen, an' when she seed de bucket ob watah, she jes grab it up an' frode it all over Miss Jennie; den she tole her she mus' done go home in de ka-age, 'cause she gwine to hab a chill."

Mrs. Bell told Victoria she thought she was excusable, but she said it with a weary, sad voice, that left Little Doctor no room to excuse herself. She went home with a heavy heart. She was old enough now to feel the conflict in her nature between the violent temper and the tender conscience that had been cultivated with such care by her parents. She related all the circumstances to her mother as soon as she reached home, and got the usual comfort from the tender, wise, patient parent.

Dolly entertained the servants, at the same time, with an account, much exaggerated and embellished now that she was talking to her own people.

Victoria's first morning at Sunday-school was one of

unmarred pleasure. Percy Tyler had been attending the
Sunday-school of St. Paul's Church for some time, and
was highly delighted with it and asked his little companion to go with him. He came over to Beechwood to
join Victoria, that they might go together. He rode a
fine spirited horse—one his father had just given him—
and he was evidently quite vain of his ability to manage
his prancing steed before the admiring eyes of his little
friend, as he rode at the side of the carriage on their way
to town. Dr. Kenyon accompanied his daughter this
first morning, and he too admired the graceful youth as
he reined in his horse occasionally to speak to them at
the carriage door.

Mammy, with her grand-children, was coming behind,
that she might be early at church herself, as well as to
see that the children behaved themselves in the class,
especially her black children. She drove a big grey horse,
in a light spring wagon with bright red wheels. This
turn-out was her own special property which her master
had given to her when he first brought her to Kentucky.
She would never allow any one else to drive it; and on a
Sunday morning she delighted in filling it with her well-
dressed family, she always driving and sitting upright on
the front seat and holding the reins on a level with her
chest. Old Mammy dearly loved authority, and would
never permit any of her own color to drive a horse if she
had to sit behind it.

The Sunday-school had not opened when the Beechwood party reached the church. Percy and Victoria
knew many of the children standing round the door, and
joined in the low-toned conversation. Presently, Victoria heard Paris' high-pitched voice, and a laugh following. She and Percy went near. A crowd of boys was
surrounding the fun-loving Paris, trying to tempt him to

perform some of his athletic tricks.

"Come, monkey! get out there, and give us some circus," said one; "Sambo, show us how you put your feet round your neck," said another; "O, he can't do that trick with shoes on," cried a third, but Paris resisted all challenges,—he stood with his back against the wall.

"No. I's got mo' 'ligion 'an to cut up at de church do'."

This very just reproof failed to restrain the boys' merriment until Victoria came forward, with Percy at her side. The boys instantly withdrew, leaving Paris master of the situation.

The pastor, superintendent, and children all gave our little one a cordial welcome. She was pleased to find herself placed in the class of Miss Wallace, a friend of her mother; also to be seated by a young friend of her own, Virginia Wallace, a child of Victoria's age, and the sister of their teacher.

As Victoria's sweet voice rose in the hymns, her face was radiant with happiness, and brought forth a sympathetic look from her teacher, who was in harmony with the music—and delighted with her new pupil.

CHAPTER IX.

Four years had passed in Victoria's school life—years of diligent, persistent study and rapid progress; and in this advancement, the old love for her father's calling had increased and become an earnest desire to adopt it as a profession.

Her first day at school, when she promptly stopped the bleeding nose, had given the children a good opinion of her skill that they had never changed.

And now, after these four years, during a morning session, the children were all assembled in their places, and Victoria absorbed in a difficult problem, when her teacher, Miss Conrad, requested her to step to the desk.

"Victoria, Mr. Ray has sent for you. One of the girls in his room is suffering with her eye. She thinks something is in it, and wishes you to relieve her."

Victoria readily consented to go, and taking a teaspoon from her lunch-basket, hastened to the sufferer. Mr. Ray met her at the door of his room, saying, with an incredulous little smile. "Victoria, your services are required in the capacity of doctor; will you be kind enough to look at Julia's eye? She will not allow me to examine it, but believes you can relieve it.

Our Little Doctor gave a modest smile in return and went to the young girl, who was holding both hands over her face. Victoria drew her head down into a position to get the light from the window, then taking the spoon, laid the handle on the upper lid, caught the lash, and gently turned the lid back over the handle. There on the

inside of the eye-lid lay a bit of sharp coal. Victoria
had given her handkerchief to Mr. Ray, who twisted the
corner into a point and now returned it. Victoria deftly
touched the surface of the lid and removed the object,
"without the slightest pain" Julia said.

Mr. Ray's smile was now one of genuine admiration.
It was, after all, a small exhibition of skill, but as no one
else had thought of the remedy, our Little Doctor became the heroine of the hour. A buzz of voices greeted
her ears, and she found herself the center of a crowd of
girls and boys all eager to show respect to one who,
even in so small a way, had distinguished herself among
them.

"I am not surprised, Little Doctor," said Mr. Ray,
"that you have won the confidence of your friends. You
certainly show a great deal of skill for so young a prac-
titioner. We are all much indebted to you."

Victoria returned to her desk, after informing her
teacher that Julia's eye was entirely relieved. At recess,
the subject of conversation with the pupils was our Little Doctor's practice among her friends and the servants
at home.

The Saturday following this incident in the school-
room, Victoria was taking her accustomed horseback
ride, Ben, as usual, acting as her groom. She was returning from a delightful canter on the river road. Ben's less
spirited horse had fallen back a little, and turning her
head to look for him, Victoria caught sight of a boy
scrambling up the bank from the river, waving his hand
as if to attract her attention. She drew up her horse and
waited. He came running almost breathless and dripping wet, shouting excitedly, "Boy drowned down there
—want a doctor—lend me your horse." With one hasty
glance behind her, to see if Ben was in sight, Victoria

dashed down a steep declivity to the river. Ben coming up and seeing his young mistress' perilous downward rush, followed in wild alarm.

Victoria was directed to the spot by seeing another boy standing over a motionless figure on the sand. She sprang from her horse, tore off her gauntlets, and seizing the limp body, she turned it over, face downward, putting one arm of the child under his face.

"Bring me that piece of drift-wood; no—the big piece, quick!"

The boy brought the log, and she raised the drowned child in her arms, and laid him across the log, gently, but firmly, rolling him on it to force the water from his mouth.

"Take my horse," she said to the boy, "run to Beechwood, and tell Mammy to bring the carriage, with blankets and hot bricks." She hesitated a moment—"Tell her to get the bricks from her fire-place, and to come as soon as she can, that Little Doctor wants them."

By this time, Ben had reached the scene. At a sign from his mistress, he took hold of the body and continued the rolling, while Victoria wiped from the mouth the sand and water forced from the lungs by this prompt action.

"Now, Ben, turn him over on his back," she said with quiet decision. Ben removed the log, and stretched the little figure on the sand. Meanwhile she took from her belt a small vinaigrette containing salts of ammonia,— "Hold this to his nostrils," she bade him; and catching the limp hands and raising them above the head, she proceeded to move them gently up and down; holding them above his head a second, then pressing the arms firmly against the side of the body, with a regular, persistent motion. Ben offered to take her place, but she shook her head and continued the motion, watching the pallid face with anxious eyes.

At length she was rewarded by a slight quiver of the pale lips, a little sigh,—and the feeble breathing was restored. Our Little Doctor's eyes brimmed over with grateful tears, as she nodded to Ben to remove the salts from the nostrils.

The carriage was just coming in sight, Paris driving and the two boys showing the way, and Mammy inside with a bundle of blankets, which she was thoughtful enough to wrap round the hot bricks. Victoria directed Ben to remove the child's wet coat, wrap him in the warm blankets, and place him in the carriage; she and Mammy taking their seats opposite. Ben drove, and Paris took charge of Victoria's horse.

Victoria rubbed the little brown hands, and Mammy applied hers to the cold feet most vigorously. Presently, the child raised his weary eyes to the sweet face before him, and tried to smile. "How do you feel, little boy?" she said, with emotion in her voice.

"I feel so good, but who are you?"

"O, I'm your doctor," she answered laughing—"and you must do just as I tell you."

They drove into town, along a back street, to a humble little cottage. The two boys had sped on before, on Ben's horse, to tell the news, and the poor mother was at the gate when the carriage drove up. Ben jumped from his seat and opened the carriage door, and Victoria stepped out as the mother came anxiously forward.

"Mrs. Blake, your little boy fell from a raft into the river—but see!" and she stood aside, "he is quite recovered now."

Ben was ready to carry the boy into the house, but the mother had him in her arms, crying excitedly over her child. The two boys had given a full account of their companion's danger, and how the young lady had restored him to life.

Victoria followed her into the house, and gave some suggestions as to the care of her patient; that he must be kept warm, and friction to his feet kept up. The poor woman glanced at the soft blankets round the child, and Victoria understood the look. "Please keep the blankets, Mrs. Blake, he will need them to-night.",

"O, I can't thank you enough, Miss Kenyon, for all you have done. Certainly the Lord sent you at that moment to save my child. I shall never forget your kindness."   ..

When Little Doctor reached home, she found her father and mother had just returned. They had been dining at the Tylers, and knew nothing of the drowning incident until Victoria came home with Mammy. She sought her father in the library, coming in with a face glowing with satisfaction.

"Father, I have something—" she stopped, for there stood Percy Tyler, whom she had supposed was at the University. He was paying a flying visit to his parents. He had arrived while the party was at dinner, and returned with Dr. Kenyon to see his former playmate. It was two years since they had seen each other, and time had made a change in the children who had parted so affectionately.

A tall, handsome youth came forward to meet the slender, beautiful girl of twelve years. The sweet bright face was suffused with pleasure, as she held out both hands to the dear friend of her childhood. Percy took the little hands, and pressed them close in his own, "Victoria, my little playmate, how you have grown!"

She glanced up at the tall figure, and with the old

childish arch look, "Well, Percy, I think you have made some progress in that way yourself."

"Ah, now I recognize Little Doctor," he said, laughing heartily. "I was almost afraid of the tall young lady who came in just now; but I see it is a riding habit you have on and not a young lady's dress—but, I interrupted your remarks to your father," and he started towards the door.

"No, no, sit down Percy. I was about to tell father of an adventure I had this afternoon, and if you will promise not to think me presumptuous, I will allow you to share it."

Percy sat down, promising to be very good indeed.

Victoria seated herself near her father, and holding his hand, told him how she saved the life of Billy. Blake. Her skill and success in her father's profession was the only thing that ever called forth anything like self-gratulation in Little Doctor.

Her father praised her prompt action, and the skill she had displayed in resuscitating the boy; saying he could have done nothing more had he been present. He was really surprised at the coolness and courage she had evidently shown in such an emergency.

Percy listened with much interest to her account of the incident, and playfully asked if she intended to confine her attention to small boys; he said he was almost tempted himself to take a tumble into the river, just to give her the pleasure of exercising her skill.

She answered that he might afford to risk the danger, as she remembered that he was an expert swimmer.

Victoria was quick to perceive a subtle change in her friend. He had not only acquired the ease and grace of manner that contact with the world of culture brings to a youth; but the five years difference in their ages was more marked, showing itself in some condescension to herself, which she was inclined to resent as an assumption of superiority. It amused Dr. Kenyon very much; his little girl was not yet familiar with the self-importance of a youth home from college.

Paris now made his appearance. "Marse Vic, des a white man out to de stable, wif a pretty young hoss. He say, will Marse please step out to de barn-yard."

Dr. Kenyon rose, with a pleased look at Victoria—"Come, my child, and you too, Percy. I have a little reward for my skillful little partner." They met Mrs. Kenyon in the hall, and all proceeded to the barn-yard, where they found a man holding the bridle on a handsome black horse, with graceful arched neck, small head, and slender, shapely limbs.

"O, you beautiful creature!" cried Little Doctor. At the sound of her voice, the intelligent animal turned a pair of soft gentle eyes towards her, and gave a low whinny, as if the voice were familiar to his ear.

They all laughed, and the man said, "Seems to be love at first sight."

"Well, my daughter," said Dr. Kenyon, "do you think he is a fair exchange for old Comet?"

"Father, I know you are jesting about Comet, but tell me, is this beauty really mine?"

"Yes, child, if you like him, he is yours. I think you may be safely trusted now with something a little more animated than the old nag you have been riding.

Victoria caught her father's hand with her childish impulsive grace, and kissed it affectionately, whispering, 'Father, dear, how can you know always just what I want?"

"Well, you know your mother is the keeper of my

memory as well as conscience, and I trust her to remind me of my duty."

Victoria patted the glossy, arched neck, and smoothed the straight nose, standing close to the beautiful spirited animal. Mrs. Kenyon was not a nervous woman, but she was a little suspicious of the swift, impetuous movements of the new horse, and warned Victoria to be on her guard.

"O, you need have no fear, Madam," said the man, who seemed to be as proud of his training as if the horse were his own. "I have been drilling him for weeks, even putting on a skirt when I went about him, so as to accustom him to a lady's attentions; and riding him with a side-saddle and long skirt."

Paris asked to mount him, and was sent in for one of Mammy's skirts. He came out with it on, trying to fasten the band round his own waist after doubling it. "Dis yer ban' will go roun' me two times," he said as he tugged at the skirt to fasten it on as an apron.

"Get inside of it, you monkey," said Percy, laughing, in which they all joined, as they saw the agile Paris drop the skirt to the ground and draw it up to his waist from below.

In the meantime, Victoria had whispered to her father, who stooped, and taking the slender foot in his hand, placed her in the saddle. Mrs. Kenyon looked anxious, but there was no prancing, no curveting; as swiftly and smoothly as a bird flies, the horse sped along the avenue to the orchard, then turned back again to the admiring spectators, coming to a halt without a perceptible jerk.

"O, this is delightful," exclaimed Victoria, as she sprang to the ground.

All talked at once, commenting on the splendid gait of the animal.

"What name will you give him, Victoria?" asked Percy.

"I hope he is already named," she said, turning to the man. "It gives him more individuality to have a name he knows."

"Yes, he has a name, and knows it too," said the attendant. "Carlisle is his name." The horse pricked up his ears and turned his proud head at the word.

Victoria repeated the name, saying, "I like that very much. Did you name him, father?"

"No, and you may call him what you please."

"No, indeed, I shall not change his pretty name."

"Mammy say hits bad luck to change de name," said Paris, with an ominous shake of the head; but no one heeded Paris' frequent quotations from Mammy.

Early next morning, Percy, mounted on Juno, was at the gates of Beechwood ready to escort Victoria on a horseback ride to town. It had all been arranged the evening before that the relative speed of Carlisle and Juno should be tested by this early canter into the city.

Percy was very proud of his beautiful companion. She wore a new habit of dark blue cloth; a velvet cap of the same color, with a puffed crown, and close band, fitting over her golden curls which fell in a shower to her waist. Gauntlets of chamois skin reached nearly to the elbow, and she carried the silver-mounted whip which Dr. Harris had given her on that eventful birthday, though Carlisle needed no whip to stimulate his speed.

Victoria returned in time for breakfast—Carlisle had won.

CHAPTER X.

One Saturday morning in October a school-boy friend of Victoria's, Lawrence Balfour, drove past the Kenyon place on his way to join Hartley Ward, who had invited him to a day's hunt in the neighborhood of Beechwood. Quail were plentiful in that locality, and the boys looked forward to full game bags.

Lawrence reached the front veranda of the Ward home just as Hartley came out, gun in hand, to look for his friend.

"What have you there?" said Hartley, as Lawrence threw aside the lap robe, a beautiful leopard skin, and jumped to the ground.

"That is worth its weight in gold," and he held the robe up to view. "See the head and face of the animal! Now you turn away, and I will give you a regular East India scare."

Hartley turned his back to his friend, who proceeded to adjust the head of the animal over his own laughing face. His hands and feet were soon covered with the paws, and the make-believe leopard seemed as real as any to be found in the jungles.

"Look!" came from the huge mouth, with its savage teeth.

Hartley was prepared to be startled, and for a moment a genuine fear seized him; the next he broke into a merry laugh and caught the extended paw, saying, "Howdy! glad to make your acquaintance. Say, Lawrence, where did you get him? Let me try it on."

After Lawrence had strutted round awhile, and given Hartley several uncomfortable hugs, he took off the robe and arranged it on Hartley, who rushed into the house, putting everybody to flight save the big house dog, who disputed the right of possession with the fierce intruder, and made a ferocious attack upon his disguised master. Lawrence came to the rescue, and held "Robin Hood" until Hartley escaped from the house, then followed him.

"You have not yet told me where you got this beauty?"

"Well, it has a history, and an interesting one too. My cousin, and name-sake, Lawrence Balfour of England, sent it to me. It arrived only last night. He is a soldier in India and killed this leopard just as he was about to dine on the Colonel of the regiment. He returned to England soon after, and was praised and toasted to his heart's content for his bravery. Even the queen made a lion of him."

"Or a leopard," suggested Hartley with a laugh.

"Well, come, let's off on our hunt. Did you bring plenty of bird shot—I find I am out?"

"Yes, enough to kill all the quail in the country."

"Bring your robe along," said Hartley, "We may have a chance for some fun if we meet any of the fellows out there.

Lawrence took his gun, and throwing the robe over his arm, they both started for the beech woods overlooking the Kenyon meadow-land and the creek winding its way across the country to the Ohio river.

The woods were filled with the pleasant voices of nature. The cooing doves, the piping robbins, and the low sweet mumur of insect life made the boys stop to listen, with a glance at each other of keen appreciation; and their eyes were charmed with the bright green and russet foliage overhead and in the undergrowth about them. A dropping nut, or a drifting leaf caused the boys to start, thinking game was near.

As they came out on the brow of a hill, leading down to a quiet shady lane on the outskirts of Beechwood, Lawrence suddenly stopped—"Ah! here is fun for my leopard. Look! Little Doctor and her black shadow coming up the lane this way."

Hartley looked and smiled as he saw the face of Victoria. She carried her white sun-bonnet in her hand, and swung a blue parasol in the other, and as she fluttered in and out of the deep foliage that bordered the lane, she sang in a sweet voice the tender song, "Annie Laurie."

Hartley took up the air and whistled it softly, watching his young friend and her maid as they pursued their way.

"Say, Lawrence, you are not really going to frighten Little Doctor, and her 'black shadow' as you call her?"

"Yes, I am," said Lawrence; and putting on the robe, he started down the hill through clumps of wild blackberry bushes, Hartley still warning him not to go. Then hearing the whir of a covey of quail, he turned off to get a shot.

Victoria approached, Chloe near her carrying a basket with a dainty napkin over the top. Lawrence noticed this as he peeped through the hedge, and said to himself, "Going to see some of her charity patients, I'll bet a dollar!"

Little Doctor turned to Chloe, "Did you bring my book, we must gather some ferns and forest leaves as we return?"

"Yes'm, hits in de basket."

A crash in the hedge, a ferocious growl, and the make-believe leopard bounded in front of the frightened girl. She shrieked in mortal terror, Chloe joining with frantic screams, which soon brought Hartley to their help. As he rushed down the hill he shouted, "Don't be frightened, it's only Lawrence Balfour."

Lawrence, in the meantime, had thrown off the mask from his face, seeming to forget that he was still in the leopard skin and was making a feeble attempt to laugh at the success of his plot; but was startled by the deadly pallor that spread over the face of Little Doctor, as she sank back in Chloe's arms.

Lawrence sprang forward, stretching out the clumsy paws of the animal in his genuine alarm. In an instant she recovered, and as the figure approached, she rushed at him in a frenzy of terror and rage, striking wildly with her only weapon, the blue parasol; but a thrust from this weak instrument brought down the would-be leopard to her feet. Lawrence sank to his knees, then down on his face with a deep groan.

Hartley now hastened up, and Victoria realizing what she had done, cried, "See! I have hurt him."

"O, no, he is only playing off," Hartley answered, laughing; but Little Doctor was already at Lawrence's side, and as she raised his head she was horrified to see his face covered with blood.

Hartley dropped on his knees, exclaiming, "What is it, old fellow! where are you hurt?"

"I fear my eye is out—but I deserved it. Victoria was fainting, and I ran to her in this guise; she did not recognize me, and tried to defend herself with the parasol. She stuck it into my eye."

"Yes, I did recognize you," said Little Doctor, "I saw

your face, and struck at you intentionally; but O! I did not mean to do this," she said, as she wiped away the blood from his features and looked into the wounded eye.

"Chloe, run quick, and dip this handkerchief in the stream yonder."

Hartley took Lawrence's arm to raise him up, but Little Doctor said, "No, no, let him lie down; and run, Hartley, to Beechwood for my father. Tell him what has happened and to bring the carriage."

Hartley set off at full speed for Beechwood; and poor Little Doctor lifted up her heart in agonizing prayer that the sight of the eye might be spared.

Chloe brought the wet handkerchief, and Little Doctor folded it and laid it tenderly on the eye. "Lawrence, give me your handkerchief to bind it on with," she said, and taking it from his breast pocket herself, bound it about his head. Then she took the little white sun-bonnet and placed it gently under his head, saying with pale, quivering lips. "Lawrence, can you forgive me? I was so wickedly angry when I saw your face, and knew you had frightened me intentionally; but it was so wrong to yield to such fierce passion, and I am punished for it."

"Yes, Little Doctor, I forgive you entirely; indeed, it was my own fault. It was—" But at that moment Dr. Kenyon came round the hedge. He had left the carriage without their hearing its approach. Victoria met him with the old look of sorrow in her eyes when she had done wrong.

"Father, I did it," she said, as she put her hand in his.

"Yes, daughter, I know how it happened—Hartley told me, and I don't blame you at all my darling."

The Doctor spoke kindly to Lawrence, although he

was very indignant at the cruel joke practiced on his daughter. He picked the great fellow up as if he had been a child, and put him into the carriage; Victoria followed her father, and Chloe got upon the box with Ben, where she let loose her pent-up rage at Lawrence. "Sarved him jis right. He went afoolin' 'bout de wrong pusson dat time."

Little Doctor was touched by Lawrence's self-control before her father, and it made her sick at heart to see the pretty hunting suit of brown corduroy soiled and stiff with blood.

They were but a few moments driving to the house. When they arrived, Mrs. Kenyon had a room already prepared for the patient. The Doctor carried Lawrence in and put him to bed, and proceeded to treat the eye. Mrs. Kenyon took Little Doctor in her arms and comforted her.

A note was dispatched for Lawrence's parents, who came in great alarm. While they were distressed and anxious about the accident to their son, they were deeply pained by his rash, foolish act in perpetrating such a cruel joke on the young girl.

Doctor Kenyon suggested that they should leave Lawrence under his care until the morrow.

As soon as her father was disengaged, Little Doctor called him aside and asked about the condition of Lawrence's eye. The Doctor thought the accident not so alarming as they had supposed, and that with great care, the sight might be saved.

This news relieved her of a great anxiety that had oppressed her heart. Her quick imagination had already pictured Lawrence with a sightless eye.

Little Doctor ascended the stairs wearily, and went

to her room, where her mother soon joined her and begged she would lie down and rest until luncheon time.

She threw herself into her mother's arms with a burst of tears, "O, mother, I am so burdened by this terrible temper. I was so angry at Lawrence for frightening me that I wanted to kill him. How can I conquer this miserable fault. It makes me shudder to think of what I have done."

Mrs. Kenyon sat down and took her daughter on her lap, just as she had always done when she came to her mother in repentance and for pardon and comfort.

"My darling child, you are now old enough to understand the blessed Saviour's teaching on this subject; The conquest is gained by prayer and fasting."

Little Doctor sprang to her feet, her form expanding as if a year had given size and strength to her being.

"Then let me begin," she said with shining hope in her tearful eyes.

"That is right, my child," and Mrs. Kenyon embraced her daughter tenderly. She went to the book-case, and taking down the Bible she marked some passages and laid the book on the table, saying, "God will help and bless you, my precious child, in your efforts," and she left Little Doctor alone to fight the first battle with self.

Mrs. Kenyon sought her husband in his office, where they could talk over their dear child's grief. They visited her many times during the day, and their love and appreciation of her heroic efforts of self-control were very precious to her.

Old Mammy was greatly distressed at Little Doctor's staying away from the table at meal times, and expressed her mind to Judy in the kitchen.

"Dat bressed chile am a raslin' wid de debil like ole

Abram, an' she gwine to git him under her feet. Dat de on'y way Marse Vic done git head an' shoul'er 'bove udder men. Dar is no foo'lin' when de debil come knockin' at de do'. Many times I's know'd Marse Vic to 'fuse goin' wid de boys sky-larkin', w'en he 'joys fun ez much ez any on 'em; but he neber had no use fo' low-down fun sich as robbin' de million patch, an' watchin' fightin' cocks."

The light burned in Little Doctor's room until after midnight; and often her old faithful Mammy would go out and kneel under the window and pray for her darling child's peace of mind.

Sunday morning the Doctor came to Victoria's door with the cheering news that Lawrence's eye was much better; that all danger to the sight was passed. She thanked her father for his thoughtful kindness and kissed him gratefully.

Little Doctor came down to breakfast that morning with a calm, sweet face, though pale and quiet. Lawrence was able to come to the table and the gloom of yesterday had passed away. Only the bandage over his eye told of the exciting scene of the previous day. Little Doctor sat near and they chatted in a friendly way of their school life.

The family drove to church, after leaving Mr. Balfour and Lawrence at their home. No worshiper in church that morning confessed her sins with more earnestness and fervency than our Little Doctor; she had won the first victories, but it had cost something in the winning.

Victoria felt much older than she had done the day before, as she rambled along the lane before she met Lawrence in disguise.

It was some time before Lawrence's eye entirely recovered, but the sight was not in the least impaired. Of course, his absence from school was commented upon, but no one except Hartley Ward knew how the accident to his eye had occurred.

The following Sunday afternoon, Dr. Kenyon asked his wife and Victoria to accompany him across the creek to see a new cottage he was building for the family of one of his wood choppers.

Mammy heard of the intended walk, and set off herself, with Paris, in the same direction. The rest of Mammy's family, seeing their leader start out, likewise joined the party; so that by the time the Doctor and his family reached the creek, there was a goodly company.

Chloe and Hayden told Little Doctor of a new bridge they had made over a shallow part of the stream, and begged her to go with them and try it.

Their bridge consisted of a broad plank reaching from one bank to the other. Little Doctor, who was always fond of adventure, started over on the precarious crossing. Mammy and her procession had just reached the creek, and stood watching the graceful creature in her pretty white frock, balancing herself on the swaying board. As she reached the middle, Hayden caught the end of the board, and raising it a few inches, said, "I's gwine to give Missy a lif'." But the "lif'" was too much for 'Missy's' equilibrium. She lost her balance, and fell into the stream. A scream went up from the whole party. Ben plunged into the water, and drew her out on the bank. She was thoroughly drenched, and the flushed face and sparkling eyes showed a rising of the dangerous temper, but it was instantly conquered. She smiled as Ben set her down, saying "Thank you Ben. It did not go over my head, but the stream is deeper than I thought it was."

Where was the sudden anger that all expected? Hayden stood trembling, expecting the punishment he knew he deserved; but seeing no sign of anger now, he grew saucy, after his kind, and ventured a bit of humor.

' "Wha's de blaze, Missy? Did de duckin' put out de fi'?"

There was an unexpected vengeance behind him— Mammy came up and gave him a stinging box on the ear that sent him howling away.

Dr. and Mrs. Kenyon hearing the excitement, came hurriedly to the scene, Mrs. Kenyon exclaiming, "Why, my darling, how did you fall into the water?"

Mammy told the story, not sparing Hayden in the least. Dr. Kenyon called him up and reproved him sharply.

"Look here, boy! I will have no more of this rude fun —do you understand?" And he took him by the shulder and shook him to give emphasis to the warning.

Mrs. Kenyon told Gip to take Victoria home at once, and change her clothing; the Doctor adding, "And rub her down, thoroughly."

Gip and Dolly each took a hand of Little Doctor, and ran as fast as the wet clothes would permit.

The Doctor and his wife sat down on a log to wait the return of their daughter. Taking his wife's hand the Doctor said, "Mildred, what an interesting study our child will be in this new life she has just begun—this self-conquest. Your wise suggestion came to her at the right moment. You have been a wise faithful mother, my dear, and you are worthy of such a daughter."

"My precious husband! our child is the reproduction of yourself, and I am the happiest mother in Christendom."

Victoria soon returned, radiant with exercise, and they

continued their walk to the cottage, all taking the old safe bridge this time; Mammy and her family following at a little distance.

CHAPTER XI

Victoria had given much of her leisure time in the last year to the study of infant cases, in her round of visiting with her father. He always encouraged her, and explained each case to her as they drove about from house to house.

An opportune time came for her to practice what she had learned. It was Saturday afternoon; her parents had gone out for a long drive, and Victoria was left to enjoy a new book. She had gone to her father's office, situated across the hall from the front parlor, where she loved to nestle down in his big green morocco chair and read. She had just finished the first page, when she heard hasty steps, loud sobs, and the piteous crying of a child. She rushed to the hall door and saw Mrs. March, the wife of a workman living on the outskirts of Beechwood, coming up the steps.

When she saw Victoria, she called out, "O, Miss, is the Doctor in? My baby has convulsions, what shall I do?"

Victoria answered quickly, "No, father is not in, but I can relieve the child."

The poor mother had no faith in a mere girl doing anything in such a terrible emergency, but she could go no further, so yielded to Victoria's request to follow her into the office.

Gip had heard the commotion, and came in to see if she could help her young mistress.

Her coming was just what Victoria wanted; "Gip,

run for a foot-tub of warm water, a blanket, and towels."

She knew the first thing was to give an emetic. She took from a shelf a bottle of ipecac, putting fifteen drops in a spoon with water, then gave it to her patient.

"What has she been eating?" she asked the half-distracted mother.

"I think she helped herself to wild grapes while we were at dinner. My husband brought a basketful home with him, and put them down on the porch where she was playing. Do you think they have caused this?"

"I have no doubt of it," answered Victoria, as she took from a closet a large washbowl and placed it on a chair by the side of the woman.

Gip came with all she was sent for, and when Little Doctor had undressed the little girl, she gently put her in the water. The medicine soon began to take effect, and it was not long before Mrs. March had positive proof that the feast of grapes had caused all the trouble. The small white face, with blue circles about the gray eyes and pretty mouth, looked less ghastly, and to Victoria's delight the muscles began to relax in the warm water. Little Doctor's voice and touch acted like a magic charm on the little sufferer, and she recovered rapidly.

When the body became soft and restful, Victoria took her out and rolled her in the blanket, deftly rubbing her dry beneath the warm folds. She then gave her to her mother to hold, who by this time had wonderful confidence in our Little Doctor.

Victoria left the room, giving a signal to Gip to follow her.

"Gip, prepare some refreshments in the diing-room for Mrs. March—tea, and something nice."

"Yes, Missy," said Gip; "I's glad ter help you comfort dat po' soul."

Victoria then hastened up stairs and opened a large trunk in her dressing-room. This same trunk had carried a part of her mother's bridal clothes to Beechwood, and now contained Victoria's infant clothes. She took out a suit of flannel underwear and two tiny skirts, also a pretty white slip, and a pair of red shoes; nor were stockings and bonnet forgotten.

When she returned to the office she took her patient on her lap, and proceeded to dress her; and to the amazement of both mother and doctor, the child took notice of the red shoes and held out her hands for them.

Mrs. March was much concerned about the pretty clothes being put on her child, and said, "She will just ruin them."

Victoria, smiling, answered, "To-morrow you may put them away for visiting clothes, if you wish."

"Do you mean for me to keep them?" said the poor woman, as if she could not believe she had heard correctly.

Victoria assured her that Ginny was welcome to them, saying, "Look how nicely they fit her."

When she had finished the infant's toilet, Ginny looked up at the face of her new-found friend, and said, "Did oo was' me cause I was dutty?"

"No," said the laughing little doctor; " 'cause you were ill."

She could not understand this answer as she had never before been put in a tub of water for being ill.

Gip came and put the office in order, and told her mistress that the tea was ready, and Victoria, in her own pretty hospitality, persuaded Mrs. March to go out with Gip and take some refreshments.

Our Little Doctor knew it was best for her patient to sleep a few hours, and proceeded to walk up and down the room with the small head resting on her shoulder.

While she still walked, Paris came to announce two young visitors, Hartley Ward and his sister Agnes. Victoria received them graciously, and explained her occupation. Both were much interested in the little patient, for they loved children very dearly.

Agnes joined Little Doctor in her walk, asking how old the child was, and many other questions.

"Two years and a half old, I believe," said Victoria. "She is so pretty and bright, I wish you could see her when she is well. I often meet her as I pass the house when horseback riding."

"I can see she is a real beauty—don't you think so, brother?"

Hartley was too deeply interested in the doctor to notice the good looks of her patient. He got up and joined the girls, saying, "Little Doctor, you have fairly earned your school title to-day. Let me relieve you of the baby—I will promise you one thing, I will hold fast."

Victoria placed her in his outstretched arms, saying, "I thank you, Hartley, I am really tired. Please put her to sleep."

He took up the sweet cradle song Little Doctor had been singing when they came in, and soon the little one fell asleep.

Agnes and Victoria sat down on the lounge to talk.

"Do tell me all you know about that pretty child— we want to adopt just such a little girl, don't we, brother?"

Hartley did not second the suggestion, but from his tender kindness to small Ginny, one would suppose he could do his share of loving an adopted sister.

Victoria gave all the information she could, but she felt sure that the parents would never give their child away, good and devoted as they seemed.

Agnes sprang to the door when Mrs. March made her appearance, saying, "Mrs. March, do give us that dear little girl; we will treat her as a sister, and Pa will compensate you for the sacrifice—just anything you ask."

The mother's face darkened, and she replied, "Do you think we would sell our child?"

Agnes was really frightened, so Hartley came to the rescue, saying, "Mrs. March, please excuse my sister, she did not mean to offend you. I admire your spirit, no true parent would part with their little one for compensation."

Agnes apologized, and went back to the lounge very much taken down.

Little Doctor told the mother she had better leave the child with her until she awoke, as she had much need of the refreshing sleep.

She consented, and as she glanced at the strong young arms holding her treasure so tenderly, she felt sure she was well taken care of by the young people. She said her husband would come for the child when he returned from work.

Victoria saw that she wished to see her alone, and went out into the hall.

"O, Miss Kenyon, I can't tell you how much I love you for saving the life of my baby." She caught her hand and covered it with kisses, and said with streaming eyes, "I know God will bless you for your kindness and devotion to the afflicted and poor. I have often heard of the generosity of you and your parents—but you, only a girl, to be able to do what I, a mother, ought to know is wonderful. If you had not acted so promptly my child would have been cold in death by this time."

Victoria soothed her, and said, "You are so worn out, let me send for your husband to take supper here, and you come and lie down."

"O no! I am quite able to go home now. The nice things your colored woman coaxed me to eat have strengthened me ever so much. "

When Victoria returned to her friends, she found Ginny nicely tucked in a little bed on the lounge, and Agnes by her side.

Hartley began—"Little Doctor, have you seen the 'Clever Six?' "

"Do you mean the juvenile Balfours?" she asked.

"Yes. They are all marvelous children, all bright and fresh as a spring morning."

Victoria had never seen them as the "Clever Six," and said, "I know the family, every member, but I have never visited the younger ones in the nursery."

"Well, there is a treat in store for you. We spent two hours with them this afternoon, and each one contributed his choicest accomplishments to entertain us. Lawrence leads them. They sing, dance, recite, declaim and perform the most astonishing athletic feats."

Agnes joined in the praise of the young prodigies, and said, "The twins sang a duet for us—they are but three years old, you know; and just think of fourteen in one family, all pretty and bright."

"Lawrence in particular," said Hartley with a smile, looking over his sister's head.

She blushed, pouted, and then appealed to Victoria for confirmation of what she said.

"Indeed, they are all good looking, everybody will admit—Lawrence included," she replied.

Agnes looked at the tiny sleeper, saying, "How foolish Mrs. March is to refuse to give us this dear little girl. They are very poor and not able to give her proper care. The man is often out of work, and what do they do then?"

The words of Agnes sank deep into the heart of our Little Doctor, and she resolved on future efforts to help them.

Hartley saw the expression, and said, "Now, Sister of Charity, don't go to puzzling your brain over the family, you have done enough to save the life of their child, so give us one of your new songs before we go."

Victoria consented graciously, and calling Gip to sit by Ginny, she led the way to the music room.

Agnes could not forget the charming young Balfours. She said, "Little Doctor, don't you wish there were fourteen in your family?"

"I would be quite well pleased with a brother," said Little Doctor, seating herself at the piano.

Hartley placed the music before Victoria, and she sang the new song in a sweet, tender voice, much to the delight of her young friends.

As the Wards were leaving, Hartley looked in at the small girl, and said, "Little Doctor, do you remember the time your father dressed my hand in that office? I came, bellowing like a calf, and you set about entertaining me, so I soon lowered my voice and listened to you —or perhaps I got ashamed of myself before the doctor. He must have thought me a baby to make such a fuss."

"I am sure he thought just to the contrary, for you held still with all the pain of having the splinter taken out and the wound dressed. It relieves suffering to weep and cry out, so always make all the noise possible and you will be the better for it.

Hartley was glad to have good authority for his favorite way of expressing pain, and said, "When I need a doctor I am going to send for you. I remember you do something else to comfort a fellow in trouble—I shall never forget the coffee, waffles, and syrup you served us that morning—I just took my benefit. You must have thought me a gourmand."

"I can assure you I like to see our guests have good appetites,—why, your father said you left home before breakfast, and it was natural you should be hungry. To convince you that I like to see people enjoy good things, I invite you and Agnes to take breakfast with us next Saturday; "And giving Hartley a smile and nod," she added, "we shall have waffles and maple syrup for your special benefit."

"O, I accept, before Ag. has time to say, 'I thank you,'" but Agnes was not slow to convince Little Doctor that she too would be happy to come.

Hartley and Agnes had taken leave of their hostess, and were just driving off as her parents advanced, and as they passed exchanged pleasant greetings.

Dr. Kenyon had seen the delighted expression on his daughter's face as soon as they came in sight, and said, "Victoria has been very pleasantly occupied while we were gone."

"Yes," answered his wife, "the Wards are congenial friends. But social enjoyment never brings that exultant delight to her countenance."

It was not the pleasure of companionship that glowed in the deep violet eyes, it was the love of saving human life that touched her great heart. She well knew the danger the child had been in, and that the prompt treatment saved her life.

She sprang down the steps extending both hands to her parents, exclaiming, "Father! mother! I have something to tell you."

After she had informed them of the case, she led the way up the steps and into the office to exhibit her patient.

"She was having terrible convulsions from eating wild grapes. I treated her, father, as you did those children who had eaten the green melons."

Her parents congratulated her, and both gave the kiss of loving appreciation; her father saying, "You are becoming a valuable assistant to take my place when I am away—how could I do without Doctor Kenyon, Junior?"

They found Ginny sitting up admiring the pretty clothes, and asking Gip many questions about them. When she saw Dr. Kenyon, she put her hands over her eyes and looked at him through her fingers, smiling gleefully, for she recognized him. Victoria induced her to put her hands down, and say "good evening" to her father, and put out her hand to her mother.

She soon grew genial, and was entertaining the family with her pretty ways when the father came for her.

He too was most grateful for the kindness to his child, and expressed himself like an intelligent man; so much so, that Doctor Kenyon thought of making inquiry about him so that he might better his condition.

Little Doctor put a warm shawl about the little one, tied the white sun-bonnet on, and saw her depart with her father with a feeling akin to Agnes' desire to adopt her; but it was not many minutes before Little Doctor and her parents were deep in planning for the good of the Marches.

When Victoria knew her parents were interested in helping the family of her patient, she gave expression in a merry outburst of song, then ran for her father's violin. She placed it in his hands, saying, "Father, please play a waltz for me."

The sweet, inspiring music filled the room, and Little Doctor fairly excelled a Fairy Queen in her grace and joy of the dance.

When she had finished, she came and knelt at her father's side, saying, "Father, do you think it is silly to sing and dance when I am very happy?"

"No, my darling child, it is a natural way to express youthful delight."

CHAPTER XII.

The Christmas holidays brought Percy home, and his coming disclosed a pleasant little coincidence. Both he and Victoria had been led to the serious contemplation of confirmation, although neither knew of the other's thought.

Percy had kept up a correspondence with Dr. Kenyon, and an occasional little note between the young people had passed through his letters; but they had not mentioned to each other the subject of their serious reflection; indeed, Percy was so reticent on the subject that he had not even mentioned it to his parents.

Percy had been deeply affected by an incident at college. While playing a game of baseball, one of his dearest friends, standing at his side, was struck in the head by a swift ball and instantly killed. The occurrence made a strong impression upon Percy's mind. As he looked upon the white face and still, rigid form of Dudley Armstrong, a deep sense of the uncertainty of life and the importance of the future took possession of his heart, and was to work out a change in his life.

Percy well knew that his determination to regulate his life in accordance with these new views would not meet with the sympathy of his parents. They were wholly governed by worldly considerations; and a brilliant future in this world was their highest ambition for their promising son. Percy felt lonely, indeed, with these new thoughts.

He returned home on the twentieth of December. On

that same day, in the evening, the Kenyons were gathered in their cozy library. A bright wood fire burned on the hearth, and a lamp, suspended over the center table, gave a cheerful glow to the comfortable surroundings.

Mr. and Mrs. Kenyon sat at the table reading, and Victoria sat in a corner by the wide fire-place engaged in cutting the leaves of a magazine; but her attention was not on her employment. For she was listening to Wiley's deep voice in disapprobation of an intruder. She waited for footsteps, which she soon heard on the gravelled carriage-way, then a light, firm step on the veranda; and strange enough, she knew whose step it was, and glanced down at the pretty crimson dress, trimmed with black ribbon, then down at her dainty feet in the bronzed slippers.

She attempted to rise, brushing back the wealth of fair curls from her face as she did so; but the long curls caught on the back of the elaborately carved chair, and held her fast. At that moment Percy made his appearance at the door. She saw him glance at her first, though he hastened to meet her mother's out-stretched hand as she rose to welcome her old favorite, then he turned to meet the Doctor's cordial greeting.

All this time, our poor little heroine was struggling to release herself from the snare of the carving. Percy, taking in the situation, laughed merrily; and coming forward, gently lifted the curls above the chair, saying, "You shall owe your freedom to me."

Victoria's delicate face was charmingly colored by the unpleasant exertion, or by the reflection of the light on the crimson dress,—though maybe something else contributed to heighten the rosy glow. However, Percy was evidently pleased to see it, for he looked with admiring eyes at her confusion, and taking a seat beside her, he began to talk with an easy grace to his host and hostess, while he managed to bestow some pretty compliments on Little Doctor.

Paris, after announcing Percy at the library door, stood outside to see and hear all he could, to carry the news to the kitchen; but Little Doctor's incident with the chair caused him to betray himself with a titter, and so he was dismissed with a wave of his Master's hand. He hurried to the quarters with his limited supply of news, but knew well how to make the most of a little capital. He rushed, breathless, into the kitchen, and soon had an audience. Though now grown to manhood, Paris retained the popularity of his boyhood, by his ability to beguile his hearers.

"Marse Percy done come home, an' he coch our Missy in a pow'ful fix. Her cu'ls done got fas' on de cheer, an' dey stick like grape vines on de tree, and hole her fas' till Marse Percy come an' say som'pin 'bouten settin' her free; an' Missy's face jes turn as red—as red as dem wintah peppers ahangen da on de chimbley."

Mammy laughed with the rest, but growing suddenly serious, she said, "Yo' jes aspyin' on de fambly, an' I's got to break yo' ob dat onmannerly way, ef yo' is growed up to de 'spectable age of manhood," and she smoothed down her apron with a threatening shake of her head, that made Paris rather uncomfortable.

Dolly and Chloe soon managed to get Paris outside where they could ply him with particular questions about their young mistress and the gentleman whom they all knew as a boy; for they had all, young and old, speculated as to the future of this favorite of the Kenyon family.

Mrs. Kenyon, at her husband's request, seated herself at the piano, and began that pathetic air, "Flee as a Bird to the Mountain." While her sweet voice filled the room with the song Victoria turned and met the kind gray eyes of Percy. She noticed a depth of expression unusual in their cold intelligence, and was moved to say what had been in her thoughts very often lately.

"Percy, the Bishop will be here next week, and will be our guest during his visit."

"Is it his official visitation to the parish?" asked Percy.

"Yes. There is a large class for confirmation."

"Who are the candidates? Do you know any of them?" he asked.

"Yes, and you know three of them, Hartley Ward, Lawrence Balfour, and—"she hesitated, but Percy continued silent; thinking of his own long cherished desire to announce to the world that he was on the side where true courage is to be found. No one knew better than Percy, what Christian boys at College had to encure from their thoughtless companions, but he did not shrink from the Christian life. Recovering himself, he said, "You did not tell me the name of the third candidate."

Little Doctor looked at Percy, and the pure, violet eyes grew misty with the recollection of the violent act that led her into the serious contemplation of confirmation. She had long before told Percy of the accident to Lawrence's eye, which her uncontrolled temper had caused.

"Percy, I am the other candidate, though I have never forgiven myself for the act which led me to think about such a thing."

Percy, who could never repress indignation at the

mention of that "cowardly assault," as he called it, was quick to answer, "Do not let that trouble your tender conscience, Victoria; you served him right. He got off well to what he would have received if I had been there."

A pause followed, and then Percy said, "I am very glad to hear that you are a candidate for confirmation, Victoria, for I too, have been thinking of it for a long time, and talked with the Bishop of Virginia the last time he was at the college."

Victoria was much interested, and said with a bright smile, "Are you really thinking of confirmation? I am so glad!"

Percy inclined his head, and taking up the magazine which lay at her feet, he whispered, "May I claim your sympathy in this matter, Victoria, even if I displease my parents?"

"Indeed you may! but I cannot think that your parents will object. They are so devoted to you, how could they oppose you when they know you are so sensible and deliberate in everything, never frivolous like some young men? I think they will be happy to let you please yourself, if nothing else."

Percy blushed with pleasure at this first serious compliment from his young friend.

"Victoria, it is not what I have been, nor what I am now, but what I aim to be in the future, that will influence my parents in objecting to the step I contemplate."

"Then you have not told them of your wish?"

"No, I thought I should like to mention it to—to—you, first. Have you told them—my parents— of your intended confirmation?"

"Yes, last Sunday I had a little conversation with your mother on the subject. She was very lovely, and said I was a good little girl; then said, smiling, 'Let us go and tell your best friend this news,' meaning your father. He, too, was very kind, as he always is. He said, laughing, 'Why Little Doctor, you will in future have more poor and sick folk to look after than Lady Bountiful ever dreamed of.' Then he asked me what I thought you would say to it," and Victoria gave a shy smiling look at the person in question.

"And what did you tell him?" asked Percy, smiling in return.

"I remembered a conversation you once had with my mother: you said you admired Christian women who had courage to do what they thought right; and I said I thought you would not be displeased. 'I don't know about that, little lady,' your father said; 'That boy of ours has some very decided opinions on the subject of a woman's independence.' But I told him I was sure you respected a woman's independence in matters of religion; then he called me a 'little bigot' and asked if I intended to proselyte you."

"That's an idea," laughed Percy, "Let me be your convert!"

Percy had brought a box of decorative articles for the Christmas tree, which he knew Victoria always provided on that occasion. He went into the hall and returned with a package, displaying a collection of beautiful new designs.

Victoria was charmed. She merrily threw them all out on a table, and the two heads bent over them, examining them, and praising their preferences like two children with new toys.

When Percy rose to leave, he took Victoria's fingers, and pressed a kiss on the pretty hand; and catching Dr. Kenyon's roguish smile over the top of his book, Percy tried to be defiant.

"Come now, Doctor, you did the same when you were a boy," but the Doctor's eyes were lowered again behind the book, and he innocently asked, "What have I been doing?"

The next evening found the Kenyons at dinner with the Tylers. Percy and Victoria had much to talk about, and the time passed rapidly. As the Kenyons were about to leave, Mrs. Tyler asked Dr. and Mrs. Kenyon to go into the library to see a new picture, one of Turner's which they had just hung above the fire-place that morning.

Victoria whispered to Percy, "Shall we tell your father now?"

Percy bowed his head, and they approached Col. Tyler, who was standing at the window contemplating the wintry view outside—the barren trees, and lawn strewn with withered leaves.

"Father, Victoria was telling me of a conversation you had with her last Sunday on the subject of her approaching confirmation. I, too, have been thinking of being confirmed for some time, and have only hesitated because I was not sure of myself."

The father turned with surprise, and looked into the frank, manly face of his son.

"You had better say, you were not sure of me, sir; it would be more to the point."

"Father, I think it is a matter one must decide for himself; yet your approbation would give me great pleasure. I came to this conclusion some time ago, but preferred to speak to you face to face."

In spite of his severe words, there was a look of tender sadness in the father's eyes, as he listened to his son's avowal of sentiments he had never inculcated; and when Percy finished, he abruptly turned again to the dreary

view outside. He was deeply moved, but was unwilling
that his son should see how little faith he had in his own
theory.

Percy nodded to Victoria, and she laid her hand softly
on Col. Tyler's arm.

"Dear Mr. Tyler, it will not make any change in
Percy's love and reverence for you, and it will make him
so happy to have your sympathy. O, I don't know what
I should do without my father's and mother's sympathy
at this time. When we feel anything very much, we
want all who are dear to us to be near us—don't you
think so?"

"Yes, little one," and Col. Tyler turned from the
window once more, and laid his hand on her head,—
"and though I cannot promise to be very near my boy in
this new course, I shall not oppose it; but I did not expect him so soon to cut loose from his father's prin-
ciples."

He turned again to his son, with something like deference, "Well, my boy, you are assuming responsibility
early; I hope you will be faithful, and stand by your
colors,—no deserting, remember."

Percy took his father's offered hand, with grateful
tears in his eyes,—"I trust I have inherited my father's
honor; and, for all else, I depend upon a strength greater
than my own.

Dr. and Mrs. Kenyon now appeared in the hall from
the opposite room, Mrs. Tyler following. When Mr. Tyler joined them, he said, "Victor, do you know, our children are beginning to think for themselves. Does it always come unexpectedly this way to parents?"

"No, not to me, my friend, but I have been expecting
this boy of yours to confound his learned, unbelieving
father one of these days."

Mr. Tyler brought his hand down heavily on the doctor's shoulder,—"O, you cunning proselytizer! I have long known your designs on my peace of mind. You will never rest till you bring my gray hairs to the chancel-rail. I expect to see this house turned into a hospital for paupers before I die, and the whole Tyler family acting as nurses."

The ladies joined in the laugh that followed this preposterous speech, and the parting of the friends was much more cheerful than Percy and Victoria had dared hope for, an hour before.

The Sunday before Christmas, the day appointed for the confirmation service, dawned gloriously bright. The ground was covered with newly fallen snow, the atmosphere clear and crisp—"real Christmas weather," as the Sunday-school children said.

Victoria was in perfect harmony with nature's clothing. Her dress was of white cashmere, trimmed with pure ermine. Her long golden curls falling over her white cloak added the only bit of color in her appearance.

The good old Bishop was looking more frail and aged than usual, but his impressive words sank deep into the hearts of the young candidates, who listened with a new interest to the feeble, trembling tones as they rose to that high pitch so familiar to his people.

The young Rector, Mr. Wallace, brother of Victoria's Sunday-school teacher, came forward, his countenance radiant with holy joy as he presented to the Bishop these young candidates—his first confirmation class.

Victoria and Percy walked together to the chancel-rail, and kneeled side by side, Lawrence Balfour on Victoria's left. Seventeen in all waited with bowed heads for the hands of the venerable Bishop.

When the ceremony was ended, all the new members walked to their seats, while the congregation sang that sweet hymn, "My Faith Looks up to Thee."

Percy's mother sat by the side of Mrs. Kenyon, and was evidently much impressed by seeing her manly son and dear young friend making the solemn promise and vow to lead a new life.

CHAPTER XIII.

"Marse Vic, please sah, I's want to speak to yo' 'bout some very 'tic'lar business."

Paris stood in the doorway of the library, where Dr. Kenyon and his wife and daughter were sitting. The Doctor glanced up from the book he was reading.

"Well, Paris, what can I do for you?"

But Paris, for once in his life, seemed to hesitate; he twirled his hat in his hands, and kept bowing his head, scraping one foot, and rolling his prominent eyes from one member of the family to the other.

Finally, his master said, "Perhaps if you would call again, Paris, you would be better able to explain yourself."

"No, I's comin' at it, Marse Vic, on'y I's not used to dis yere kind o' business."

Dr. and Mrs. Kenyon exchanged glances of amusement. They were expecting a visit of this kind from Paris, and waited patiently for him to control his unusual nervousness.

"Marse Vic," he began again, "ef yo' hab no ser'ous 'jecuons, I's gwine to get mar'ed. Bliky Tyler an' me hah been a-sparkin' a long time; an' Bliky, she think she ole 'nuff to judge fo' herse'f, an' Marse Tyler, he done gib his 'sent."

'Certainly, Paris," said his master, "you have my consent to marry whom you please. How soon will the wedding come off?"

"Some time 'twixt dis an' Christmas."

"But, Paris," said Mrs. Kenyon, "as Christmas is only a few days off, you have very little time for preparation."

"But, Mistis, dat am de bride's business; I's spec' Bliky done got all her fixin' ready."

They all laughed at Paris' irresponsibility in the matter.

"Well, you will want a suit of clothes, at least," said the Doctor, and he opened his desk and gave Paris a bank note that caused a smile to spread over the black, happy face, showing the strong white teeth.

"What does Mammy say about it?" said Victoria.

"O, she say we bofe fools to put our neck in de halter; but she am mighty glad to hab a weddin' in de famtly, jes de same."

Paris still stood irresolute. At last,—"Marse Vic, don' yo' tink a pinchbeck ring would do to be mar'ed wid? Buky, she say she mus' hab a gol' ring, kase it mo' 'spectable."

"Bliky is right," replied the Doctor

"Father," said Victoria, "let me give the ring,—do you like a broad one, or a narrow one, Paris?"

"I's spec' Bliky would like de broad one, kase da is mo' gol' in it."

As Paris finally left the room, Gip made her appearance through another door. She glided up to her mistress with her soft swaying motion, and knelt down at her side; taking up the pretty ribbons that adorned her mistress' gown, she smoothed them out, glancing up at the sweet face.

"Miss Millie, dem folks am pow'ful happy bouten dis weddin', but me an' George hab been keepin' comp'ny mo'n two year, an' I think we'uns ought to marry fus'."

"Why have you not told me sooner, Gip? You may marry as soon as you like."

"Well, Miss Millie, me an' George t'ought we would wait awhile, but we'uns didn't know dat dem niggers was goin' to git ahead of us."

Her mistress laughed heartily, saying, "I really don't know how you can manage it, Gip, unless you will both be married the same evening,—how will that do?"

"Dat is jis what I want, Miss Millie, but I's got no frock. I's been makin' my weddin' things fo' a year, an' all I need is de weddin' frock."

Her mistress gave her the keys from a little basket on the table,—"Go to my wardrobe and bring me that white alpaca dress."

Gip hurried upstairs, and returned, radiant with happiness, carrying the pretty white alpaca, trimmed with folds of satin. The truth is, Gip had this dress in her mind from the first; and her thoughtful mistress was not unmindful of this very occasion when she put the dress aside.

"It will not require any altering, Gip; but I will buy you some nice lace for the neck and sleeves, and you will want some white ribbons and flowers."

Gip assented to all these delightful suggestions with a beaming smile. She was tall and slight like her mistress, and there was nothing she rejoiced in so much as wearing her mistress' cast-off dresses.

The day for the double wedding was fixed for Christmas Eve, and that morning was heralded long before dawn by the cheerful whistling of Paris. For several days before, the kitchen had been a scene of cheerful bustle, and now was a blaze of light-hearted, merry darkies hastening to and fro with jokes and laughter.

Mammy presided over all, with good-natured authority.

Outside, the men and boys whistled and sang old
negro melodies; and the cocks crew in lively sympathy
with the stir going on within hearing of the barn.

The new barn was just finished—a large interior with
nice smooth floor, and this was to be the scene of the
festivities. It had been decided that the two wedding
parties should hold a joint reception; and servants from
both houses were busily engaged in decorating the walls
with evergreens, and bright red holly berries gleamed
among their shining leaves.

On each side of the wide room, long tables were
spread with white cloths, outlined with green vines.
Mammy and Judy superintended the setting of these
tables, while Biiky and George represented the Tyler
family in the cheerful work.

The ceremony was to take place at eight o'clock in the
evening, and long before the hour crowds of black people were waiting at the church door. Mammy, in su-
perintending the arrangements at the church, had white
ribbons drawn across the aisle separating two pews for
the acccommodation of the master's families. At the appointed hour, the Kenyons and Tylers filled these reserved seats, while the others rapidly filled with the
gaily attired wedding guests.

The family carriages had been sent back for the bridal
p rties, and Mammy's little wagon did good service
carrying the attendants.

Gip, by her superior right as lady's maid took prece-
dence of Bliky, who was a house servant, and advanced
with George up the aisle, Paris and Bliky following.

The rings were given, and the ceremony for each
couple proceeded very impressively to the end. Paris

and George could not resist a happy smile at each other as each produced his real gold ring at the proper moment. They knelt down and received the minister's blessing, and then marched out to the joyous notes of the organ.

If Gip had been first in the ceremony, Paris was first in the merry-making at the barn. All looked to him as a social leader in the entertainment for young and old.

The fiddlers were stationed on a platform at one end of the great room; a lively strain struck up, and Paris whirled Bliky out into the space prepared for the dancers, George following with Gip. No others yet joined them, but all looked on, and with restless, moving feet kept time to the music as it grew faster and faster, and the swaying figures mingled in the dizzy whirl. At last they stopped breathless, but laughing gaily.

The next dance was joined in by as many as could find room on the floor.

Supper was served in the midst of the jollity.

Christmas morning had dawned when the party broke up, and all was quiet at Beechwood.

Before breakfast, Christmas morning, gifts were distributed among the servants, and George, too, was included in Mammy's family, but before he joined the other servants Mammy took a slice of bread, and sprinkling a little salt on it, she gave it to George, saying, "Eat dis bread an' salt an' den yo' will be one ob us."

George performed the ceremony very seriously, for he had abiding faith in Mammy's superstitions, and was proud to be one of her family.

Percy was the happiest boy in Kentucky that Christmas morning. At breakfast he was unusually thoughtful; there was something on his mind, and he hesitated to do what his conscience dictated. After awhile his native courage and candor prevailed, and going to the back of his father's chair, as he still sat at the table he said, "Father, do you want to make me very happy this morning?"

"Why certainly, my boy, what can I do for you?—but I thought the time for Christmas gifts was only early in the morning."

Percy laughed, and said, "O, no, father, it is not a gift —you have been most generous—I want you and mother to go to church with me this morning."

Mr. Tyler turned to his son with some surprise, and meeting the earnest. solemn eyes, he hesitated a moment, and then returning to his usual courteous manner,—"Why, yes, I am at your service, my son."

Percy suddenly threw his arms around his father's neck,—"Now, you are the noblest of fathers," he said, with emotion.

The old gentleman was unwilling that his son should see that he too was somewhat moved, and said with his old humor, "O, no, I am only in my dotage, or I should not allow you and that small saint, Victoria, to have me in leading strings."

Percy turned to his mother, who rose to meet him. She clasped her boy in her arms, as she said with a tender smile, "My darling child, I think I am as happy as you are. I have long desired to go to church with you, but had not the courage to approach your father as you have done. I think we shall all be better for it."

Percy ordered the carriage, much to the coachman's surprise, for Percy usually went on horseback. On their way, they overtook the Kenyon carriage, and all exchanged their Christmas greetings. The Doctor called out, "I wish you a pleasant drive."

Mr. Tyler returned the compliment,—"But, say, Victor, you mistake, we are not out for a drive, we are going to our doom—the church. "This young man," glancing at Percy, "has come to the conclusion that he can instruct his father, and since my wife, too, is making common cause with him, of course I have to yield."

"No, father," said Percy, "I will leave the instruction to our pastor."

Doctor Kenyon was very much gratified, but he simply said, "You will find a hearty welcome in our pew. —there will be room."

The ladies exchanged some little pleasantries, and Percy's gray eyes sought Victoria's as the carriages moved on.

They all enjoyed the service,—even the "sinner," as Mr. Tyler called himself.

"I was really very much entertained. That young parson is a born orator, and your music is fair. I like the idea of a boy choir, I never heard one before."

Dr. Kenyon smiled at the idea of being "entertained" at church. He was too wise to make any comments, but he hoped for better things for his old friend.

CHAPTER XIV.

Dr. and Mrs. Kenyon had been well-pleased with the theory of the public school system of education for girls, as well as for boys; and were now more than satisfied with the practical results as shown in the advancement of their daughter over the young girls of her acquaintance who had, at the same time been under instruction in private schools and with governesses. A thorough foundation for an education was not their only object; Dr. Kenyon had long been of the opinion that children should be educated with a view to doing the most possible good to others, as well as securing the greatest advantages to themselves; and contact with nearly all classes of children he considered essential in developing this quality.

Victoria was a splendid product of this system, and her father knew that his child's influence had been felt and recognized throughout the years she had been associated with the children of the public school. Of course Victoria's parents knew that Home Culture was of the greatest importance and they had faithfully discharged that duty. She was taught and encouraged to be kind and courteous, compassionate and generous to all; and she had succeeded in winning the love and esteem of all her school-mates notwithstanding her unfortunate temper—indeed, those who had felt her displeasure most, were won by her forgiving spirit and her frank admission of error in herself.

Now that Victoria was fifteen years old, her parents

decided to extend her advantages of culture and send her to a school in the East distinguished for its high standard of learning; so this was to be her last year at the high school.

An aunt of Mrs. Kenyon's was teaching in St. Mary's Seminary in Virginia, and to her care they intended to commend their daughter.

It had been their rule to keep Victoria from general social entertainments, except those they accepted for her among their friends; but they were now desirous of promoting the influence she had gained over the young girls and boys in the school, and took the first step toward it during the holidays.

One evening, they were seated as usual round the library table. Doctor and Mrs. Kenyon were reading, and Victoria sat on a low stool at her mother's side, leaning the pretty, curly head against her mother's knee.

Mrs. Kenyon closed her book, and resting her hand on the curls, she said, "Daughter, we have been considering your wish in regard to entertaining a few of your school-mates before this term closes; and I think an evening party during the holidays would give the most pleasure to your friends."

"Mother dear, I am so glad," said Victoria. "I have wished very much to have them all at our house. You know I have declined all invitations since I have been in the school, and it has given offense to some. It really hurts me for them to think that I feel myself superior to them in any way, and it would be very pleasant to have a real party. I thank you so much, mother, I would indeed like the evening party."

"You know, my darling," said her mother, "that I have never approved of your going anywhere without

me, but in this way you may make a return for all their
courtesies."

The following Thursday was fixed for the entertainment. Besides the natural pleasure a young girl would
feel in the anticipation of her first party, her generous
nature delighted in the opportunity of removing at last
all restraint that had been caused by her "exclusivenss"
as the girls termed it.

Percy was early informed of the proposed entertainment and came over to offer his services in the preparations. He entered into all the plans with enthusiasm.
Mrs. Kenyon told them they might go to the library and
write the invitations. Victoria wrote them and Percy
directed the envelopes, dropping them into a basket at
his side; all the time keeping up a running comment on
the names as he read the list. At last, Paris was dispatched with the basket to deliver the dainty invitations.

That morning, as Cass McLean, one of the school
girls, was just leaving her mother's cottage for a walk in
the brisk air, she met Paris at the gate in Mammy's
wagon. Paris had been taught to read writing, and was
very proud of selecting the proper name to give the
young lady.

With a face flushed with pleasure Cassie hurried back
to the house.

"Mother, I have an invitation to the Kenyon's to a
party; what will happen next? None of the girls at
school have ever been invited there except Virginia Wallace, and she is of their own set."

"It is certainly very kind of the family," said her
mother, "and I am pleased for my daughter to be recognized by well-bred people, as the Kenyons assuredly
are."

"O, yes, I am immensely pleased myself," said Cassie,

"but I don't at all understand why they should so suddenly let down the barrier."

"My daughter, I do not like to hear you talk in that flippant way. I know we are poor, but I was accustomed to refined surroundings when I was young, and I know that much of what is called pride and aristocratic exclusiveness in well-bred people, is only self-respect, and quiet, refined taste that is repelled by rude intrusion; but we must think about your dress, I can make something pretty for you in time, I think." But Cassie was still thinking of this unusual condescension, as she regarded it.

"Victoria has always been a puzzle to me. She is as good as a saint, but has a temper like a cyclone; she is not proud, and yet one never feels that she is quite one of us; and she is as generous as sunshine—she will assist any girl with her lessons, give all her luncheon away, and if any one is hurt or sick—well, I will not count that to her credit because she positively revels in the delight of relieving suffering. The boys all just worship her; always appeal to her in matters of religion, morals, etiquette, and medicine. There is not a boy in school that would not fight for her."

"I can't imagine a person of her character needing any one to fight for her," said her mother.

"Well, lovely as she is, there are some of the girls who speak very ill-naturedly of her. There is Julia Osborne—who is jealous of her, of course, as we all are—she is always saying disagreeable things to her. I must say, Victoria generally hears it like a martyr, though the temper sometimes flashes out. She joined the church lately—that may have something to do witht her self-control. I want to run over and see if Julia has received an invitation."

She found Julia at home, and was surprised to find that she had not received the coveted invitation. Julia took the card in her hand, and read aloud,—"From eight to eleven,' dear me, what provincial hours! regular baby party!"

"Indeed, I am amazed," said Cassie, "that it is not in the afternoon, from three to six."

"I wonder if she has invited the boys," sneered Julia.

"Of course, for an evening party, and then—they are all so devoted to her majesty, they would 'Eat a crocodile,' as Hamlet says, to gain her favor."

"You are always so ready with your quotations, Cassie, but—" Julia at that moment saw Paris with his basket coming towards the door. She waited for him to ring the bell and then went to receive her invitation.

Paris made a pretense of looking over the names, but he had already spelled out the one he was to deliver, and had it at hand.

"Here, let me find it," and Julia stretched out her hand towards the basket.

"I's got it right here, Miss," and Paris drew it from its corner.

Julia would have liked a glimpse of the few remaining cards, but the wily Paris was too well trained to stop when on an errand, or disclose his business to strangers.

"Aren't you glad?" said Cassie, a little maliciously.

"Of course. I knew I should get an invitation, if you did."

"Well, I must be going home," and Cassie hurried away.

Both girls felt that they had not been generous in their conduct to the young girl who was so desirous of giving them pleasure, and in their hearts resolved to be worthy of her friendship in the future.

Elaborate preparations were making at Beechwood. Mrs. Kenyon was a woman of generous hospitality, and she resolved to make this an occasion full of pleasure to her daughter and her guests. The parlors and hall were already decorated from the Christmas festivities; but some fresh, bright berries were added, and the choicest flowers in the greenhouse were gathered to decorate the table, and to provide a delicate bouquet for each of the girls, and a button-hole flower for each of the boys.

The evening came round at last. Clear weather and fine sleighing added to the pleasure of all. Paris, in his best suit, with white gloves, waited in the hall; Hayden attended the guests in the gentlemen's dressing room, while Gip and Dolly assisted the guests of her young mistress in the finishing touches to their toilets. On a table in the dressing room, the little bouquets were arranged, and the maids presented each lady the flowers as she was about to leave the room.

Sleighs from Beechwood, and also from the Tylers, were sent into town to bring out the guests. The long avenue was lighted with Chinese lanterns hung among the trees, and the galleries were a blaze of light. The hall door stood open, displaying the beautiful decorations of palms and jars of rare hot-house plants.

Dr. and Mrs. Kenyon stood within the drawing-room, and Victoria, with Percy at her side, waited to introduce the guests to the host and hostess.

The dancing hall was handsomely decorated, and the waxed floor in perfect condition. An orchestra of stringed instruments, played by skillful negro musicians, was ingeniously arranged behind a screen formed of delicate vines and clusters of red berries.

Victoria and Percy led in a beautiful dance. They all

soon caught the new step, and joined merrily in the pastime. For the second dance, Percy engaged Julia Osborne, and after it was ended, he sat by her in pleasant conversation.

"We are so much obliged to you, Mr. Tyler," said Julia, "for your kindness to my little brother. You have become his hero, he talks of you constantly. Did he tell you how he came to be in the wood?"

"He said he had started out hunting, and lost his way," said Percy.

"O yes, he had a day of adventures. He started before daylight, without any luncheon with him. In his wanderings he fell into the creek and was thoroughly drenched that cold day, and was in that condition until late in the evening, when you found him."

Percy turned his eyes to the girl, with real interest.

"Why, he was a little hero himself. He said nothing about his mishaps. He was a brave little fellow. I found him sitting on a log, shivering with cold; but not a word of complaint. I put my overcoat round him, and took him up behind me on my horse and hurried him home as fast as I could."

The music struck up once more, and Percy bowed away to seek his partner for the next dance.

At supper time, the large dining-room presented a scene of brilliant light and flowers, and the table was spread with a feast of good things. Gaily dressed girls, and bright, fun-loving boys assembled round the table, while servants moved noiselessly about, serving the guests with oysters and coffee, their smiling faces showing their enjoyment of this part of the entertainment.

The gay chatter went on; all was animation and sparkling wit,—Victoria the happiest among the gay crowd. She had a sweet smile and charming manner with all.

The girls thought they never really knew her before, and the boys were more than ever pleased by her grace and loveliness.

Eleven o'clock came all too soon for the happy merrymakers, and there was more sincerity than we generally find in the expression of pleasure, as they bid their entertainers good-night.

When Reginald Page, one of the boys (usually called Rex), reached home, he sat down, thinking over the events of the evening, and soliloquized—"It makes me rage to see that Percy Tyler lording it over the other boys, and behaving with that assured manner towards Victoria Kenyon, as though she belonged to him; though, indeed, old Mammy told Aunt Bonney that they were betrothed to each other when they were little tots —but I don't believe it, the Kenyons are too sensible for that Old World humbug. But Percy has always acted as if it were so. I remember how he used to scowl at dancing school if any other boy danced with Little Doctor, as we used to call her,—and what a sissy he was! dressed in velvet and lace like a girl."

Rex's mind was still running on these things, when sleep nearly overcame him; he went to bed to dream of whirling in the merry dance, holding a big cake instead of a partner; then he was presenting a beautiful bouquet to a smiling lady, when, suddenly he discovered it was Mammy's turbaned head he was offering, and then awoke, and laughed at the vagaries of sleep.

CHAPTER XV.

New Year's Day came cold and clear, with crisp air and brilliant sunshine. A heavy snow had fallen the day before on the frozen ground, making the roads most favorable for sleighing.

It was the general custom to keep "open house" on the first day of the year, and the fine sleighing promised a larger number of visitors than usual. Mrs. Kenyon always observed the custom with lavish hospitality. Great fires were early made in the drawing room and hall, but there was no shutting out of the glorious sunlight as was the fashion at that time—darkening the windows and making artificial light with wax candles.

On that day no dinner was served. The dining-room was appropriated to tables, set with refreshments for the callers. Gip, Bliky and Dolly were arrayed in blue and white striped frocks, white aprons and caps; all employed as serving maids in the dining-room; while Mammy and Judy kept up the supply of refreshments, Mammy coming in occasionally to see that "Dem young darkies don't git to frolickin' roun' dem tables an' upset somepin."

The road leading to Beechwood presented an animated scene; sleighs drawn by two, sometimes four, horses, with jingling bells and swiftly flying feet, passing each other in whirling drifts of snow, the occupants of the sleighs just catching the merry laugh and happy greetings of each other as they dashed on in an abandon of delight.

Late in the afternoon, two young friends of Victoria's, Reginald Page and Lawrence Balfour, came to pay their respects to Mrs. Kenyon and asked to see Victoria. She was not receiving with her mother, but Mrs. Kenyon sent for her to come to the drawing-room. Chloe followed her carrying her white embroidered cloak which she wrapped round her young mistress.

Victoria thanked her maid, and said smiling, "Chloe treats me like a baby, and mother encourages her in it. Now I should like to harden my constitution, for I want to go to the North Pole some day."

"Let me know," said Reginald, "when you get up your expedition, and——"

A loud scream, and calls of "Missy! O Missy!" came from the stairway. Victoria ran into the hall, and to her horror, saw Chloe in a blaze, rushing down the steps. She fled past Victoria, who called, "Lie down, lie down, throw yourself on the floor."

Chloe was too frantic to heed, but fortunately she slipped on the tiled floor and fell prostrate. Victoria was instantly at her side, and snatching from her shoulders the cloak, which poor Chloe had just brought her, she wrapped it round the girl; then seeing a fur rug near the door, she seized it, and soon succeeded in smothering the flames. Mrs. Kenyon and the gentlemen hurried to the spot, and at Victoria's request they carried the shrieking girl to the smoking-room at the rear of the hall; Mrs. Kenyon preparing the lounge for Chloe's comfort, while Victoria sped away to the office for proper remedies.

Chloe had been standing with her back to the fire in her young mistress' room after she had carried the cloak down stairs, when the back of her apron caught the flame. The foolish girl ran down the stairway, catching the draught. The back of her head, neck, and both hands were severely burned.

Victoria returned with lime-water, linseed-oil, bandages, and scissors. Mrs. Kenyon cut away the burnt clothing from Chloe's neck, while Mammy removed them; and Little Doctor set to work, rapidly, but tenderly, to dress the wounds, Lawrence and Reginald assisting by holding the remedies. She clipped away the scorched wool from the back of the head, then pouring some lime-water into a small bowl, she bathed the burns with a soft sponge; and saturating some linen cloths with the oil, laid them gently on the wounds, then bandaged the head and neck, carefully pinning the bandages in place. Afterwards, the hands were dressed in the same way, each finger being dressed separately.

Victoria betrayed no nervousness, no hurry. She spoke occasionally in a soft tender tone to her patient.

Old Mammy, standing by, was distracted by poor Chloe's continued screams, and said, "Yo' mus'n holler dat way, yo' will make Missy narvous."

"No, no, Mammy," said Little Doctor, I do not mind it at all."

As Victoria finished the treatment of her patient, an old gentleman, Mr. Chase, said in a whisper, as he withdrew with a friend, "I never saw such skill and tenderness combined. The child is a marvel—how old is she?"
"Not more than fifteen," said the friend.

As they departed, Dr. Kenyon and Percy drove up in a sleigh. Paris was ready to take the horses, and quite as ready to tell the news.

Mrs. Kenyon met her husband at the door. "Mildred, is our child burned in saving the girl?"

"No, Victor, she is not hurt at all, and has been most heroic in saving Chloe."

Victoria caught her father's out-stretched hand, kissing it, as she always did when she was grateful to him, and whispered, "Father, it was your teaching and example that gave me courage to save poor Chloe—but, father, she needs an anodyne; will you give her something?"

"Yes, daughter, at once," and kissing her forehead, he led her with him into the office. Taking her hands in his, he said, "What is this? I thought my baby was not burned?"

"I really did not know it, myself, father," and she laughed nervously, for the strain was over, and Little Doctor was but a child after all. Her father dressed the palms tenderly, and took her to her own room.

The Doctor came then to examine Chloe, and found everything done as skillfully as he could have done it himself.

Chloe had heard that her young mistress was burned, and she began to cry and sob, "O, my bressed Little Doctor, she don' got burnt herse'f, and dat bu'ful white cloak all spiled, jes kase I's stan' too close to de fi', and Granny she tole me neber stan' wif my back to de fi'." But Chloe soon yielded to the soothing potion Dr. Kenyon had given her, and fell asleep.

Percy enquired anxiously for his young friend, and the Doctor said she was just a little over-wrought and very slightly burned and he had left her in her own room with her mother.

As Rex and Lawrence drove from the door, both were very quiet and went some distance before either spoke; then Rex said, "Victoria Kenyon has marvelous courage and nerve; I never saw anything like it."

Lawrence was too busy with his own thoughts to reply at once. After a moment he said, "Yes, she is of the material that heroes are made. I expect to see her a second Florence Nightingale, some day, or something greater."

"It has always been something of a mystery to me why Dr. Kenyon should send his only daughter to the public school."

"I believe his theory was to educate his daughter for a life of usefulness, and I think he has proved it a success. She is the most popular pupil in the school, and every girl and boy in it has felt her influence for good."

"That is true, she has left her impress on us all."

"What do you think of Percy Tyler?" asked Rex, after a pause.

"O, a very fine specimen of apron-string rule. He never went to school a day, and knew nothing of boys until he went to college."

"Well, I can tell you, he is not wanting in manliness now," said Rex. "I have talked with him several times since he came home, and I find him a splendid fellow. He is the best scholar in the country for his age."

The boys separated with a sense of improvement, a broadening of mind. Not that they analyzed this condition, but there was a feeling of elevation and gratification in recognizing noble qualities in others, and Percy and Victoria were well qualified to raise their standard still higher, if they followed their example.

Later in the evening, Mr. and Mrs. Tyler and Percy came over to Beechwood to enquire after Victoria's hands, and to learn whether Chloe's burns were very serious.

Percy brought a large cluster of fragrant white pinks, and presenting them to Victoria, "An offering to heroism," he said, smiling.

Victoria knew how he treasured these flowers; they

had watched their growth in the green-house. "O! she said, "You have cut all your lovely pinks. I counted them a few days ago, and every one of them is here." She inhaled their fragrance, exclaiming, "You precious creatures!"

"They only bloomed for Little Doctor," he said gallantly.

"Your skill to-day entitled you to the name 'Little Doctor; don't you think so, mother?" and Percy turned to his mother with a glowing face.

Mrs. Tyler looked at Victoria with eyes beaming with affection, "Yes, I think Mammy was certainly prophetic when she gave you the name the day you were born."

The Doctor had removed the bandage from one hand, Victoria insisting that it was only slightly blistered, and that she could not endure being swathed like a mummy.

Victoria went with her father to pay a visit to Chloe before they retired. The Doctor gave another dose of the soothing medicine, and left her in charge of her mother, Judy.

Little Doctor did not sleep soundly that night—she was restless; while the burns on her hands were not severe, they made her too uncomfortable to sleep. About midnight she arose, and wrapping herself in a warm white robe, and putting on her slippers, quietly descended the stairs to the room in the back of the hall, to see her little black patient.

She entered softly, but roused Judy, who was nodding in her chair. She looked up at her stately young mistress in the long white robe, the golden curls gathered to the top of the shapely head like a crown of spun gold, and murmured, "Sholy de angels do walk in white robes!"

Chloe slept soundly. The young black face resting

on the pillow looked very pathetic surrounded with the white bandages. Little Doctor looked long at the face of her devoted little maid, then telling Judy to put more wood on the fire she drew an easy chair to the bedside, and sat down to watch with the nurse; but Judy was soon nodding again, and finally she, too, slept, and Victoria watched alone, busy with her own crowding thoughts.

When the early dawn came, she put out the oppressive lamp, and opened the doors to the hall to let in fresh air. She crossed the hall to the East room, and drawing back the heavy curtains, looked out on the familiar scene, and listened to the sounds of cheerful domestic life.

Mammy stood in the kitchen door, (she had taken Judy's place in getting breakfast), calling cheerily to Paris to leave a pair of chickens in the hen-house. Hayden was chopping wood at the open door of the wood-house, scattering a shower of chips with each stroke of his ax. Ben was riding away to town to market, his basket on his arm. "Quiet old faithful Ben!" she thought, as she remembered that he had been going every morning, just the same, since she could recollect. She could see Dolly and Bliky having a stolen game of snow-balling, behind the barn, in the distance.

Victoria heard another sound—a movement in Chloe's chamber. When she returned, she found both mother and daughter awake, and much surprised to see their young mistress at that hour.

"Good morning;" she said, as Chloe tried to smile her pleasure at the sight of Little Doctor, and she took her wrist in her hand to feel her pulse.

"O, you are doing nicely," she said cheeringly,—"no fever at all. You will be up in a few days and ready to play snow-ball—I saw Dolly and Bliky enjoying a game

cut there just now; but Chloe, I think I shall have to
make you a cap, for do you know, I had to cut your hair
behind so I could dress the burn, and it will be pretty
cold for you for awhile."

Chloe asked what time her mistress came to her room,
and she and Judy were distressed to know that Little
Doctor sat up while they slept.

"Now, Chloe," she asked, "what would you like for
your breakfast? You shall have something nice."

"O, Missy, don't yo' go botherin' yo' sweet se'f bouten
me, Mammy will git me a bite bime-by."

But Victoria sent Judy to get a dainty breakfast at
once, then she suddenly thought of something,—"Chloe,
you like apple-fritters, and you shall have some."

She called Judy back and told her to prepare Chloe's
favorite dish—fritters.

When Victoria sought her own room, she found a
bright wood fire burning on the hearth, and Gip sitting
on the warm rug in front of it.

"Now, my Missy mus' go right to bed. It's two
hours 'fore breakfas', and yo' kin git a fine sleep; an'
ef yo' still is asleep. Mammy will git yo' a fresh breakfas' when yo' gits up."

"Yes, Gippie, I will," said Victoria. "I'm tired and
stupidly sleepy; but you may bathe my feet before I lie
down, they are so hot and tired."

Gip got a small tub of warm water ready, and she was
soon down on her knees before her idolized little mistress, rubbing her feet, and wiping them caressingly, as
if it were indeed a work of love. She covered Victoria
comfortably in the warm bed, and softly went about the
room restoring it to perfect order, and then lay down
on the rug before the fire.

An hour after, Little Doctor awoke and asked the

time. Gip got her watch from its little velvet pocket, where it always hung just beside her bed, and told her the hour.

On chairs by the fire hung fresh clothes, warming. A pretty Scotch plaid dress was ready, the shoes and stockings, too, near a low chair by the fire, and the warm bath-robe ready to put around her.

After a refreshing bath, Victoria sat down before the fire and Gip, with her combs and brushes, began the toilet, while she indulged in a little gossip. She dearly loved this hour with her young mistress. It was a kind of privileged time for Gip, and the little mistress enjoyed it too.

She began now, as she brushed the long curls, "Marse Percy done been in de lib'ray some time. He came ovah to ax how is yo' alls, and I tole him all de fambly was in bed yit; den he ax fo' my young Missy," and Gip smiled to herself, "an' I tole him yo' had been up wid Chloe all night and was jes gittin' a little sleep. He kine o' look sorry, an' say, "Why didn't Mammy or Judy sit up wid de patient?' " This was said in unconscious imitation of Percy's vexed voice.

"Now, Gip, you may run down and tell Mr. Percy that I am able to go down, and will see him soon and that we shall expect him to take breakfast with us."

Percy met Victoria in the hall. Taking her free hand, which happened to be the left one, he examined it critically, as if looking for the burns; then taking the other hand, "O, this is the poor little wounded one!"

Victoria laughed merrily at his playful manner. She knew it was his nature to suppress any feeling; and from what Gip had just told her, she knew he really sympathized with her.

Then he asked gravely, "Victoria, how are your hands, and how is your patient?"

"Both doing well. Gip dressed my hand, under my direction this morning, and did it nicely, too."

"Now, that is unpardonable," said Percy, "when I came over so early, and went directly to your father's office, hoping I would have the pleasure—no, the—pain of dressing that hand."

Again Victoria laughed, the clear, ringing, happy laugh of girlhood. She had never before seen Percy in such a mood, and it was such a delightful relief from the painful strain she had been under for nearly twenty-four hours that she entered into the spirit of his pleas-antry with an unexpected lightness of heart; but they soon settled down to a serious discussion of the accident, and then Percy said, "Do you know, I had important business with you this morning, and not knowing that you had turned nurse, as well as doctor, I expected to find you up—by the way, I must report you to the head physician for unprofessional conduct—condescending to the role of nurse!"

"But what is the important business that brought you out 'so early' this freezing morning?"

"I have a favor to ask," said Percy. "You know Dr. Kenyon has invited my father and mother to join him and your mother in a sleigh-ride this afternoon, leaving us out altogether, do you understand. Now, Victoria, will you do me the favor to let me take you out in my new cutter? It is a beauty—you did not see it when I brought your father home yesterday evening; you had something more serious on hand than looking at my new Christmas toy. Will you go with me—the sleighing is perfect, everybody will be out to-day, and we shall have such a merry time?"

"I shall be delighted to go, Percy," said Victoria, "if mother approves,—but come, breakfast is served, I see Paris going to announce it, and we shall discuss it at the table."

Mrs. Kenyon approved of the young people trying the new cutter, and Percy left after breakfast in exuberant spirits.

As Dr. Kenyon was about to leave the dining-room, he called Victoria,—"Your mother and I are going to the city this morning, my daughter, and I shall leave Chloe in your hands. You know, as well as I, what to do for her—she is your patient," he said smiling.

"But, is there anything else you would suggest, father?"

"Nothing at all. I have confidence in your skill and faithfulness, and I wish to see the result of your unaided treatment. Good-bye, my child," and the Doctor kissed his daughter's cheek as he hurried away to join his wife, who was already in the sleigh at the door.

Victoria went directly to Chloe's room, and with Judy's assistance dressed the burns carefully. She told Judy to raise her up from her pillows, Victoria herself arranging them comfortably; then giving Chloe one of her own old picture books, she left her to amuse herself while she went to her own room with an unusual expression of concern on her face."

"Gip," she said, "what shall I wear this afternoon? I have just thought about my cloak. I don't like to wear my old last winter's wrap, it is so small for me now, and besides it is dark,—I like something light and fluffy for sleigh-riding."

Gip was busying herself in the wardrobe, and said in a doleful voice, "I's 'spec' yo' got to war dis un, Missy. It sho do look shabby fo' a fine sleigh-ride a-sittin' up aside a young gemman, all wrapped up in bu'ful furs."

It had never been necessary for her to give a thought to her attire, and she was a little surprised at herself that it should trouble her now; but when she thought of the gay new turn-out, and somebody sitting beside her in a handsome fur-trmmed coat, she looked at the last year's cloak with a sigh.

Dr. and Mrs. Kenyon returned from the city in time for luncheon. As the sleigh came up to the door, announcing its approach with the merry, jingling bells, Victoria ran down the steps to meet her parents.

Paris was just taking from the sleigh a big pasteboard box; "Wha mus' I take dis yer box, Marse Vic?"

"To the library," said Mrs. Kenyon; then taking her daughter's hand, she said, "Darling, that box is for you; come with me to the library."

Paris put the box on the table, and Victoria hastened to untie the tape strings, and remove the cover. Inside, nestled a wealth of pure white fur; on the top lay a dainty cap, then a muff, and at the bottom of the box, an elegant wrap, all of the same beautiful ermine.

As Victoria lifted them out, one by one, and examined each article, her delight increased.

"O, how beautiful!" she exclaimed: "They are the most exquisite things I ever saw, and I never before wanted anything so much—and just in time for this glorious snow. What shall I say to my precious mother and father—you have made your little girl so happy?" and she kissed them both affectionately, they returning the caresses with glad hearts.

Victoria was not a vain person but loved things with the true appreciation of the beautiful.

At two o'clock, Ben brought round the sleigh, drawn by the high-stepping chestnut pair; and a few minutes after, Percy drove up in his new cutter, his bright face aglow with health and happiness.

Dr. and Mrs. Kenyon soon made their appearance, followed by Victoria. Percy sprang from the sleigh to greet them, and as he glanced up the broad steps, he pretended to be quite overcome by the lovely vision in white fur, Victoria laughing merrily at his gestures of admiration.

He caught the pretty muff, and putting the tips of his fingers into it, he mimicked an affected lady carrying it. Victoria was in a humor to be amused, and Percy's playfulness was highly enjoyed.

"I like the cap immensely," he said; "you look as if you might be the daughter of Santa Claus—or, is there a Miss Santa Claus?" No one had ever heard of the mythical person.

He assisted Victoria into the gay little cutter, and drove out towards the main gate, while the Doctor and Mrs. Kenyon crossed the meadow to the Tyler home, and pulled up at the door where they found their guests for the drive waiting. They were soon all wrapped in the warm fur robes and again dashing off towards the main road.

Percy and Victoria were waiting at the gate for their parents to take the lead.

Mrs. Tyler complimented Victoria's handsome furs: "Fortunate little lady," she said; "you look like a Russian Princess in ermine."

Mr. Tyler looked on awhile, and then said, "I suppose the list of adjectives has been exhausted by my hopeful son, so I will only say, you look very happy, and—warm." Victoria bowed in acknowledgement of the cheerful greetings.

"Take the lead," cried Percy; "age before beauty." Dr. Kenyon and his party led off, Percy following, his horse pulling on the reins impatiently, unused to being behind.

This was a merry ruse on the part of Percy; for, with a word intelligible only to Juno, the cutter passed the big sleigh like a bird on the wing, which, indeed, it represented—a peacock, the out-spread wings forming the sides of the cutter, while the breast answered for the dashboard.

On they went! Juno seeming to borrow swiftness from the wings behind her; but it was not long before Guy and Dan were close on her heels.

They had gone several miles, when Percy said, "There is a sleigh just ahead of us. I think it is Peter Benson with Miss Cassie McLain—shall we pass them?" and before Victoria could reply, he said the significant word to Juno, and swift as an arrow, the cutter whirred by the sleigh in front.

"O, who is that," exclaimed Cassie; all in lovely white fur?"

"It is your friend Little Doctor," said Peter.

"Are you sure, for the Kenyons are so conventional, Victoria never drives alone wthout"—at that moment Dr. Kenyon's party passed the sleigh.

"There's my answer," laughed Peter; "the chaperons are not far behind, you see."

"But did you see that exquisite fur? It is the same set that Mamma priced at the merchant's while it was on exhibition,—Victoria is certainly a fortunate girl.

Peter had not recovered from the astonishment caused by the handsome new cutter, and answered vaguely, "Who is a fortunate girl?"

"Why, Victoria Kenyon, of course, with that extravagant set of ermine—but you seem bewildered."

"Excuse me," said Peter; "I was thinking of that stunning sleigh. Yes, Little Doctor looked as lovely as a blush-rose."

"I did not ask for your opinion of her looks," said Cassie, with pouting lips.

Peter adroitly changed the subject, and they finished their ride in a very cheerful mood, in spite of the little wounded vanity in both.

The Tylers and Kenyons closed the day with a family dinner-party at the home of the latter.

As Gip was brushing her young mistress' hair that evening Victoria said, "Gippie, this has been the happiest day of my life, for nothing has occurred to mar the perfection of our sleigh-ride. You know, Gip, when one is very happy, something unpleasant is almost sure to come in the way. I suppose it is because we forget ourselves, and do something to cause it."

"No, Missy," said Gip; "I's think it is de debil. Wheneber he thinks folks is havin' a good time, he jis gits jealous-like an' comes a trompin' wid his big hoofs, a tarin' up everything—jes like he made Chloe cotch fire on New Year's an' break up de jolly time in de parlor, an' spile yo' pretty cloak, and have de smokin' room all dirty an' mus' up wid Chloe in dar."

"Why, Gip, don't you think it was far worse for poor Chloe to have to suffer, than it was for us to have the trouble?"

"Yo' see, Missy, de debil didn't count Chloe no how, he was jes a thinkin' 'bout tormentin' yo'uns, an' kine o' frode Chloe in."

CHAPTER XVI

One cold afternoon, soon after the sleigh-ride, Victoria was sitting before the blazing logs trying to make up her mind to brave the cold and run out for her accustomed exercise, when Gip entered.

"Missy, Bro' Ben say he got somepin in de hay-mow dat yo' would like to see."

Victoria knew that quiet Ben never exaggerated a fact, so this news decided her to go out. Gip got her cloak and hood, and putting them on her, they started out together.

On their way to the barn, they met Hayden carrying a basket of corn on his head: "Missy, I's seed Marse Reginald dis mornin' as I's comin' from de sto', an' he ax me, how is my Missy; an' I say, I's knowd yo' was well, kase yo' a snow-ballin' wid Marse Percy."

Victoria was displeased; there was something saucy in the boy that never failed to irritate her more or less. Unlike Paris, who was fond of fun, there was in Hayden a spirit of mischief that provoked Victoria more than she would have been willing to acknowledge, even to herself. She never appreciated his gossip, and would not allow him to chat with her as she did some of the other servants.

He walked away, balancing the basket on his head; and with a cunning look of mischief in his eyes, he said, "Marse Reginald 'mires our little Missy, dat he do; I's foun' dat out by a-watchin' him."

Victoria turned with an indignant face towards the

darky; but Gip saw the look, and before her mistress could speak, she dealt Hayden a blow in the back that sent the basket off his head, scattering the corn over the frozen earth.

"That's right, Gip; he deserved that," said Victoria, as she walked on, followed by Gip who kept an eye over her shoulder, though she had no fear of her nephew's resenting the blow while she was with her mistress.

Victoria recovered her composure in a few minutes, and felt vexed with herself for allowing her temper so to get the better of her dignity in the presence of her servants; then came the thought—was it worthy of a Christian to get angry at a servant for so slight an offence?

She turned round and saw Hayden picking up the corn with his stiff, cold fingers; and, going back, she said, "Gip, you must pick up this corn, and I will help you; and Hayden, you may go to the kitchen and warm your hands."

"O, Missy, I dassent go whar Granny will see me, she'll say I's ben in mischief agin."

He went on picking up the corn, while Victoria and Gip joined in the work. Just as the basket was re-filled, Ben came up, and saw at a glance that Hayden had been in mischief. Not waiting for inquiry, he took up a barrel stave. Hayden seeing it was for him fled to the orchard without a word. He would run from his father's wrath if opportunity offered; if not, though he was eighteen years old, he would take a thrashing like a boy of ten. Ben pursued him some distance, then came back out of breath.

In the meantime, Victoria, with Gip, had ascended the ladder to the hay-loft, and there saw a large flock of snow-birds holding council in a noisy fashion. Ben found them in possession when he went to get hay in the morning, and they were still in a loud discussion.

Ben looked on a while, then said, "Dey minds me ob a camp-meetin' of darkies, all jawin' at onct."

Ben's natural repose of mind was always disturbed by the wild clamor of his people assembled at camp-meeting.

Hayden returned for his basket after awhile, and carrying it to the kitchen he slipped in behind the great cooking stove, and began shelling his corn for the chickens; but when Ben came in to supper, Hayden thought the better part of valor was to withdraw, which he did with precipitant haste.

Victoria was still walking, when she saw Hayden running from the kitchen, and asked what it meant.

"Dad jis come in, and he's not done walloped me yit."

The grin that accompanied this speech did not show much fear of the "walloping."

"But it is too cold for you to stay out here, and you must have your supper;" and Victoria went to the kitchen door.

They were all at supper, Mammy at the head, and Ben at the foot of the table, while the fumes of hot boiled food rose from the dishes—bacon, with turnips and cabbage; delicious golden corn-bread, in a great pone; and a pot of strong coffee.

Victoria explained to Ben that she had pardoned Hayden for being saucy, that he really meant no harm, and she hoped they would let him have his supper at once. Hayden walked in behind his mistress and took the vacant chair, glancing shyly at his father. Mammy gave him a big cup of coffee, and Ben was so far conciliated as to fill his plate with the hot food. Little Doctor said good-night, and went to her own room.

Gip had made up a large fire, and drawn her mistress' favorite easy chair to the hearth. A lamp was burning on the table, throwing a warm glow over the moss green carpet, the pattern a wild profusion of blue, white, and pink morning glories; the heavy silken curtains were drawn to shut out the bleak winter twilight, giving warmth to walls, pictures, and furniture, and the book she had been reading lay open on the table with a clean folded handkerchief beside it. Gip was an admirable lady's maid; no detail of her office was so small as to be forgotten or omitted.

Victoria looked around her with something of a new sense of comfort. Her favorite Maltese cat purred softly on the rug before the fire. As Victoria took her seat, she put out her hand and stroked the cat's smooth fur. With this encouragement, pussy made bold to creep into her mistress' lap—only to be put down instantly. Victoria was fond of animals, and enjoyed having them about, but she was early taught never to allow them to lie on her lap. Her father thought the practice of allowing cats and dogs to be about one's person, or in one's bed, very unhealthful, and also unrefined.

Victoria was thoughtful. The tender conscience that had been so newly awakened by her recent confirmation had suffered some twinges since the sudden rising of temper at Hayden's impertinence; that act had opened a door to serious reflections on the responsibility she owed to God for the welfare of her servants. Her parents had inculcated this from her childhood, but she had never before felt a personal responsibility in the matter.

She thought of Hayden's subjection to his father, though himself a man in size; that he would, at her command, submit to being "walloped" as he said, for what seemed to her now such a small offense. Dr. Kenyon had always allowed Ben the privilege of punishing his own children, no matter what the cause might be; but this did not relieve Victoria's mind of a deep sense of accountability.

She rose with a definite purpose in her mind, resolving to be watchful over herself, and less exacting of others. She went to her book-case and selected a story book and sought Chloe's room down stairs. She found her patient restless and fretful; the healing burns were irritating, and Chloe had not much experience in suffering. Little Doctor dressed the wounds very tenderly, and bid Gip make her comfortable for the night; then taking the story book she sat down to read Chloe to sleep. Gip lay down on the rug by the fire, and listened with as much interest as the patient. Afterwards she went to the kitchen to repeat to her family, gathered round the big stove, her version of the story of "The Daisy Chain."

The following Sunday was the last day of Percy's holidays. He drove with his parents to church. It was the last of the snow too, so they went in their sleigh. At the church door they met the Kenyons, who had just arrived in a sleigh also. Percy hastened forward to assist the ladies from the sleigh; but Reginald Page, who was standing near, stepped in before him, and offered his hand to the ladies. This was too much for Percy's equanimity; "The fellow is always getting in my way," he muttered to himself. It was true, Rex had a habit of turning up at the right (or wrong) moment.

As Percy was leaving the church, Rex came up with out-stretched hand: "I suppose this is the last time I shall see you, Percy—I hear that you leave to-morrow."

"Yes, early in the morning," said Percy.

"I am sorry," said Rex, "that I shall not have an opportunity to discuss that passage in Horace with you. I should like your opinion as to the correct translation."

Percy could not resist this direct appeal, and after hesitating a moment, he said, "I shall be disengaged this afternoon. Come out and take dinner with me, and we can give it an hour or two."

"O, thank you! I shall be very glad to do so."

Early in the afternoon Rex made his appearance and was shown to Percy's room. They spent the time before dinner over their Horace. Percy was very kind and helpful. Rex found his friend much more advanced than himself, and was glad to avail himself of his assistance.

As they were coming down stairs to dinner, they heard a sweet voice singing to the organ accompaniment, and Rex learned that Victoria and her parents were also guests at dinner.

It was one of his lucky days—as the boys would say—and he enjoyed it thoroughly; and when he found Percy's sleigh at the door, with George to drive him home, he felt that the pleasure was complete.

Monday morning came with dark clouds. It was raining heavily, and the snow had melted on the roads making them almost impassable; and this was the first school morning after the holidays. Victoria looked from her window and thought of the many school children destitute of the blessings she possessed, and ran down to breakfast with heart and mind full of plans for the day. "Father," she said: "I should like to have the carriage all the afternoon, after school is dismissed. Many of the girls in my room have a long way to go, and if I could carry some of them home, it would save them a miserable walk."

"Certainly, daughter, your mother never uses it in such weather. Give Ben your orders."

Mrs. Kenyon smiled and said, "I am glad for my child

to feel this sweet consideration for her school-mates."

As Victoria was leaving the breakfast-room, her mother said, "My dear, tell Mammy to put up an additional quantity of luncheon for you to-day; some of your companions, I dare say, will be glad to share it with you, rather than go out in such weather."

"O, I forgot," and Victoria turned back; "I intended to ask you about that. Thank you, mother dear," and Victoria ran away feeling a delightful sense of gratitude for the means of making others comfortable.

It was Dolly's duty to carry the books, luncheon, and the medicine case, and put them into the carriage before Victoria came out. This morning, she was astonished at the size of the basket Mammy had ready for her.

"Why, we uns don't want all dat lunch, an' we kaint hab a picnic in de slush."

Vctoria, laughing, told her that they could have a picnic on the school desks.

As the carriage passed the Fox cabin, Victoria looked out to see if she could give any of the children a ride to school. Ducy made her appearance, dressed ready to walk into town, and was taken into the carriage.

As usual after a holiday, the pupils were slow in getting settled to study this morning. They all gathered round Victoria's desk, discussing the events of the two weeks—the party, thc accident to Chloe, and the lovely sleighing, till the bell rang, and all quietly separated and took their accustomed seats.

At noon all the girls who were not obliged to go home were invited to join Victoria in her bounteous luncheon. They borrowed a table from another room, and Dolly spread the repast—cold turkey, ham, buttered biscuit, with mince pie and apples for dessert. In the meantime, a quantity of milk was heating on the stove. This Dolly served in cups. She was much disgusted to find that two cups must serve the company, but she consoled herself with the reflection, "I's not gwine to let my little Missy drink outen de same cup wid udder folkses, kase Granny says it not healthy nohow. Dar is de tumbler what had de jelly in. I will jis wash it out, an' put my Missy's milk in dat."

While the girls were exercising in the hall, Victoria saw one of the little girls sitting in a corner crying piteously.

"What is the matter, Hulda," she asked.

"My ear aches so badly," and she burst into a wail of distress.

Victoria sent Dolly for her medicine case, and brought the child into the school-room to the fire. When Dolly brought the case, Little Doctor took some of the cloth used for bandages, folded it into a compress, then saturated it with laudanum, and warmed it thoroughly by the stove. She placed the child in proper position, and laid the compress around the ear. Taking a silk handkerchief from her pocket, she folded it and covered the ear, carefully excluding the air.

The girls and boys looked on with interest, and Lawrence Balfour said, "Do you really take pleasure in that kind of thing? I declare, you look as if you were in your element. It's fascinating, I admit, the way you do it. Your skill in dressing that young darky's burns was really scientific."

"O, yes," said Little Doctor; "I do indeed enjoy giving relief to suffering. I think I inherit the love for it from my father. He is an enthusiast in his profession."

Lawrence examined the medicine case with curiosity; "I have a fancy for the profession myself. Do you take regular instruction?"

"Only such as my father gives me when I ask him questions on some difficult point. He does not thnk it advisable for me to take up the study until I have finished my education."

When school was dismissed for the day, Victoria first gathered up the younger children who lived at a distance, and had Dolly pack them into the carriage, as many as it could hold, and told Ben to take them to their homes. The little Hulda she took on her lap, and carefully protected her from the cold wind.

Mrs. Davis, Hulda's mother, came out to the carriage and thanked Victoria for her kindness to her little girl. She said the child had been so much exposed to the weather during these cold days,—hinting at their poverty, which was but too apparent in their mserable abode. Little Doctor returned in time to take many of the girls in her room to their homes also.

She brought the circumstances of the Davis family to the notice of her parents, and the next morning Dr. and Mrs. Kenyon drove out to see the family, that they might relieve their wants. The woman's husband was ill, and had no medical attention. The Doctor asked if she would like him to prescribe for her husband, and went in to the poor room where he lay.

Mrs. Kenyon learned what was most needed, and that afternoon she sent Ben with the big farm wagon filled with provisions and wood for present use, and a bundle of blankets and comforters piled on top.

Chloe recovered rapidly under the faithful care of our Little Doctor, and before the end of February was able to go to the "quarters." She was very happy to be out among her people once more; but her pleasure, like most things in this world, was marred. The wool had not yet grown out on the back of her head. Hayden took advantage of this, and made it a source of fun for himself and vexation to poor Chloe.

The first morning after she was able to be with her family, Hayden was as usual baking an extra pile of buckwheat cakes for himself. When Granny's back was turned, he held one of the cakes on the back of his head and danced around Chloe making signs to remind her of the bare place on her head.

Chloe watched him with tearful eyes, not even crying out to get Granny's notice; but the fun was not to last long. Granny did see, and punished, too. She took up a strip of red calico from the table, and in her own amusing way tied the buckwheat cake to his head, saying, "Now yo' kin jis tote dat cake about fo' Chloe ter laugh at yo'." He was amused at first, but when Mammy, Judy, Gip, and Chloe began to laugh, he grew desperate and rushed out of the house to hide, leaving the feast to Chloe, who enjoyed it in peace.

During the early spring there had been much sickness among the school children. Little Doctor generally went with her father in the afternoon when he made his round of visits. Sometimes he permitted her to go in and see the children he visited. She always brought books and pictures, and sometimes delicacies when it was allowed.

One boy was on the Doctor's list of patients who had been making brave efforts to enter the highest grade at school, and was taken ill with fever. He aroused Dr. Kenyon's interest by his intelligence and patient submission to treatment. Victoria always took something to please and entertain the sick boy, which she sent up to his room.

One day, as she was waiting in the phaeton as usual for her father to pay his visit, a window opened above her, and looking up she saw the sick boy, Jay Lightner, himself. The Doctor had drawn his bed to the window that he might enjoy the lovely spring day. He thanked Little Doctor for her kindness to him, saying, "The books and other things you bring me are the only comforts I have."

"Do the school boys not come to see you?" she asked, in surprise.

"No, I have seen no one but my own family and my kind doctor," he said, trying to smile.

Victoria thought of the strong, healthy, happy boys in her room at school and of the comfort they might be to Jay, and resolved to try and interest them in the sick boy's welfare.

As soon as her father was seated in the phaeton, Victoria mentioned the subject to him, and asked if he thought it would be practicable to organize some system of visiting the sick children. He told her it was practicable and commendable, except in cases of contagious diseases; and that he would give her a list of his own patients with whom it would be perfectly safe to begin their work of charity.

The next morning, Victoria went to school with mind and heart full of plans for carrying out her newly formed project. As her companions gathered round her as usual, she said, with a bright smile, "I have some work for our Dramatic Club.   I should like to interest all our members in a real work of charity. Several of the girls and boys of this school are ill, and confined to their lonely rooms without anything to interest or cheer them. Some of them need substantial help; and it seems to me that we might all do something for our school-mates."

The boys and girls gathered closer around her, and asked what they could do.

"I have been thinking a good deal about it," said Victoria, "and my idea is to have some system about visiting."

Just then the school bell rang, and Victoria had only time to propose that they all, the "Dramatic Club," meet at her house that evening to discuss the plans.

Reginald Page whispered to Peter Benson, "I wonder if she will give us refreshments?" and Peter replied, "I would rather she would let us finish with a dance."

A merry party met at Beechwood that evening. As it was an informal meeting of the Club, they proceeded at once to discuss plans for visiting. The boys were to visit their own companions, and among the first, Jay Lightner must have a call. Each boy was to call on a sick companion each day, the girls to call on their friends, and all to report at the next meeting of the Club.

Rex said, "I always thought this kind of work was for old church members, but Little Doctor can make anything popular."

Neither Rex nor Peter was disappointed in his expectation of some reward. Cake and hot chocolate were served in the way of refreshments, and Mrs. Kenyon kindly consented to play some dance music for them.

They all went home well pleased with the work laid out for them, and were all most faithful in the duties assigned them.

At the next meeting of the Club they made a very creditable report of the work done; the number of visits paid, the books read, pictures and flowers bestowed. None of the sick ones happened to be members of the club, but all felt nearer together. The bond of human sympathy was greater than the bond of talent, which at first had bound the members together.

Jay Lightner and many other boys and girls had reason to love the twenty members of the "Dramatic Club."

The round of visiting and happy meetings at Beech-wood were continued, and other members of the high school were added to their number, giving a permanent plan to the good work begun by our Little Doctor.

CHAPTER XVII

The month of June finished Little Doctor's last term at the public school. Arrangements were made for her to enter the next term at St. Mary's, where Victoria's aunt occupied a prominent position. She was to take charge of her little niece and complete her education.

The last day at school was a sad one. The members of Victoria's classes all felt that her absence would be a loss, and were grieved to part with her for her own sake. They vied with each other in kind attentions and little acts of special favor. Her teachers, too, were unusually tender and considerate.

Victoria's heart was very full, and tears could no longer be restrained when the last lesson was recited and the books laid aside.

This day was not the final parting. Little Doctor and her parents had planned a delightful entertainment for the entire school. A lawn party was to be given at Beechwood before the family would leave for the East. Victoria had invited Mr. Ray and the other teachers, and the Dramatic Club was invited to assist in receiving and entertaining the other children.

Percy arrived home in time to lend a helping hand in the elaborate preparations.

The lawn party was to be given on the Fourth of July, Dr. Kenyon's birthday. The day dawned gloriously bright and beautiful. The sun shone resplendent on Beechwood. Every tree and shrub seemed to offer a welcome to the little guests. The great gates stood wide open long before the hour. Two o'clock was appointed, but many impatient little ones were already gathered under the grateful shade.

Exactly at the hour, the Club, twenty in number, arrived. All wore white, and each member wore a badge —a pale blue satin ribbon, with "Little Doctor" embroidered in gilt letters surrounded by a wreath of violets in their natural color. The girls were dressed in white, with blue ribbons, and the boys in white linen suits and blue cravats. Victoria was much pleased with the pretty compliment paid her in the selection of the badge.

Victoria received the Club with cordial delight, and graciously assigned them a part of her duties as hostess. They all entered into the gaiety of the occasion; leading in all the games provided for the little ones, swinging the timid ones, and drying the tears and soothing the feelings of any who were unfortunate enough to meet with any mishap.

The tables were placed under the trees, and spread with every delicacy dear to a child's taste.

Victoria, and Percy too, were untiring in their attentions to the elder guests, showing them over the beautiful grounds, and through the green-houses.

The happy day came to a close with a grand display of balloon ascensions and fireworks, as the guests departed.

Mammy, who was at the tables, surrounded by the other servants, remarked, "Bress goodness! dem chillens won't want no suppa dis night."

The tenth of July was fixed for the departure of the two families—the Kenyons and Tylers—for their Eastern trip.

It was an understood custom that Mammy was always to go back to Virginia with the family each year; but Chloe was to make her first visit this time, and to remain with Victoria at St. Mary's. She was of course overjoyed at the honor of serving her young mistress as maid, and had promised her parents to watch over "Missy" every hour of her life while away at school.

Ben and Paris drove the travelers to the railroad station where they met the rest of the party. They had seats in the coach together, and formed a cozy family party.

Just as the train was moving, who should jump aboard but Reginald Page. At the last moment he had received a dispatch from his wealthy aunt in Washington, consenting to bear the expense of a college course for her favorite nephew; and as Rex was never troubled with a superabundance of baggage, he was not long in deciding to join his friends on their journey.

Good-natured, audacious Rex was a welcome addition to the party. His sources of entertainment were exhaustless, and his merry wit irresistible. He carried a newspaper in his hand, and before he was seated he asked, with comical assurance, if he might sit by Victoria while he read aloud an article—"an account of the lawn party"—written by himself.

Percy was still disposing of his numerous traveling conveniences, and had not had an opportunity more than to speak to Victoria, and this unlooked for appearance of the irrepressible Rex was anything but agreeable.

There was a natural antagonism between these two youths, but Percy was too polite, and Rex too politic ever to allow this difference of temperament to amount to hostility. These sudden intrusions, as Percy called them, were a strain on his usual self-control, and Rex's self-assurance always irritated him; but on this occasion Rex showed his good manners by withdrawing to his own seat as soon as he had read the article.

From time to time, however, he joined his pleasant neighbors, and with one of his original speeches caused a burst of merry laughter, the older travelers enjoying the quaint sallies of wit as much as the younger ones; but once in awhile he was taken down in his lofty flights of fancy by one of Percy's common-sense remarks. He was always the first to acknowledge his defeat and join in the hearty laugh at his own expense. His friends used to say that Rex had three characteristic qualities— wit, audacity, and a good appetite. He certainly proved the latter on this journey, much to Mammy's amusement. She had provided a bountiful supply of eatables, and when she saw it rapidly diminishing, she whispered to Chloe, "Sho, Marse Rex am got a healthy appetite."

About half-way on their journey, when once the train stopped, Rex jumped off and ran into an eating house. As he disappeared, the train started. Our party all exclaimed, and put their heads out of the windows just in time to see Rex rushing towards the car with his hat in one hand and a paper bag in the other. He made good time, but failed to get on.

"Too late!" shouted Percy from the platform of the car, and he laughed with unconcealed satisfaction.

It was very amusing, but our travelers soon missed the untiring source of their entertainment, and lamented the mishap that deprived them of their lively companion.

During the course of the journey, Dr. Kenyon had invited Rex to visit Gray Cliff before the vacation was over. The Doctor was well acquainted with Reginald's family and had taken a fancy to the bright, interesting boy.

A few days after they arrived at Gray Cliff, Rex put in an appearance, and was cordially welcomed by the family. Old Senator Kenyon especially enjoyed the

fresh young vitality of his boyish guest, and made him
heartily welcome to guns, hounds, and fishing tackle;
but Percy won the old man's admiration by his strong,
manly physique, as well as by his dignified, high-bred
manner.

After a few weeks spent at Gray Cliff, and Poplar
Grove, the home of Victoria's grand-parents on her
mother's side, the entire party again set out. Saratoga,
Newport, and Niagara were all visited. Six weeks
slipped away, and the Kenyons were again at Gray Cliff
for a few days before vacation would end, and the parents
would have to part with their darling child.

It was a trying time to all. Victoria had never been
separated a day from her parents in all her young life.
She had thought more of the parting than her parents
knew, and had braced herself to bear it with as much
composure as possible for their sakes.

The journey to the Seminary was made in a day, and
a night at the hotel had refreshed our Little Doctor so
that she felt equal to the ordeal of a first day at a new
school. She was much pleased with the appearance of
the large building and beautiful grounds.

The trying moment had come; they were all in the
great drawing-room of St. Mary's, where the principal
and Aunt Charlotte had received them.

The final arrangements were completed, and Dr. and
Mrs. Kenyon were about to leave, when a gentleman with
his wife and daughter, a girl about Victoria's age, came
in. As it happened, the gentlemen were acquainted—
Mr. Willington was an old collegemate of Dr. Kenyon's
and they met cordially. Each introduced his wife and
daughter.

The two weeping girls looked shyly at each other, and
then Victoria timidly extended her hand to Claire Will-

ington, and each smiled through her tears, though
Claire's lips instantly pouted into an angry protest
against the smile. She drew Victoria aside, and whispered, "You are very nice to me, but I don't want to stay
here; I hate it already. Pa would let me go back home,
but Ma is so head-strong," and the willful girl scowled
in the direction of her mother. This conduct quite
shocked our well-bred little girl.

When Victoria's parents turned to say good-bye, she
embraced each in turn and kissed them through blind-
ing tears, but no word escaped her lips. She followed
them to the gate, holding a hand of each one; and as
the carriage drove away, she stood under the big weep-
ing-willow tree and kissed her hand to them as long as
they were in sight.

While Mr. Willington talked to the principal, Claire's
mother tried to comfort her daughter. She drew her
tenderly to her side, but Claire only pouted her pretty red
lips, and jerked her hand from her mother's clasp.

When her father at length turned towards her, she
threw herself into his arms with passionate pleading: "Pa,
if you will take me back home I will promise you never to
defy my governess again. I will study diligently, and—
and I will practise my music two whole hours a day."

Her father spoke tenderly to her, whispering softly in
her ear; but he was evidently not yielding, for she broke
from him, crying, "I won't stay here," and rushed out of
the room, her parents following her.

Victoria had returned to the veranda, and was standing on the steps when Claire passed her. She was
holding her hat by a ribbon, while her long red curls
fell in confusion around her flushed face. She walked
to the gate, and climbed into the carriage that was waiting for her parents, and took her seat in bold defiance.

Her parents came out, and a few words in a command-ing tone from her mother, brought the rebellious girl to something like submission. She got out and walked to-wards the steps, while the carriage drove off.

She glanced back and said "Good-bye, Pa," but not a word to her mother; then throwing herself down on the steps, she sobbed out, "O, I am the most miserable girl that ever lived!"

Victoria looked down at the strong, beautiful young creature with pity and wonder.

At this moment, her Aunt Charlotte came out, and taking her niece in her arms, she said, "My darling, you have behaved with commendable self-control—I am proud to call you my niece."

Victoria leaned her head on her Aunt's shoulder, and wept showers of tears.

Claire stopped her wailing, and looked up at the digni-fied lady before her, and said, "I suppose, then, you have not a very flattering opinion of me."

Miss Dorcey looked at the young girl in surprise—she had left the room before the scene with Claire. She hesitated a moment, and then turned to her niece: "Come, my child, I will introduce you to Professor Field's wife; you will find her very lovely."

After the introduction to the lady, Aunt Charlotte whispered a word to Mrs. Field, who at once went out to Claire. She then led Victoria to her room, which was adjoining her own apartments.

Poor Chloe, left to herself, sitting in the hall, was not much less miserable than her young mistress. At a sign from Victoria as she passed up the stairway, Chloe fol-lowed her mistress to her room.

Mrs. Kenyon had secured a room with a small apart-ment attached which Chloe could occupy.

Victoria was pleased with the large cheerful room. Shelves projected from the bay window on which plants were growing in pots. These plants were a gift from her Aunt, to add to the brightness of her niece's surroundings.

Aunt Charlotte took from the wardrobe in the room a dress of dark purple cloth trimmed with gold braid, and said, "This is the uniform of St. Mary's, Victoria; on dress occasions you will wear white. I hope you will like both.

"O, very much indeed, Auntie Charlotte; purple is my favorite color; though I suppose we are not expected to indulge in such preferences," she added, with a sad little smile.

"Yes, my child, you may admire it as much as you like; but I fear we could not indulge a taste for some other color. Now I will leave you to dress for dinner. The hour is five o'clock. I am glad you have Chloe with you," and she patted Chloe on the shoulder.

As soon as the door closed, poor Chloe gave way to her loneliness in a burst of tears. Victoria caught both hands of her faithful maid in hers, and their tears fell together.

But there was no time for indulging in such weakness. Victoria bathed her flushed face, while Chloe opened her satchels and arranged the toilet articles on the bureau.

When Victoria sat down to have her hair dressed, Chloe began brushing the long golden curls over her fingers; "O, no, Chloe," said her mistress; "I am not to wear curls here; it is the rule of the school to wear braids. Please plait it smoothly in two braids; and look in the drawer—I think you will find some purple ribbon to tie it with."

Chloe stood back, dismayed at this announcement; she

had never seen the beautiful hair restrained—it was next thing to cutting it off—but Victoria smiled at her reluctance, and said they must hurry with the toilet—something else Chloe was not accustomed to hurry. She consoled herself, however, with the reflection that she would "Jis let a bunch of de curls go nat'ally like at de ends."

The ribbon was found in the drawer, and fastened to the thick braid and Chloe stepped back to take a survey of the result. She was better pleased than she had expected to be; "Wal, honey, yo' looks mo' like a young lady, an' its gittin' 'bout time now to war yo' har tucked up wid a comb."

Chloe unlocked the trunks, and, to Victoria's surprise, she lifted out a large music-box, which her Uncle Howard had sent as his contribution to her comfort. The sweet tones soothed and rested her—nothing could have been more acceptable at the moment.

Aunt Charlotte was evidently pleased to find Victoria ready, and complimented her upon looking well in St. Mary's uniform. She took her niece down to the pupils' parlor, where all assembled before going to the dining-room.

In the meantime, Mrs. Field had persuaded Claire to go to her room, which was one adjoining Victoria's. After giving her instructions as to her dress and arrangement of her hair, Mrs. Field left her, and sent a maid to assist in the latter operation.

Claire was really a sensible girl, and saw that resistance was useless. She only protested that she would not have her hair braided, saying, "I would rather be guillotined than submit to it."

The maid paid no attention to this extravagant language, but began to obey orders, and soon had the curls in neat braids, while Claire sat in sullen submission.

The two hundred pupils had all assembled when Mrs. Field appeared with Claire. She merely introduced her to one of the teachers, who would take her to dinner.

As the girls rose to form in procession, one tall, graceful girl, with large, elfish-looking eyes and heavy black brows that almost met over her shapely nose, stepped towards Victoria and said, "I am appointed to escort you to dinner." Then she whispered, "I am glad I was asked, for, do you know, I quite fell in love with your violet eyes as soon as you came in. I hope we shall be in the same class."

Victoria thanked her simply, and said, "I did not hear your name distinctly, I always like to know one's name correctly at first."

"Well, at home, my name is Maryland Carroll, but here among the girls I am called 'Baltimore Blue,'" and she laughed with a twinkle of mischief in the gray-blue eyes.

The pupils were all allowed an hour for social intercourse immediately after dinner. All were again gathered in the parlor, none of the teachers were present at this hour, and the girls enjoyed the little freedom to chat among themselves. It was something new to Victoria, and she became interested in the gay, bright faces, and turned her head from one merry group to another trying to distinguish the voices, but it was all a confused babble to her.

The young girl who had taken her to dinner came up and engaged her in conversation, but her heart was still too lonely for companionship, so she excused herself and found her way to her own room.

She was telling Chloe about the girls and what they were doing down stairs, for the old habit of a confidential little chat with her maid was very strong, when she heard a heavy sob in the room adjoining hers and remembered that it was Claire's. She hesitated about intruding upon her, but her kind, helpful nature overcame her instinctive reserve, and she went into the hall and rapped at the door.

A moment passed, and then a low voice said, "Come in." Victoria found the unhappy girl lying on the bed, her face in the pillows, sobbing bitterly. She looked up, with, "O, it's you, is it? I was not sure it was you, but I did not think any one else would come to me; you were so kind to me when we were in the drawing-room; but how did you know I was in this room?" "Mrs. Field told me my room joins yours," said Victoria; "and I heard you—" she would not say "crying"; but Claire finished the sentence.

"Yes, I am so miserable, I just gave way to a big cry when I came up here away from those hateful girls; they stare at me as if I were a queer specimen from a menagerie."

Victoria laughed heartily, the first time for many hours. "But," she said, "you have not told me whether I am intruding."

"O, dear, no! I am dying of loneliness and disgust with everything and everybody, but you."

This rather equivocal compliment encouraged her visitor to stay. They were both excused from study-hour this first evening, and Victoria sought to overcome her own loneliness by trying to cheer her neighbor, who still lay on the bed.

"Well, Claire," she said, "don't you think you will feel better if you rise and sit in a chair by the window?"

"I look so horrid," she answered, as she sat up and turned her flushed face towards Victoria.

"Come and bathe your face, and you will feel ever so much better," Victoria said in an indulgent tone, as if speaking to a child.

Claire rose to her feet and took a straight-forward look at Victoria; "How can you tolerate yourself with your pretty curls done up in this hateful Dutch style? I saw your hair when I came, and it was lovely. It does not matter so much for mine, for it is horrid anyway."

"O, you mistake," said Victoria; "artists would rave over your hair—it is real Titian red."

"Well, I don't know what kind 'Titian red' is, but I do know that it is not pretty. I wish Ma could see it now—

she admired my curls—she would think she had put me into an orphan asylum instead of a first-class young ladies'—how many more qualifying words are there?"

Claire was very amusing to Victoria, though at any other time she would not have encouraged this flippant talk. Victoria was shocked at the disrespect to her mother that Claire's tone implied. She noticed Victoria's change of countenance for a moment, then she tossed her head, saying, "O! I suppose you are one of those 'goody, goody' girls that we read about in the Sunday-school books, who are always translated at the end of the last chapter."

Victoria rose from the side of the bed where she was sitting, and said, "Good-night Claire!" But before she could reach the door, Claire was holding her fast.

"O, please don't leave me! I did not mean to offend you; indeed, I did not! I am used to saying just whatever comes into my mind. I did not think you would mind just that little bit of irreverence to a Sunday-school book.

Victoria was amused in spite of herself, but she was determined not to talk to Claire in that strain.

A happy thought came to her—"Are you fond of music?" she asked.

"O, yes, I adore music when I do not have to play it."

"Excuse me a minute," Victoria said, and left the room to get her music-box.

She found her Aunt in the room waiting for her, who said, "My child, you must not sacrifice yourself entirely for that willful, spoiled girl."

"Auntie dear, she is so miserable, and I am just going to carry my music-box in to her for this evening, I thought it would soothe her better than conversation."

Her Aunt assented, and she returned to Claire, to find

her standing before the mirror holding two long, thick braids of hair in her hands. She had cut them off close to her head.

"I cut them off to spite Ma," she said, with a dangerous glitter in the large, blue eyes; "and I am going to send them to her in the morning. O, won't she weep over them!"

Victoria was speechless with disgust and indignation. She stood, with her music-box clasped in her arms, staring at the shorn head, and at last burst out, "You cruel, wicked girl! to do such a thing to pain your mother. I brought you my treasure—my music-box—to soothe and cheer you this evening, but I will—" Victoria checked herself, for Claire had thrown herself again on the bed, and covered her head with the pillows.

Victoria set the music-box on the table, started a low, soft air, and quietly left the room. Here was a patient beyond our Little Doctor's skill.

Victoria told her Aunt of the shocking act, and Miss Charlotte went at once to Claire's room. She gently, but firmly, took the girl off the bed, and with a few kind words undressed her. Claire made no resistance but got into bed, and turned her face away from view.

Aunt Charlotte took a seat, and quietly watched beside the unhappy girl until she fell asleep, then taking up the braids of hair, she carried them out of the room.

The next morning Claire awoke before the rising-bell sounded. Gradually, the events of the past day were recalled, and as she thought of her hair, she jumped up and looked around the room. The braids were gone, and, in looking about for them, she caught a glimpse of her face in the mirror and was startled by the woeful aspect she presented. The heavy locks of hair falling over her ears and cheeks, one side longer than the other, seemed to turn her face awry, and the lngering scowl on her pretty features made her look repulsively ugly.

Her first thought was, "What will the girls say?" Then, if she could only fly from the place before any one should see her.

"I'll do it," she said, and hurriedly dressed herself in her traveling suit, tied on her hat, and softly fled down the stairway. No one was in sight; she was unlocking the front door, when Professor Field stepped from his office, which was near the door and said, "Miss Claire, where are you going?"

She looked around with a frightened air, and dropped her head as she met the calm gaze of the principal.

Seeing that her escape was cut off, she again became defiant: "I am going home, Professor Field—it is no use to try to keep me here."

"Certainly not, my child, you are quite at liberty to go, but you must wait until I notify your parents; I cannot permit you to leave St. Mary's alone. I will write to your father at once, and as soon as I hear from him, I will send you home."

"O, please sir, let me go now, I am so miserable here!"

"I know you are, poor child! There is nothing makes one so miserable as yielding to violent passions. But come with me to Mrs. Field's room; we will entertain you as our guest until your father comes, for I am sure he will come, himself, for you."

She suffered herself to be led back, for she remembered that she had not enough money to pay her traveling expenses even had she escaped from the institution.

Mrs. Field exchanged glances with her husband when he brought Claire to her room, and then putting her arms around the reluctant figure, she drew her into the room, and took off the hat that partially concealed the disfigured head. She was about to exclaim, but checked herself, at the unevenness of the hair, suspecting how it came about.

Claire answered the amazed expression on the lady's face: "I cut my hair off last night, I was so angry at being left here."

"It was a pity to spoil your good looks, but it can't be helped now, and we must try and make both sides of your locks agree; come, sit down here before the mirror, and let me trim it evenly."

There was something controlling, as well as playful, in Mrs. Field's words, and Claire obeyed with a keen sense of shame.

The hair was soon made even, and brushed behind the ears.

"Now," said Mrs. Field; "you had better change your dress and then come down and take breakfast with me this morning."

"You are very kind to me, dear Mrs. Field, and I am grateful to you, but you do not know how miserable I am here," and she burst into a piteous cry.

"O, yes, child, I know all about it; I have seen hundreds of homesick girls. Why, the young girl whose room is next to yours is an only child—her parents live away off in Kentucky, and yet she bears the separation from them like a little heroine."

Claire wiped her eyes, and said, "I will try and endure it until Pa comes for me."

After breakfast, Victoria knocked at Claire's door; not seeing her in the dining-room, she was anxious about her.

Claire opened the door at once. She was pacified with the hope of her father coming for her, and she met Victoria almost cheerfully: "I am going home," she said,

"but how can you be so brave? Mrs. Field was telling
me that you live away in Kentucky, and yet you have
been so heroic—I don't believe you have cried a tear."

"O yes, I have cried like a baby," Victoria admitted;
"but I tried to control my feelings because my parents
were so unhappy at parting with me. I know I must
have my education—it is not done in any unkindness to
me, and why should I make them more miserable by resistance?"

"But have you no pleasure at home—parties and
operas and theatres?"

"I have rarely attended anything of the kind," said
Victoria; "My parents think it better for me to wait until
I leave school."

"Well, they are all I care for, and I am going to have
them."

"But how can you study after being up so late at
night?" Victoria asked innocently.

"O, I don't trouble myself about that. I sleep in the
morning, and the governess reads to Ma."

Claire did not like the expression of the violet eyes before her, and hastened to say, "Your Aunt was very
kind to me last night. I would like her very much, and
Mrs. Field, too, if they were anywhere else than in this
prison. Did your Aunt say anything about my hair?"

"No, I was asleep when my Aunt returned from your
room—but I must go—would you like me to leave my
music-box with you while I write my letters?"

Claire was willing enough to have something to entertain her while impatiently waiting for her father to come
or send for her. The willful, rebellious girl always succeeded in having her own way, as she said, and had no
doubt that Professor Field's letter would decide her
father to recall her at once.

But Professor Field knew what Claire did not, that Mr. and Mrs. Willington were to go abroad immediately after placing their daughter at school; but he hoped a letter would reach the father before the vessel would sail, and detain them until they could remove Claire.

The music-box could not make Claire forget her hair. She went to Aunt Charlotte's room, and with faltering tongue and downcast eyes, said, "Miss Dorcey, did you take my—my braids?"

"Yes, Claire, I have them; let me keep them until you are ready to leave St. Mary's."

"Please give me the hair, I want to see it."

Aunt Charlotte went to a table and took up a box and handed it to Claire, saying, "Child, your hair will soon grow out again, and will be long enough to put up before you leave school!"

"I am not going to stay here; I expect Pa will come for me in a few days."

Miss Dorcey was astonished at this news but said no more.

Claire went to her room and taking out the long, thick braids held them up to view. They shone like burnished copper in the sunlight; but she had no admiration for them. All the rage and resentment towards her mother returned. She quickly put them back in the box and wrote a note to her saying:

"Ma:—I send you this hair to remind you of your unhappy daughter.   Claire."

She directed it to her mother, put on the stamps, and then went down the back stairway and out into the garden, hoping she could get the gardener to mail the box.

She had not waited long in her hiding place, among the rose bushes, when the postman came up the avenue, much to her gratification. She stepped out in the path and handed him the box, saying "Please mail this for me."

He shook his head, and said, "Miss, it's against orders to do it."

"O, you see it is to a lady—my mother; do take it."

He reluctantly put it in the mail bag, muttering, "This is irregular, but I don't want to be disobliging to a lady."

Clairethanked him, and ran to the house and up to her room without being seen by any one.

In due time the box was delivered at the grand house on Chestnut street; but its arrival was not at a fortunate time for Claire. Her father had been so miserable about leaving her unhappy, that he had decided to go for her, and was on his way out when the box was handed him by the postman.

Mr. Willington, seeing it was from his daughter, turned back and went upstairs to give it to his wife. She smilingly said, "Some little peace offering from darling, I suppose."

She took the cover from the box, and seeing the hair she dropped it, almost overcome by the shock.

Mr. Willington quickly picked it up, and seeing the note, he said, "This is an explanation, Cornelia; shall I read it to you?"

He read it aloud with indignation, and said, "She is a cruel daughter, and does not deserve such a mother as you are. This act settles the matter, she shall remain at school instead of going to Europe with us. My dear wife, forgive me for doubting your good judgment; you are always loving and wise in your management of our children.

Mrs. Willington was greatly worried at the loss of Claire's hair, and deeply wounded in sending it to her.

Claire's first day of waiting was a trying one to her restless, pleasure-loving nature. Victoria had made her a little visit just before she went to the school-room. As she left, she kissed Claire's cheek, saying, "Do change your mind and stay here, you will soon get used to regular study; I find so many sweet girls here, I am sure you will be as pleasantly entertained as if you were home in society."

Claire smiled as she said, "You dear, unsophisticated child, you don't know anything about the glorious times I have had at home. Pa always takes me along when he goes to grand entertainments, and I have my own set when Ma gives parties; but I would never see anything if Ma had her way—she always says to Pa, 'Claire has lessons to study and should retire early.' "

"Well, Claire, I am quite confident that girls should study and sleep. I am going to leave my treasure with you to make you forget all about going away; I must hurry, I hear the call for tardy pupils, so good-morning."

Claire called out to Little Doctor, "You look charming in the gown and cap."

Victoria kissed her hand in reply, and hastened down the corridor.

Claire started the music-box, and sat thinking of the places where she had heard the beautiful airs, and sighed for a return of the gay life and freedom. She picked up a book Miss Dorcey had sent her; but soon tired of the first chapter and laid it aside with a yawn, saying, "That young saint Victoria would read it and be highly pleased; it bores me dreadfully to read any kind of book, but I am sure there are some that are funny, for brother laughs until he is tired, then will say, 'O, this is a boy's book and would not entertain a girl.' "

Mrs. Field had brought Claire a bouquet of fresh flowers, gathered by herself. These sweet creatures held out inducement in the way of color, form, and odor to entice Claire to notice them. She picked out a handful of rich carnations, with a sprig of lemon verbena, and fastened them in her dress; then took her seat in the open window.

The view was pleasing, indeed, in rural beauty. Close to her window-sill a family of robins dwelt in happy ignorance of their new neighbor. They flitted in and out of the branches of a big cherry tree, making sweet melody in their busy life, much to Claire's surprise. She chirped and whistled to them trying to coax them within; but they took fright, not being used to neighborly customs, and soon flew away to outspreading boughs where they could take notice of the intruder.

The orchard, in sight, with its bountiful harvest of golden quinces, bright red apples and russet pears, attracted the lonely young girl. She took advantage of the permission to walk about the grounds, and descended to the hall, where she saw many of the advanced pupils in academic gowns and caps crossing to the recitation rooms. They were certainly quite attractive to her, and she stood behind a piece of statuary looking at them until the last one disappeared, then went to the orchard.

A small black boy was picking up the fallen fruit, and putting it in a wheelbarrow. He plucked off his old straw hat and greeted her: "Good mornin', Miss."

Claire nodded to him, and began to feel the pears to see if they were ripe enough to eat. He looked at her

with very wide open eyes, saying, "Yo' mustn't pinch
dem pars, yo' spile 'em sho."

Claire did not condescend to answer, but continued
her investigations until she found a luscious one, then,
seating herself on the wheelbarrow, began to eat it.

The boy's glance at the self-satisfied young lady was
not in the least friendly or complimentary, and turning
over in his woolly head some saucy questions he wanted
to ask, he watched her closely. He brought his hands
full of pears and put them down near Claire, then resting
his hands on his knees, he began, "Say, Missy, what fo'
yo' crop yo' head, I seed yo' yesterday when yo' com'd,
and yo' had long cu'ls?"

Claire instinctively put up her hand to her head, for-
getting that the curls were gone, and she was without her
hat.

The boy grinned, and put out his tongue, saying,
"Dey am gone sho as yo' sot on dat wheel-bar'."

Claire got up and threw the half-eaten pear at the boy,
striking him in his capacious mouth. He shouted and
laughed, much to Claire's vexation; but she was soon
avenged by the boy's father, who came from behind a
tree, and boxed his ears until he changed his tune.

Claire sought entertainment among the flowers; all the
walks were trodden, all the varieties of blooming chrys-
anthemums and roses counted and admired, but nothing
could quiet the unrest that had taken possession of her
heart.

"O, but I am sorry I cut off my hair," was forced from
her pretty lips; "I suppose every rude servant on the
place is laughing at me, and I shouldn't wonder if everybody in school has heard by this time of what I have
done; but the worst part of it is, I sent it to Ma."

She sank down on a rustic seat, and burst into a passionate flood of tears, saying, "After all, she had a right to do as she pleases with me—I am her child. Pa will be very angry with me when he sees her weeping over those hateful red braids, and I doubt if he will come for me when he sees them, for he will think I look just horrid."

Claire did really love her mother, and well knew her judgment was always just and right for others; but when she was the subject of discussion with her parents, she felt bitter, and acted in an unbecoming way towards her mother.

"It is all Pa's fault; he will let me do as I please, and then reproach me for displeasing Ma. O, I wish I were dead, I am so miserable I cannot wait until he comes for me."

She got up and walked to the house, As she ascended the steps of the veranda she heard merry voices; a door opened into the hall, and a crowd of girls came out. Among them she recognized Victoria. She ran to Claire, and taking her hand led her up the wide flight of stairs to the second story.

Little Doctor's heart was deeply touched by the tearful eyes and quivering lips of her new friend; and pressing her hand, she asked, "What is it, have you heard from your father?"

Claire shook her head, not venturing to speak until they reached her room; she then broke down, throwing herself on Victoria's shoulder, and sobbing out, "No, he will not come for me, I am sure, because I sent that hair and a—a—note to Ma."

Victoria did not reply, for she was too indignant at Claire for being so cruel to her mother.

Claire was quick to interpret the silence, and straightening herself up with wounded pride, she said, "O, I ex-

pected you would despise me for it; but I am real sorry
that I was so unkind to Ma."

Victoria kissed her flushed cheek, saying, "Now I do
sympathize with you, I knew you could not be indifferent to your mother; but you must cheer up, you will
be ill, fretting in this way. Write at once to your mother,
and tell her you are so sorry you grieved her."

Claire was silent for a time, then with scowling brow,
she said, "If I do that she will think I—I—have got
religion."

Victoria could not suppress the laugh that this expression called forth.

Claire smiled shyly as she glanced at her, and added,
"I just hate canty people."

Victoria's face grew serious, as she replied, "Are you
not sincere in being sorry that you gave your mother
pain?"

"Yes, I am, or I would not tell you so."

Victoria drew her to a lounge, saying, "An honest confession of doing wrong will convince your parents that
you are worthy of their devotion. Now, bathe your face,
while I go and ask Mrs. Field if we can take our luncheon together in your room.

Victoria soon returned, with Chloe carrying a large
tray with the luncheon. Chloe spread a cloth on the table
then set the tempting food on in her dainty fashion.

When they were alone, Victoria induced Claire to eat
a little; but she was very miserable, and Little Doctor,
knowing what was best for the heartache, put her to bed.
After she had darkened the room, she said a few cheering words to her and went out, telling Chloe to stay near
the door to prevent any one from disturbing Miss Claire.

After school hours, Victoria went to Claire's room, and
found her refreshed by sleep and rest.

Mrs. Field took her down to dine with her, and by bed time she quite regained her cheerfulness under the genial influence of our Little Doctor.

Claire awoke very early the next morning—with the robin family in her room; they were investigating the premises to see if she was still in possession.

The moment she raised her head she put them to flight. She jumped up, thinking she might capture one, at least; but all went through the open window with fluttering wings and throbbing little breasts. Claire looked into the mirror and smiled, thinking it was no wonder the birds had taken "French leave" of her.

She walked to the window eastward, and sighed, as she noticed the station a half-mile distant, and wondered if her father was on his way to St. Mary's.

"O, I do wish I had not sent that box and note to Ma —I am confident Pa will not come for me. If I had the money I would start right off, and they would have to keep me with them."

She took out her purse and counted the silver pieces, then sat down, resting her head on her hands.

A thought flashed through her mind—why not go to the University, to her brother Lenox, just half way home; she felt confident he would take her the rest of the way if she wept and begged.

It was five o'clock and the train passed St. Mary's station at six. She quickly dressed, putting on her pretty pearl-grey traveling dress, then brushing her unruly hair, she put a few toilet articles in her satchel, with her purse; and this, with her hat, she dropped out of the window. Then climbing out on the tree close by the house, she slid from boughs to branches until she was four feet from the ground, then jumped the rest of the way.

She was not in the least the worse for the squirrel-like

fashion of descending. She picked up her satchel and hat, and ran out toward the orchard. She remembered seeing a large gate on the outskirts of the place, and counted on getting to the road in that direction.

She was passing the last row of trees when the woolly head of her little tormentor of yesterday popped from behind a currant bush. The fright was mutual.

Claire jumped, saying, "How you scared me! what are you doing there?"

He shivered with fright, and stammered out, "I frought yo' was my dad. He is gwine to dress my jacket, an' I's hidin' from him."

Claire recovered herself, and said, "You come and go to the station with me, and I will give you fifty cents."

His eyes rolled with delight, and he answered, "Suttinly I kin go. Yo' a-runden off?" he looked at the locks of curly hair clustering about the face, remembering the offence he had given yesterday, and feared her displeasure, as the fifty cents might be in danger.

They started off in the direction of the station, reaching it just as the train whistled. Claire gave the boy the promised half-dollar, and got into the coach with a loud-beating heart.

Joe, the boy, called out, "Thanky fo' de money; good-bye."

Claire nodded, then made her way to a vacant seat near a good-natured looking woman with a small boy by her side, thinking she was safe in sight of the motherly person.

After the train started, Claire was at her ease; she had watched the road to St. Mary's with a nervous dread, fearing some one would discover her flight, and overtake her.

Claire started when the conductor reached out his

hand to her, saying, "One fifty, Miss," but she recovered her presence of mind and gave the money with some little independence in her manner.

The ride to the University was long and tiresome to our young traveler. At noon the train reached the station, and to Claire's great delight, her brother was standing ready to help her off. She greeted him with joy, saying, "How did you know I was coming?"

He kissed her, then led her to the small waiting-room.

She could not wait the proper time to talk, and said, "You don't seem to be surprised at seeing me."

He smilingly said, "No, I am not; here is a dispatch from Professor Field." He took it out and read aloud:

"Mr. Lenox Willington:—Your sister will pass the University at noon to-day on her way home. Please be at the station to meet her.   John R. Field."

Lenox took Claire's hand, as they sat down on the bench, saying, "Little sister, did you run off from St. Mary's?"

With tearful, pleading eyes, she acknowledged she had.

"Well," said her brother, "Father is coming for you to-day; here is the dispatch I received last night; he will be along here in a half-hour. Come and have some luncheon, you are hungry, I fear."

Claire jumped up with delight, laughing merrily as she looked out of the small window to see if the train was in sight.

As she turned to tell Lenox how good she intended to be when at home once more, the telegraph operator handed a dispatch to her brother. He read it, and from the expression on his face, Claire thought it contained bad news.

She caught hold of his arm: "Do tell me what it is," she exclaimed in a panting whisper.

"It is from father, and he is not coming for you." He read aloud to her, while her heart ached.

"Lenox Willington:—I will not go to St. Mary's. Claire has decided the matter. Will stay at school until we return from Europe. Go to your sister at once to comfort her.   Henry Willington."

Lenox looked puzzled, saying, "I can't understand it."

Claire comprehended all its meaning in a second, and bowed her head in silent weeping. Her hat fell off, and for the first time Lenox noticed the wealth of shining curls were gone.

"What does this mean," he said, laying his hand caressingly on her curly locks: "Its an outrage for them to have cut off your hair."

Claire lifted her tear-stained face, and said, "I did it myself to spite Ma, and sent it to her with an unkind note. This explains Pa's saying that I have decided the matter."

As Lenox put his arm around her, she made an honest confession to him that she deserved to be left behind. The hours on the train had mellowed her heart towards her good mother, and she was miserable indeed.

But her curosity soon suggested, "I didn't know they were going to Europe."

Lenox smiled, "They have thought about the trip for some time."

"Why didn't they tell me?" she said with indignation.

Lenox patted her cheek, saying, "They could not count on our little girl's self-control. Now, I hope you will be sensible and go back to St. Mary's and show us how good and studious you can be while our parents are gone. You know your education has been neglected by irregular study, and you can now make up for lost time. How do you like the principal, teachers, and pupils?"

"I like them well enough, but I hate to stay in that prison and study all the time—never going to the opera and other nice places of amusement."

"Now you are old enough, my sister, to understand that a lady must be educated and accomplished; and you can never do anything at home when you are disturbed by amusements and society. Come, the train is in sight," and he led her out.

As they got on, Percy Tyler came out of the express office with a package in his hand. He nodded to Lenox and lifted his hat to Claire, wondering with all his mental power where Lenox was going with the pretty young girl.

Before they reached St. Mary's, Claire was persuaded by her brother to make up her mind to submit to the requirements of the Institute, and devote her time to study.

She said, "It would be intolerable but for one person there—a beautiful girl, bright, good, and lovely. She has been like a guardian angel to me since the moment I arrived, only when I—" Claire hung her head, and said in a whisper, "I talk ugly about Ma; then she gets real angry with me."

"I don't wonder she does. I admire her for that," said Lenox.

It was after nightfall when the travelers entered the gates of St. Mary's.

There was a light in the chapel, and some one singing a solo—a sweet, young voice full of melody. Lenox stopped.

"Sister," he said, "listen to that charming voice—what does it mean, is she singing alone?"

Claire remembered Victoria had told her about the

pretty custom at the evening service—one of the pupils always sang a solo after the benediction, and she told her brother about it.

Both were much interested, and walked to the chapel door, which was open. Professor Field knelt at the chancel, and the teachers and some two hundred pupils knelt in their seats. Mrs. Field played the accompaniment on the organ and Victoria stood at her side with clasped hands and uplifted face and eyes. She sang her mother's favorite hymn—she did not need the notes, for she had known it by heart for years.

"Who is she?" asked Lenox in a whisper.

"Why, she is my dear friend, my angel."

"But what is her name?" demanded Lenox.

"Victoria Kenyon," replied Claire with a faltering voice. She was deeply touched by the voice and appearance of Victoria; and it is possible that Lenox also was impressed, for they stood until the congregation of pupils formed into line and left the chapel by an entrance at the rear, adjoining the seminary.

Brother and sister escaped without being seen, and walked to the front entrance, hand in hand. Lenox sent a servant for Professor and Mrs. Field.

Of course they were gracious to Lenox and Claire, and received the apology made by the pretty penitent, assuring her of their good will.

Lenox was invited to be the guest of the Professor for the night, and Claire bid him a tearful good-bye, as he was to return on the early train.

Claire was accompanied to her room by Mrs. Field, who made everything pleasant and comfortable for her, sending a delicious supper to her, as she knew she must be in need of refreshment; but she could not retire until she had seen Victoria.

She stepped to her door and tapped gently. Little Doctor opened it, and they flew into each others arms, glad to be together again.

"O, I am so glad to be with you once more, I have had such a dreadful day," said Claire, trying to keep back the tears.

She told Victoria all she had done since she left, then added, "Now, you will be good to me, when I am going to try so hard to be brave, as you are?"

"I will, indeed, and help you all I can," answered Victoria.

Lenox arrived at the University at noon and the first person to greet him was Percy Tyler, who called him to account for his surprising movements.

"First thing, what were you doing with a young lady at the station yesterday? And most mysterious to contemplate, you got on the train wih her, and did not return until noon to-day. Please give an account of yourself."

Lenox was much amused, as it was the first time he had ever known Percy to play the roll of inquisitor. He first laid aside his duster and hat, saying, "Father Confessor, I am willing to lay bare my heart to you."

He then told him all, adding, "It would have been impossible to leave her so very unhappy, had she not become devotedly attached to a young girl, just her own age, who entered the Seminary the day my sister did; and she laid aside her own grief at parting with her parents to comfort Claire. I don't wonder she has led her captive, for she is a grand beauty—golden hair nearly a yard long, and a voice like Parepa's."

Percy was more than interested, and smiled as he recognized Little Doctor.

Lenox gave him a quizzical look, saying, "What does that winsome grin mean? Who would believe you were an amorous lad?"

The expression of Percy's face was exasperating to Lenox. He sprang at him, giving him a rough shake-up; "Say, tell me all you are thinking about or I will annihilate you."

When Percy found himself, he answered, "I was thinking about the young lady you have been describing; perhaps you will take me along the next time you go to St. Mary's."

Lenox laughed long and loud. "Take you along! why, you have to have a sister there to gain admittance— why, the President of the United States couldn't take you in; so be contented with what I can tell you about the inmates of St. Mary's."

Percy made no confession, but decided to go to St. Mary's.

In due time a letter came from Philadelphia and Professor Field read the following:

Dear Sir:—I exceedingly regret the trouble that the insubordination of my daughter has caused you. Our passage is already taken, and the vessel sails in two days. May I count upon our friendship for your forbearance with my little girl? I feel sure that she will submit obediently to the rules of your school when she learns that we have gone abroad. I must admit that it was scarcely fair to ignore her feelings in regard to our plans, but her violent temper made it unavoidable. I have already written her, commanding entire compliance with the rules of St. Mary's.

Yours faithfully,
HENRY WILLINGTON.

Claire received her father's letter next morning, in-

forming her of their departure for the Old World.
She read no further than this news. She tore the letter into fragments, hurling them from her. Thrusting
her hands through the thick red locks, she clutched and
shook herself in her frantic rage. She had still too
much self-respect to cry out, but vented her impotent
fury on the objects round her. The toilet articles were
hurled to the four corners of the room; then catching
sight of a beautiful Bohemian glass vase that her mother
had brought and filled with rare flowers to brighten her
room, she rushed at it and struck it a violent blow with
her hand. A cry of pain now burst from her lips. She
had cut her hand frightfully on the broken glass.

Victoria heard the cry, and hurried in. Claire was
standing near the mantelpiece, the blood streaming from
the wound. Victoria caught her by the wrist, looked a
second, and then ran to tell some one to bring the Doctor. She came back and wetted a towel and pressed
it on the wound to stop the bleeding.

"How did it happen?" she asked in real alarm. "I
think it will require a few stitches."

At this Claire drew her hand away and would have
fled from the room, but Little Doctor was once more in
her element, and caught the hand and held it tight.

Professor and Mrs. Field came in, followed almost instantly by the physician of St. Mary's.

Claire was on the bed, and Victoria pressing her fingers above the wound.

The Doctor glanced at the patient, then at her attendant. Victoria rose and withdrew to a distance.

The Doctor examined the wound, and then looking
up at our Little Doctor, "Why did you think to press
above the wound as you were doing?"

"Because it is an artery that is cut, Doctor."

The Doctor held his own finger on the same spot.

"Open my case, will you, my dear," he said to Victoria. "This cut needs a stitch or two."

Again Claire shrieked out, "I won't have it sewed up, I'll never live through it," and she jerked her hand from the Doctor's hold.

But he laid a firm hand on her arm, "Come, my child, it will not hurt you half as much as you are hurting yourself."

Victoria opened the medical chest, and taking out a needle she threaded it with deft fingers, knowing where to find the white silk in the familiar case. She handed the needle to the Doctor, as Professor Field took Claire's hand in both his own. Then Victoria got the roll of bandages and held it ready.

The Doctor gave his young assistant a searching look as he took the bandage from her hand. The wound was soon dressed, and Dr. Brentano gave Claire a composing powder, and sat holding the wounded hand in his.

It was not until the patient was quiet that the Doctor asked how it happened. Victoria nodded towards the fragments of the vase. The Doctor saw nothng more than an accident; but Professor and Mrs. Field looked inquiringly at Victoria.

In the meantime, Victoria had wiped the needle carefully, and was replacing the articles in the medical chest. The doctor watched her with a pleased smile.

"You make an admirable assistant, my little doctor," he said. "Where did you learn so much about my profession?"

"My father is a physician, and I always assist him when it is a case in which he will take me with him."

"Ah! that accounts for your familiarity with the instruments of our trade. What is your father's name?"

"Dr. Kenyon, of Hamilton County, Kentucky."

"Victor Kenyon?" asked the doctor.

"Yes, Sir. He is a Virginian by birth."

"I know him, or used to know him, very well. We were at Medical College together, in Philadelphia. I am glad to meet his daughter. He has been more fortunate than I, for I have no little doctor to follow in my steps," the doctor said kindly, taking Victoria's hand as he withdrew from the room.

Claire's wounded hand was nursed very tenderly by the gentle Mrs. Field and Victoria, and was soon well enough for her to have an interview with Professor Field. It was a long, solemn talk she had to listen to. No one knew just what passed; but she came from his study subdued and composed, and became a diligent, conscientious student.

Though never popular with her school-mates, she clung to our Little Doctor with affectionate dependence.

CHAPTER XX.

Lenox Willington was an intelligent, handsome youth, and distinguished more for his physical strength and athletic accomplishments than for mental acquirements.

His parents, before sailing for Europe, visited him at college, and charged him to be attentive to his lonely sister and to visit her as often as possible. Lenox loved his pretty, spoiled sister very dearly. Indeed, she was a model sister to him; she learned while yet in the nursery that she could not dominate him as she did her over-indulgent parents. Whenever she yielded to her violent temper with him, he would leave her with quiet dignity, only saying, "You may play with your dolls and I will go and play with boys," giving such emphasis to the last word as to impress her with its importance. This discipline had a very beneficial effect as far as Claire's intercourse with her brother went.

Lenox was a courageous boy at College, but he looked forward to his visit to St. Mary's with a sinking of heart. He was not acquainted with the rules governing young ladies' boarding schools, and supposed he would be obliged to sit at table with several hundred pairs of curious eyes upon him. It became appalling the more he thought of it.

He had allowed several weeks to go by before fulfilling his promise to his parents. It was Saturday morning. He had gotten permission from the Chancellor to spend Sunday at St. Mary's, and was looking over his wardrobe to make a selection of the most becoming suit for the occasion.

Nothing pleased his fastidious taste; the coat, made at the best tailor's in Philadelphia, he discovered did not fit perfectly in the back, not considering that the wrinkles between the shoulders were caused by twisting himself round to view his back in the mirror. But time was passing, and he hurriedly packed his valise, and rushed for the station, with anything but a tranquil mind.

Imagine his delight upon seeing his friend, Percy Tyler, quietly sitting in the waiting room. They laid hands on each other's shoulders, with mutual inquiries, laughing boisterously, as boys will when the occasion affords them nothing else to do.

Lenox admitted that he was on his way to St. Mary's to visit his sister, but Percy was not so frank. He had received permission from Dr. Kenyon to visit Victoria once or twice a year, but when it came to taking any one into his confidence about this privilege, he found himself a trifle embarrassed; but finally condescended to say that he, too, was going there to visit a young friend of his family.

"Did you see Rex before you left?" asked Lenox. "The fellow actually had the audacity to ask me to take him along and introduce him to some of the young ladies. I should enjoy his company very much—I don't know any one with such an exhaustless fund of entertainment; but I would not dare, of course, to make myself at St. Mary's responsible for any one but my humble self."

"I saw him yesterday," said Percy; Rex is a capital fellow. I knew him at home. He is a little aggressive, but he is always a gentleman. He knows I have permission to visit St. Mary's, and wanted to go with me;

but, like yourself, I have no merit to count for another."

The versatile Reginald was not long in devising a plan to outwit his more fortunate companions. He knew they were both to spend Sunday at the seminary, but thought they were to go together. Learning this the day before, he set to work to evolve a means of getting there before them.

He suddenly recalled the fact that he had heard his aunt in Washington speak of Mrs. Field as an intimate friend, and at once decided on his plan. He would leave for Washington that afternoon, make a plea to his aunt of visiting in the neighborhood of St. Mary's, and secure a letter of introduction to Mrs. Field, and then present himself at St. Mary's before the others could reach there.

His aunt was easily imposed upon. She not only gladly gave him the letter, but added a big shining gold piece, that her favorite nephew might furnish himself with a new suit of clothes, in which to pay the visit to her dear friend.

Sunday morning Reginald made his appearance, was graciously received by Mrs. Field, and invited to take breakfast with them.

He mentioned casually to his hostess that he was acquainted with Miss Kenyon, who was a neighbor of his at home, and an old acquaintance. Thereupon, Mrs. Field invited Victoria to join her at breakfast in her private dining-room. She wished her to meet a guest.

Reginald was cordially received by Professor Field, and as usual made himself very interesting.

Victoria was surprised to find that Reginald was the guest she was to meet, but she welcomed him kindly, and asked how he left his friend Percy.

His merry black eyes flashed with fun, as he said, "He

was very well, and on the eve of making a journey when
I saw him last."

Victoria was puzzled to know what could call Percy
away from College almost at the beginning of the term,
but she said no more; though Reginald watched her perplexed countenance with secret amusement.

After breakfast, Mrs. Field proposed that Victoria
should go with her to the chapel, and of course invited
her guest to join them.

Percy Tyler and Lenox Willington had gone to the
hotel on their arrival the evening before, and on Sunday
morning presented their letters to Professor Field, apolo-
gizing for calling on Sunday as it was their only day.

Professor Field welcomed the young men heartily, and
invited them to accompany him to the chapel as his family had already gone.

So, it came about that as Percy and Lenox entered the
chapel they saw their companion, whom they had so
coolly snubbed, composedly sitting beside Victoria in
the principal's pew. Both saw him at the same moment,
and turned incredulous eyes to each other.

Lenox whispered to Percy, "As I live! he is no ghost,
but real flesh and blood."

Percy replied. "There's no doubt about his corporeal
presence; but, how did he make it!"

The organ voluntary ceased and the clergyman began service.

We must pardon these youths if their eyes sometimes
wandered from the chancel, and their minds from their
devotions.

Lenox soon discovered his sister sitting near the beautiful girl, at whose side the irrepressible Rex was seated;
then finding Percy's eyes fixed in the same direction,
he asked in a whisper, "Is she your friend?—the girl

with the golden braids?" but Percy was reverently silent at that moment, and Lenox had to content himself with the fact that his sister knew her and would probably introduce him.

Claire was by no means the fright her brother had expected to see. Her hair had the same pretty habit of curling, and was more becoming than the long braids.

Reginald seemed very much attracted by the beautiful head covered with short curls, the delicate fair complexion, and eyes like the blue corn-flower. There was a gentleness in her manner and attitude that her brother had never seen before, and which, he thought, added much to his sister's improvement.

Service over, Victoria turned to come out, when she caught sight of Percy some distance behind her. Suddenly she looked as if under a canopy of La France roses, the glow of pleasure was so real.

Claire saw her brother, and with her old impetuosity, dashed down the aisle to greet him. With outstretched arms they met—the brother and sister. Lenox was quite as demonstrative as his sister. They did not heed the many sympathetic eyes that were upon them. It was always a charming episode to the girls to see one of their number meet with some dear one.

Reginald had officiously taken up Victoria's prayerbook and walked down the aisle at her side. Percy advanced up the aisle to meet her. There was genuine pleasure in the clasping of hands, and the old familiar look into each other's eyes.

"This is a real surprise, Percy," Victoria said, with a charming smile.

"Not to me." he answered. "I have been thinking about this visit ever since we parted at Gray Cliff."

As he took the prayer-book from Reginald's hands,

Percy whispered, "You made good time, old fellow, but haste is not always gain."

"At least, I have the art of anticipating my friends," Rex quickly returned. "It is strange that you fellows should turn up here just as I ran down from Washington to have a pleasant Sunday."

Then he dropped back to Lenox's side, and whispered, "Out-witted, eh?" and passed out of the chapel gate.

Mrs. Field invited the three young men to dinner, and besides Victoria and Claire, she invited Maryland Carroll to join the party.

As usual, Rex was the life of the company. No one ever thought of the dark, swarthy face, with the heavy black brows, the short, square figure, and ungraceful movements, when under the fascination of his eloquent tongue.

The dinner passed off happily to all. With all Rex's power of absorbing attention, he had cultivated the art of drawing out the best ability of others. It was this amiability, as his friends called it, that made him so popular, even with those whom he threw into the shade.

At five o'clock the three young men made their adieu to their host and hostess. The brother and sister had spent an hour together before dinner and now all were assembled on the wide gallery to say good-bye to their guests. They parted reluctantly.. The pleasant day was over.

During the winter months, Victoria had learned to skate, and by Christmas was quite an expert. A large pond in the grounds of St. Mary's afforded fine skating for the pupils, and their hours of recreation were generally spent in that sport.

One afternoon about fifty girls were on the pond, chaperoned by two of the teachers. The ringing laughs and little shrieks of real or affected terror were heard on all sides, as the timid ones, clinging to the stronger skaters, made ludicrous attempts to "strike out."

Victoria enjoyed the exercise with all her young vigor, curving round and round the pond, with the sure, swift motion of a bird on the wing. Just ahead of her a young girl was making her first attempt to skate alone. She made two or three successful strokes, when she fell heavily on the ice. Victoria skated to her, and attempted to assist the girl to rise, but she shrieked out with pain at the attempt. "My arm is broken!" she cried in alarm.

Little Doctor took up the arm, and finding it hung limp and powerless in her hands, she knew that it was, indeed, broken. Dropping on her knees, she quickly unbuckled her skates, then removed the cord with her muff from about her neck.

The other girls had gathered round by this time, and two of them supported Helen Adair, while Little Doctor prepared a substitute for splints. She gently put the arm through the muff, and then bound a skate on each side, with the cord, to hold the arm in place until they could get Helen to her room.

One of the girls had gone for Professor Field, who came at once. He took the girl in his arms, while Little Doctor supported the arm, as he carried her to the house.

The doctor had been sent for, and met them at the door. Poor Helen was suffering almost as much with terror as with pain. The doctor was very tender with her, and as he assisted in carrying her to her room, he noticed Victoria, and smilingly said, "Ah, my little doctor again on hand to assist—well, you could not have

done better under the circumstances. You improvised
a very good splint."

Victoria stood by while the arm was being set, and
with ready tact and skill assisted Dr. Brentano in the
operation, often anticipating his need of an article by
having it ready at his hand. Professor and Mrs. Field and
Aunt Charlotte were present, and all bestowed hearty
praise on our Little Doctor for her commendable self-
possession, as well as for her skill.

Victoria asked permission to sit with the patient an
hour or two each day. She read to Helen her favorite
poems. One day she said, "I would rather you would
talk to me, Little Doctor,—tell me how you ever became
so much wiser than other girls."

Victoria smiled at the name, "Little Doctor." It was
odd to hear the familiar name applied on account of
some quality she possessed, for no one at school knew of
her title at home.

"Why do you smile?" asked Helen.

"O, I was only amused at my little old home title find-
ing me out. I have always been called 'Little Doctor.'
My nurse gave me the name when I was born because
I resembled my father, who is a physician."

"Well, I think your skill merits the title now," said
Helen. "But you are in many ways different from
other girls. For instance, you sit here with me, when
I have no claim upon you, instead of being out on the
ice this glorious day. Why do you take this interest in
others?"

"Helen, I do not think the highest object in life is to
gratify one's own selfish desires; I mean, I don't believe
one is the happier for it. I do enjoy skating very much,
but 'taking an interest in others,' as you call it, is as
much pleasure to me as the skating. It is a real happi-

ness to me to see you smile, as you are doing just now. O, I can't explain it, Helen, only my heart prompts me to do what makes it the happiest.

"But my hour is up, and I must leave. I'll put your Browning where you can reach it. Shall I raise the shade a little more?"

CHAPTER XXI.

During the second year of Victoria's sojourn at St. Mary's many opportunities came to develop her uncommon strength of character, and aptitude for benefiting others in time of peril and accident.

One night in early spring of this year, after all the inmates of the seminary had retired, Victoria awoke with a slight sense of suffocation. She got up and opened the door leading into the corridor, where a light was burning. She perceived there was a fire in the building from the smoke and odor of burning wool.

She quickly drew on her dressing-robe and slippers, and rushed down to the rope communicating with the great bell in the tower, and pulled it with all her strength. It rang out loud and clear, giving an alarm to all within the building, and for miles around the neighborhood.

She was startled, and for a moment stood with tightly clasped hands pressed to her heart. Looking up she saw the smoke puffing from the open transom of room No. 20, Miss Van Allen's apartment, the teacher of music.

She sprang to the door and pushed it open. To her horror she saw that the foot of the bed was one smouldering heap of burning bed clothes. She caught hold of the blankets at the head, not yet burned, and whirled them over the fire to smother it.

Miss Van Allen lay on the carpet close to the window. Victoria caught her out-stretched hands and dragged her out into the corridor, then opened a window near by. She was unconscious and breathing heavily. Little Doctor knelt down by her side, feeling her pulse and rubbing her hands vigorously.

By this time the entire household was aroused. Opening of doors, loud shrieks, crying, talking, and rushing to and fro filled the long corridor with discordant sounds. Victoria heard all as in a troubled dream, yet retained her consciousness, and her desire to save Miss Van Allen. .

Professor Field directed and urged the servants to bring water and put out the fire. Mrs. Field, Doctor Brentano, and many of the teachers and scholars grouped about our Little Doctor and her patient. Doctor Brentano assisted in resuscitating Miss Van Allen. He asked Little Doctor to go for stimulants. She rose up to obey, then fell forward, overcome by the smoke and exertion.

A wail went up from the sympathizing pupils. Mrs. Field lifted her head to her lap, and brushed back the golden hair. The Doctor suggested taking her to her room, and lifting her up in his strong arms carried her to her own apartment.

Aunt Charlotte and Chloe were greatly alarmed at missing Little Doctor from her room, and had been searching for her in the rushing crowd. When they saw her limp body and pallid face, they were terrified.

The Doctor laid Victoria on the bed, saying, "Wet her face and hands with cold water, while I go for stimulants."

Miss Dorcey quickly applied the remedy, and by the time the Doctor returned Victoria had recovered consciousness. He put a tablespoonful of brandy in water, and gave her a little as she could swallow it, then left her in her aunt's care while he went to Miss Van Allen.

Victoria's first thoughts were to ask after her patient.

"Chloe," she said feebly, "go and ask after Miss Van Allen." Chloe was shedding some big tears for her young "Missy," but went as she was told.

She soon returned with Doctor Brentano, who gave the information himself that she had recovered. When he saw the violet eyes wide open with inquiry, and her smile of welcome, he exclaimed, "Hurrah for our Little Doctor! You have been playing a double role this time. I will wager my new carriage and horses that you gave the alarm. The pulling of that bell was like your energetic touch." Then with a humorous twinkle in his brown eyes, he added; "O, I can vouch for your fine dramatic appearance in the play—a graceful young maiden kneeling over the prostrate form of her patient, arrayed in a flowing robe of pale blue covered with golden curls, and—"

Little Doctor closed her eyes, which was a signal to the Doctor to cease his amusement at her expense, and prompt him to a serious discussion of what filled her mind with anxiety for the safety of all in the building.

He felt her pulse, and laid his hand on her forehead, saying, "Well, my child, you showed yourself a heroine. Do you know you saved the lives of more than two hundred people?—for you gave the alarm, there is no doubt."

"The smoke gave the warning, and I responded readily—let me ask you, is Miss Van Allen burned?" she answered.

"No, not a bit. It is a marvel to me how she escaped," said Doctor Brentano.

"She had evidently tried to open her window, for she

was lying just under one when I saw her," replied Victoria.

The Doctor settled himself back in the chair with a grim smile, saying, "Miss Van Allen will not likely go to sleep again with the candle burning on her bed. She said she had been reading until late, and does not remember anything about putting out the light; but the fire occurred by her carelessness, there is no doubt, and if it had not been for your timely assistance, she would now be numbered with the dead—and all the rest of us most likely owe our lives to you. The fire occurred at an hour when sleep is the soundest, and all would have been stupified in a few moments."

The loud ringing of the door-bell caused Doctor Brentano and Professor Field to go down stairs. Mrs. Field and many of the teachers and scholars came to inquire for Victoria. The alarm given by our Little Doctor had been heard far and near, and the kind neighbors came to render assistance. All expressed their sympathy and admiration for our heroine. One gentleman in the group asked many questions about her, and began to write it down. Professor Field declined to give Victoria's name, saying, "She would not like the publicity of her name appearing in print, I can assure you."

As the stranger left the door, he heard one of the scholars call her "Little Doctor." He smiled with satisfaction to himself, saying, "That name will do."

After the neighbors dispersed, and order was restored, Mrs. Field, with the assistance of the teachers, persuaded the pupils to go to their rooms.

Aunt Charlotte could not be induced to go to bed, but sat by Victoria until morning. She had company, for Claire begged with tearful eyes to be allowed to lie beside Little Doctor and hold her hand.

Our brave little girl could not sleep. She thought of her dear parents, Percy, and his kind mother and father, and of Mammy and all the rest of the devoted servants at home, thinking how distressed all would be if they knew the peril she had been in, and of their words of loving approbation of her in doing all she could to save others.

Little Doctor finally fell asleep in the early dawn, while listening to the sweet songs of her feathered pets congregated about her window. Aunt Charlotte led Claire from the room to her own apartment and tenderly put her to bed, then returned to her dear charge. She darkened the windows and put out the lamp so that she could sleep soundly.

It was late in the day when Victoria awoke—too late to join her companions in the class-room. After she had taken her breakfast, Doctor Brentano called to see her, bringing her a basket of sweet violets.

Victoria was delighted with them, and thanked him most heartily, adding, "I have been looking for a week for just one pretty creature but have not found even a bud."

"These came from Castle Hill where they were well protected by the trees," explained the Doctor. "I have a treat in store for you and your aunt—I am going to take you for a drive, it is just what you both need," he said, nodding to Miss Dorcey.

Victoria was over-joyed, and expressed her thanks, then turning to her aunt, she said in a pleading voice, "Can we go, Aunt Charlotte?"

"Yes, my dear, it will do you good, and we shall enjoy the Doctor's new team."

Doctor Brentano had invited Mrs. Field to accompany them also. When he left the room, he said to

Victoria with a pleasant nod, "You may bring your driving gloves with you; I am sure you can drive as you are a country lassie.

"O, I can indeed; our good Ben taught me to drive the carriage horses before I was ten years old."

It was not long before the Doctor's guests were ready, and admiring his beautiful team to his heart's delight. Little Doctor went to their heads to pat and smooth the gentle, intelligent faces. They were evidently pleased with the wearer of the broad-brimmed leghorn hat, and the purple dress fluttering in the breeze.

"What a perfect match they are!" she said; "The white stars in their faces are exactly alike, and they have such small erect ears."

They were large, shapely animals, dark iron-gray, with flowing tails and manes, and "swift as the wind" the Doctor said.

Mrs. Field and Miss Dorcey took the back seat in the carriage. Victoria sat on the front seat with Dr. Brentano. He looked very happy, and well-pleased with the skillful way his young friend took up the reins and started off.

It was a glorious day in spring. The birds sang and piped from trees and fence, while the shy wild flowers bloomed in sheltered nooks. The road was fine, and the trial trip of "Storm and Tempest," the horses, was a splendid success. They went many miles without slackening the swift pace.

Finally, Victoria's quick eyes caught a glimpse of a quiet little figure by the roadside, sitting on a log. She drew in the team, saying, "Did you see that forlorn little boy back there?"

"No," answered the Doctor.

They stopped, and Dr. Brentano looking back recog-

nized the "forlorn little boy" as one of his young country friends. He called out, "Dewey, come here." The
small boy limped up to the carriage, wiping the tears
from his face with his shirt sleeve. He had brave eyes,
and an honest freckled face. He was evidently ashamed
of the tears, for he averted his head when he saw the
ladies looking at him.

"What's the matter, my lad," said the Doctor; "are
you in trouble?"

He gulped down the sob in his throat, and said, "I
have cut my foot, and can't get to the hotel,—you see
they won't buy my spargrass after one o'clock."

"Well," said the kind-hearted Doctor, "we can take
you there long before that time, so get your basket and
jump in."

The small face brightened up, and he limped back for
his basket. When he returned, the Doctor took it in,
then gave a helping hand to the owner, saying, "It was
lucky we drove this way, wasn't it?"

"It was that. You see I would o' lost ninety cents if
I didn't get there in time for dinner."

He looked up at Victoria and smiled at her expression of interest in him, saying, "You saw me first, didn't
you, sis?"

Little Doctor was much amused at the familiar,
friendly little fellow, and reached out her hand to him,
saying, "I have good eyes for looking up little people.
How did you hurt your foot? Just see, Doctor Brentano,
how it is bleeding?"

The Doctor drew out his medical case from under the
carriage seat, and placed it by the side of Little Doctor,
then taking the reins from her hands, said, "Let me see
you dress that wound."

The look of gratitude and pleasure in her face was

pleasing to both doctor and patient. She made room for Dewey to sit by her side, and when she took up the small brown foot, he made a feeble resistance.

Little Doctor said with pleading tenderness, "'Do let me look at it, I won't hurt you."

He gave a shy little laugh, answering, "It aint that, I was afeared I would soil your nice frock."

"O, you are so considerate. I thank you for reminding me to put something over my dress."

She took the Doctor's morning paper and spread it over her lap, and then proceeded to dress the wound. She took a piece of lint and drew it over the cut very tenderly until it was cleansed from dust, then pressed the edges of the wound together, put a fresh application of lint on, and tied a double cloth over to protect and keep it in place.

Dewey watched her with intense interest, evidently admiring Little Doctor from her hat down to her slender boots. Once he caressed one of the golden braids lying near his hand on her knee. He shyly looked into the violet eyes and said, "I never saw hair shine like gold before."

Little Doctor laughed one of her mirthful laughs, saying, "My old nurse would tell you that it caught this color from a comet."

"What's a comet?" asked Dewey with a perplexed brow and coaxing eyes.

"O, a great star that came the morning I was born, and then went away."

Not only Dewey but all listened to the sweet voice of Little Doctor, and marveled at the simple words that suggested so many deep thoughts.

Dewey Grant took his foot from Victoria's lap, saying, "You did that business well nigh as good as the Doctor—ain't you a Doctor's girl?"

"Yes," answered Victoria with a merry laugh, and a pinch of his ruddy cheek.

He sat at her feet during the drive to the hotel, taking notice of every word and act, evidently storing them up for the entertainment of the dear ones at home, for she was a rare specimen of girlhood to Dewey Grant.

They reached the hotel in time for Dewey to dispose of his asparagus, much to his relief; then on their return, drove up a lane to let him out at his home.

Dewey's "Thanky for your kindness to me" expressed but poorly the gratitude of the throbbing young heart. When he saw the carriage turn and drive back, he called out, "Mother, mother, come here, quick!"

A heavy-set woman, with black hair and eyes, came to the door.

"Look, mother, there she is!"

"Why, sonny, what's the matter with your foot?"

She had glanced at the carriage, but the wounded foot was more attractive to her.

"She did it," he exclaimed, pointing at Little Doctor, who was looking back with a parting smile for her patient.

"She hurt you? It is just like rich folks to trample on the poor," and she cast a threatening frown at the retreating carriage.

"O, no, you don't know what you are a-talking about. She doctored my foot after I hurt it, and was so very nice to me."

Mrs. Grant's face softened, and she said, "You said she did it."

"No, no, I meant she tied it up for me. You just ought to see her drive them great big horses of the Doctor's. She is awful purty and nice, and I reckon she is smart and rich too. I'll bet she can spell 'biscuit'—we had it at school yesterday, and we all stuck fast."

When Doctor Brentano and his guests returned to St. Mary's the girls were out for recreation. Maryland Carroll saw the carriage first, and ran to greet Little Doctor. All the rest followed, gathering around with glad faces and kind words for their heroine—indeed, they lifted her from the carriage steps, and carried her to the veranda in a funny fashion, all laughing merrily. They placed her on the top step, then grouped about her, standing, sitting, and kneeling, to discuss the all-absorbing subject of the past night. Claire Willington rested both hands on Victoria's lap, and had a humorous story to tell of herself and others in their fright and excitement—"O, I am going to write to brother Lenox and tell him we have a real heroine in St. Mary's."

Birdie Brice, the tease of the school, grinned at Little Doctor, and said in a droll way, "I am going to write to your—your beau, and tell him—."

A flash of Victoria's indignant eyes cut short the sentence, and a titter went the rounds—all but Claire. She was vexed, as she knew Victoria would not tolerate remarks of that kind; and besides, it would cause her to leave them.

Little Doctor left her companions, and went to her room. She had been taught that her boy acquaintances were friends, not beaux—young ladies had beaux, children had boy friends.

She never harbored unkind thoughts, and was quite her sweet self again when she picked up a book and went to Miss Van Allen's room to read aloud a story which that lady had selected for their mutual entertainment.

CHAPTER XXII

The Saturday after the fire at St. Mary's, Percy Tyler was leisurely looking over his New York weekly, when a familiar title caught his eye, then riveted his attention. He read and re-read the article, then rushed from his room to Lenox Willington's apartment. He thrust the paper before Lenox's face, saying, "Read that."

Lenox took the paper, at the same time glancing up at his friend, for excitement in Percy Tyler was uncommon, and the article must be of great importance to arouse him thus. He read the account of the fire at St. Mary's, which gave the title of the chief figure "Little Doctor," but no other name.

Lenox had forgotten that Victoria Kenyon was called by this name. He looked up at Percy, saying, "She is a brave girl, I suppose Claire knows her. It makes me weak in the knees to think my little sister was in such peril. Have you an idea who 'Little Doctor' is?" he asked.

Percy hesitated for a second. Lenox looked up, then sprang from his chair, and laying a heavy hand on Percy's shoulder he demanded, "I can see you know all about the heroine—tell me who she is."

Percy laughed heartily, saying, "Don't break my shoulder and I will tell you that I know 'Little Doctor' and have known her since she was a few days old—."

Lenox anticipated him by saying, "O, I know her myself, and it was just like her. Claire adores her, and I am under everlasting obligations to Miss Kenyon for her kindness to Claire. She took a great burden from my heart when my sister entered St. Mary's. Claire calls her 'Guardian Angel.' I tell you, that little fire-brand of ours was able and ready to master principal, teachers, and matron, and your sister too—an unintentional compliment, but I always think of her as your sister."

Percy's face shone with pleasure, as he exclaimed, "You paid me the highest tribute in your power. She has been to me like a sister—I wish to heaven I had one as noble as she is. You are a lucky boy to have one."

"Well, Little Doctor captured Claire in the first battle. She melted her right down by telling her she was cruel to mother in cutting off her hair to spite her. Then she had the audacity to send the long curls to mother as a present; but it was the most fortunate thing in Claire's life, for it was the cause of her being left at school."

"Well," said Percy, I must be off to ask permission to spend Sunday at St. Mary's—will you go with me?"

"Of course I will. I have been waiting for you to make a move in that direction. I would rather face the wild sons of Africa than those pretty girls, unless you were along to act as a target."

Before an hour had passed, our boys stood on the platform at the station. Each had valise in hand containing his best clothes. As they jumped on the moving train, Rex Page returned to his room from a tramp in the woods, with some rare "specimens" in his possession. He glanced out of his window as he put his treasure down on the table. He looked again, for he saw his companions making demonstrations of good-bye.

His black eyes grew fierce as he shook his fist at them, causing them to laugh heartily as the train moved along.

He soliloquized, "Sly dogs to sneak off from me, I bet

my last dime they are going to St. Mary's to spend Sunday."

He proceeded to walk up and down his room, with his short fat hands crossed on his stout back. "I wish I had a sister there. In the name of common sense what did my parents want with five boys—and no girls?"

He went to the mirror and looked at himself—"We are not bad looking." He drew his heavy brows together over his straight nose, saying aloud, "But if we had a sister she would be like the rest of us—black—black, too black for a girl. I should like one fair like Little Doctor—'twould have been a pleasing variety, one with blue eyes and golden hair."

"Well, well, I can't go this time, but I will get even with them before a month."

The rare specimens had taken leave of the box; crawling, hopping, and wriggling reptiles covered the table. Rex was not in the least disconcerted. He proceeded to put them back into the box with tender interest, talking to them in a friendly way about getting left. This habit had often given his companions much amusement at his expense, but Rex was a character able to stand alone, even in eccentricities.

Percy and Lenox arrived at St. Mary's just before dark. Professor Field and his wife received them most cordially, assuring them that Claire and Victoria were both well and not in the least the worse for the excitement of Monday last.

It was a fortunate time for the boy's visit, as the first Saturday in the month was the usual time for the girls' dancing party.

All were in the assembly room having a pleasant time when the boys came. Mrs. Field conducted them to the scene of gayety, where they stood looking on until the dance was finished, but they were not long in recognizing the ones they knew best of all.

Maryland Carroll saw the guests first, and dancing up to Victoria, she whispered, "Some one is looking for you."

Little Doctor turned her head towards the door, and saw the tall, graceful youth she had known so long. Their eyes met, then both advanced. As Percy took her hand, he said, "I am glad you are safe—of course our Little Doctor was the heroine."

She laughed merrily at Percy's assurance, saying, "How did you hear of the fire?"

As he led her to a divan, and they seated themselves, he answered, "It is not difficult to find out the news when it is in the papers."

The look of amazement on her face was amusing to Percy, and he smiled gleefully.

"I wish I had thought to bring my Weekly along to let you see the interesting article—O, it is glowing with praise of 'Little Doctor.' I must send it to you, with the permission of the Professor."

"Did it give my real name—you know how annoying it would be to my parents?"

"No, just calls you 'Little Doctor.'"

Victoria asked with a puzzled expression, "Can you imagine how they heard the name?"

"Yes," said Percy; "Professor Field told me a reporter for the New York weekly was here the night of the fire and jotted down the incident. Fearing he would publish the article, the Professor refused to give your name, so he caught up 'Little Doctor' from some of your companions in the hall, I suppose."

Claire and Lenox now joined them.

After the first words of greeting between them

Lenox said, "Come, let us go to the supper-room and get some cream, I am half famished. Sister says there is a feast of good things out there." He gave his arm to Victoria, still holding Claire's hand.

Percy glanced at Claire, then gently parted the hands, saying to Lenox, "Your selfishness would be intolerable if I did not know your sister would take pity on me."

Claire took Percy's outstretched hand with a smile, saying, "He thinks we both belong to him; indeed, you too he includes in his possessions."

Percy and Claire discussed the all-absorbing topic, the fire, Claire relating in her amusing way how completely beside herself she was, saying, "I ran to my window to climb out on a big tree (the same one had done service before)," and the merry twinkle in her eyes brought the runaway scene to Percy's mind, "when I discovered I had a pitcher of water in my arms—not knowing I had it, yet drenched with the contents."

"It is hard to keep a clear head at such times," he said, with amusement.

"But Little Doctor did, and saved us from a terrible death," said Claire with a shudder.

"You see," answered Percy, "she has been taught to be brave and useful, and has a natural love for helping others. Of course she has marvelous presence of mind, and good common sense, or she could not always be doing good at the right time."

After a feast of ice cream, cake, and fruit, our young friends returned to take part in the dancing,—thanks to Mrs. Field for the invitation.

Percy and Claire, and Lenox and Victoria were partners for awhile, then the boys changed partners; Little Doctor now suggested that the boys be introduced to some of the other girls.

It was truly a pretty sight; nearly two hundred young lassies all in white, all merry, and dancing with evident pleasure. Of course the boys were much in demand, and did enjoy themselves to a great degree.

At ten o'clock the dancing ceased. Our party was standing in a group having a last chat and laugh, when Professor and Mrs. Field joined them.

Mrs. Field said ,"Children, we have planned a pleasant Sunday for you. We shall be glad if all will join us in a drive to the city to attend service. As we return, we will stop in some pretty place and have luncheon."

All were delighted, and expressed their hearty thanks to their kind hostess.

Claire clapped her hands, saying to Percy, "A real picnic."

"A capital idea," he answered. "I will offer my services as cook," he added, bowing to Mrs. Field.

"I accept most gladly, if you can make good coffee, for we shall not have any other cooking."

"I can indeed, Madam, the best you ever drank; strong, clear and delicious."

All laughed at Percy's good recommendation of his accomplishment.

Lenox asked if he might be the water-carrier—"That is all I can do, except eat!" said he.

"Eating is the one thing obligatory," said Mrs. Field, with a smile, and a friendly nod.

Professor Field had been talking to Victoria about the drive. "By the way," said he, in an under-tone, "can you tell me if both boys ride horse-back?"

"Yes, I am sure they can, for I have often heard Claire say her brother kept a saddle-horse at home, and Percy has ridden all his life."

"That's fine. We can manage it beautifully to take

Miss Van Allen with us." Then, addressing all, "Children, we will start about nine o'clock in the morning, and get there before eleven."

Bidding the girls good-night, he took the boy's arms, and conducted them to the resident apartments, where Mrs. Field had rooms prepared for them.

Of course, the pleasant trip and treats were not confined to our young friends; all the other pupils had their turn in time, when it was thought best by their elders in authority.

Long before nine o'clock next morning, old Uncle Oscar had the big family carriage at the gate; Joe brought two fine saddle horses from the stable, and hitched them near by. Not long after, Doctor Brentano drove up with his iron-grays, for he too was to go and take some of the party.

Our girls and boys met on the front veranda to await the rest. There was much sparkling chat, and conjecture as to how they were to be disposed of in the various conveyances.

Little Doctor's solution of the matter pleased the boys. "You are both to go on horse-back," she said, looking very decided.

Lenox's nerves were a little unstrung towards the time to start. He had asked Victoria to present him to Miss Dorcey, when she came down stairs. He wanted to thank her in person for her kindness to Claire.

Now he had pictured Aunt Charlotte a real "blue stocking," with blue eye-glasses, and, most likely, "blue laws" for boys and girls; in age, a few years younger than the "Father of our Country," tall, thin as a rail, and not having an atom of good looks.

He took Victoria's sun-shade from her hand, and toyed with it as he watched the hall door anxiously.

Presently, the fit of blues was forgotten in looking at a beautiful lady coming up the steps from the garden with a cluster of white lilacs in her hand. She stopped to return Dr. Brentano's greeting, and to answer some inquiry.

She was splendid in height and symmetry, had a pretty complexion, with golden brown hair waving back from a fine brow, and coiled in a braided crown on the top of her shapely head. She wore a brown silk dress, just the shade of her hair, with lace frills at the throat and wrists.

She saw Lenox's frank interest in her, and smiled in answer. Coming towards him, she extended her hand, saying in a musical voice, "My dear Lenox, we need no introduction, I already know you through your sister Claire, and your pretty letters to me."

She gave him the lilacs, saying, "In remembrance of our meeting."

Lenox dropped the sunshade, turned as pink as a cabbage-rose, saying, "I beg your pardon, Miss Dorcey, I imagined you—you were a 'Blue-stocking.' "

She laughed merrily, saying, "I wish I were literary. Come, and let me present you to Dr. Brentano, he knows your father."

Her charming freedom with him put him at ease, and heightened his admiration for her, making him forget his embarrassment.

The Doctor was cordial in his meeting with Lenox, saying, "My dear boy, your father is one of the most congenial friends I have in the world. Where is he now?"

Miss Dorcey left them to talk, while she went up to her room for her bonnet. When she came down a few moments after, Dr. Brentano stepped up to her with a courtly bow, saying, "Miss Dorcey, will you confer a real pleasure on me, by being one of my guests in the drive? And with your permission, I will ask these two children to accompany us," laying his hand on Victoria's head.

Miss Dorcey accepted for herself, and added, "You know you have my consent for these two to be of our party."

Professor and Mrs. Field made their appearance with Miss Van Allen.

"Doctor," said the Professor, "will you lead; those greys of yours are very impertinent behind my team?"

"Most gladly; I was wishing you would let me lead off."

Then to the boys, "Boys, those saddle horses are for your convenience." As he saw the smile of pleasure on the youthful faces, he added, "When I was a boy, I loved riding better than going to a circus."

Just then Percy and Lenox preferred it too, as it was Sunday morning, and a delightful ride lay before them, to say nothing of the pleasant chat with the girls as they rode along.

All descended to the gate. Doctor Brentano helped Miss Dorcey to the front seat, the girls to the back one; and the boys, mounting, took up their positions on either side of the carriage. Professor, Mrs. Field, and Miss Van Allen followed, driven by old Uncle Oscar.

Some one else went too, but not until the teams were out of sight of the house; then Joe climbed up on the back of the family carriage, with a tin pan on his head, bound for some contraband pleasure.

The weather was as perfect as all young people look for in May; the road was one of those winding white turnpikes so common in the "Mother State," leading through green meadows and forests, and passing grand old homesteads nestling among shade trees, shrubbery, and flower beds; occasionally they caught a glimpse of a shining river in the distance.

The younger members of the party were much pleased, asking the Doctor to drive over to let them get a better view of the river.

"We shall return by the river road, and take luncheon on the bank—will that satisfy all of you?" he said, looking back with a smile. All expressed willingness to wait.

Lenox was of a speculative turn of mind, and as he rode along chatting to the girls, he frequently looked at Doctor Brentano and Miss Dorcey, thinking they must have been created for each other, both splendid in physical good looks, and apparent congeniality. He whispered his thoughts to Claire, but was fairly stunned by the silent rebuke of his sister. No one at St. Mary's had ever been bold enough to intimate that the Doctor admired the dignified Miss Dorcey. But Lenox was too much interested in the future of his new friends to be put down in this way, so indulged in many possibilities for them as they drove along in front of him.

Our party reached the city in time for church, and all enjoyed the uncommon privilege. Even Lenox and Claire were deeply impressed by the solemn service, grand music, and the humble devotion of Percy and Victoria.

As our company left the church, many of the Professor's friends gathered about asking questions concerning the fire at St. Mary's, and of "Little Doctor."

Mrs. Field introduced her young friends to some of them, saying "Victoria is our 'Little Doctor.'"

Victoria extended her hand with a sweet smile, and accepted their compliments with the pretty modesty and self-possession natural to her.   Aunt Charlotte and Percy were truly proud of her, and watched her with admiration.

When they were about to drive off, Lenox put his fair curly head inside the carriage, and said, "You have been holding a levee on the side-walk. Who was that handsome fellow with the cane, who stayed longer than the rest? He wanted to go along with you girls, any one could see that."

The girls laughed at Lenox's curiosity. "He is the brother of Birdie Brice," said Victoria, "he often attends service at chapel when he rides over to see her."

The drive along the river road was grand in wild, rugged scenery a part of the way, then changed to sloping green hills, interspersed with great forest trees.

One of the hills had been beautifully terraced by nature. "Giant Stairway" it had been called, time out of memory. As they drove in front of the steps, thirty or forty feet wide, all exclaimed with admiration.

"Are we to eat luncheon here?" asked enthusiastic Claire.

"Yes," said Doctor Brentano, halting on the lowest step. "This is the 'Stairway of Giant Fancy.'"

The boys sprang from their saddles to help the ladies to alight, while the gentlemen held the teams, giving Uncle Oscar time to take out the baskets of luncheon, carriage robes, and feed for the horses.

Percy spread the robes down on the grass, under a big maple tree, saying, "This is our 'drawing-room.'"

It was inviting indeed, as he arranged cushions from the carriages about in cozy spots at the foot of the tree.

Joe tried to make himself very useful, feeling that he must justify his stolen ride with the white folks.

He had been "out foragin" he said, for dry sticks to

make a fire for the coffee; and came back in quite a state of excitement. When he saw that his stolen ride was condoned he grew confidential with the boys, and told them of an adventure he had with a "crazy calf."

"He come down dat hill jis a raren and a pitchen and chase me clean in de riber."

"Yo kin see fo' yosefs," he said, smoothing down the blue cotton trousers, and giving his woolly head a solemn shake to impress his hearers with the truth of what he said.

Little Doctor and Claire spread the cloth down on the thick velvety grass, putting pebbles on the corners to keep it straight; then set the table with taste and care.

Lenox pretended to be very busy, spending his time between the cook and the "waiting maids," as he called the girls. When Percy asked him to bring a dish of cold meat, he took up the cover of the luncheon basket, covering it with a small napkin, then decorated it with parsley.

"That is the first useful thing you have done since we took up our residence here—let us give him a medal for invention," said Percy, calling to Claire.

When all was ready, Little Doctor went to the "drawing-room" to tell the grown people to come to luncheon. As they neared the table, Joe rushed up, with arms thrown above his head, shrieking at the top of his voice. "Hims a-comin', hims a-comin'."

All looked at the excited Joe in alarm. He pointed up the hill with both hands. There posed the "crazy calf." One loud bellow, and both hind feet went up, head down, then a leap sidewise and down it came at full speed, clearing the table at a bound, notwithstanding the outspread arms of the gentlemen, and the shrieks of the ladies. It kept on its mad course down into the river, where it drank eagerly, then came out with heaving sides, and twitching ears, and galloped up the road.

Not a thing on the table was harmed, not even a bit of dust or spear of grass to tell of the funny freak of the "crazy calf."

The feast went on, seasoned with merry laughter and witty remarks at the interruption.

The sun was going down behind the distant mountain top when our happy party drove up to the gate of St. Mary's.

Before nine o'clock the boys took their departure, and the rest of the company retired to their rooms to sleep soundly and dream about church drives and a crazy calf.

CHAPTER XXIII.

One week after "Happy Sunday," as the girls called the jaunt to the city church, a new love came into the life of Little Doctor, giving her heart a sweet song of thanksgiving. The tidings came rattling over the railroad in a locked car, shut up in a mail bag—a letter, sealed by her father's hand, and directed in his bold, well-known handwriting.

She took it from the servant's hand at the door with her usual flutter of anticipation. Seating herself at the open window, she broke the seal and read the first line, then reread it—could she really believe in her eyesight, or was she not dreaming?

She got up quickly and ran to her Aunt's room. Holding out the letter she said with faltering voice: "Auntie, please read to me what father says!"

For an instant Miss Dorcey was alarmed, but took the letter and putting her arm around Victoria said, "What is it, my darling, is any one ill at home?"

"No, no, not ill—but, I am so bewildered at that," pointing to the first line in the letter. " Please read."

Miss Dorcey looked at her niece for some clew, and seeing a pleading smile on her face, she took courage to read the letter aloud.

"Beechwood, May 4th, 18....

"My darling daughter:—You have a little brother—he came this morning at sunrise. I am confident you will rejoice with your mother and me, in this, our greatest blessing since your advent. He looks as you did on your first birthday, only that he has dark hair and eyes like your mother. He is a large, fine looking child, with most powerful lungs. Of course, Mammy is jubilant over his arrival, and faithful as ever.

"We will postpone his baptism until we go to Gray Cliff, so that the ceremony can be performed by your Uncle Howard. We shall call him "Dorcey" for your mother's maiden name. You shall be his god-mother; Percy, one of his god-fathers—I am sure he will be delighted to take the precious responsibility. I will write him to-day.

"It is possible that we may go to Virginia the middle of July. Your mother and Dorcey will stop at your grand-father's while I go to St. Mary's for you.

"My dear child, you have the hearty consent of your mother, and mine too, to invite your friends, Claire and Lenox, to spend the summer with us at Gray Cliff. It was quite proper for you to write your grand-father and Aunt Mary for an invitation for them, but I can assure you of their hospitality for all of your friends.

"Your mother joins me in sweetest love to you, saying she wants to see you more than your loyal heart can echo. Little brother spreads his small hand out on this sheet of paper for you to kiss—it is the best he can do for sister to-day.

"Your devoted father,
"VICTOR KENYON."

Little Doctor listened with intense interest, her happy eyes brimful of tears.

Aunt Charlotte held out her arms, saying, "I congratulate you, my dear child. I well know how much you have always desired a brother."

Victoria seated herself on her Auntie's lap, resting her head against her cheek, just as she had always done with her mother, when they had joys or sorrows in common.

Little Doctor gave a little sigh, saying, "It will be about two months before I can see him, and hold him in my arms."

"Yes, my pet, but the time will soon go by when you are so happy; and I have something really interesting for you and Claire to assist me in for your vacation."

Little Doctor could not help feeling a pleasant wonder at her Auntie's words, as she well knew they meant much; but she was content to await her Aunt's time to tell her all.

Victoria's unselfish nature soon suggested sharing her joy with others. Calling Chloe in, she told her of the dear young brother.

Chloe was jubilant, saying, while she showed her big white teeth, "I's powerful glad dar is a baby in our family once mo'."

Claire displayed her delight by hugging Victoria with rapture, saying, "I hope he will be as lovely to you as my brother has always been to me."

Professor and Mrs. Field congratulated Little Doctor, and wrote a letter of happy greetings to her parents and the young heir of Beechwood.

Being Sunday morning, Victoria asked her Aunt to go with her to chapel before any one was there. Miss Dorcey gladly consented, knowing Little Doctor wished to go to God's house to give thanks for the priceless treasure that gladdened her home.

After silent prayers, she asked her Aunt to play an accompaniment on the organ while she sang the 103rd Psalm—"Praise the Lord, O my soul; and all that is within me, praise his holy name."

The solemn strain filled the building and reached the procession of pupils standing in the corridor ready to go to chapel for service. Claire recognized the tender, thrilling voice of her friend, and whispered to the teacher in charge, "May I be excused?"

"Yes," said the lady, with a pleasant nod; "I understand."

Claire hastened to the chapel, and for the first time in her life, of her own free will, knelt in prayer. Tears of real contrition dimmed her pretty blue eyes. It was the beginning of a new life for the spoiled child of wealth and self-indulgence.

Victoria's asking Claire and Lenox to spend the vacation at her grand-father's came about in this way—Claire had many times said she expected her parents back in time for her to spend the summer at home, and had counted on a very gay time in the dear old home once more; but, early in April, she and Lenox received word from their parents saying they would not return until the next winter, and that they had made plans with Professor and Mrs. Field to have them both spend their vacation with them at their home.

Lenox, as usual, was ready to obey, and wrote his sister that they would have a pleasant time, boating, fishing, and hunting—hoping to interest Claire so that she would be content to stay.

She shed some indignant tears, then under the good influence of Little Doctor, answered the letters with respectful submission—even saying she hoped her parents would enjoy their sojourn in Rome.

Victoria was deeply touched by Claire's disappointment, and thought of bringing about a visit to Gray Cliff for her and Lenox. She took Aunt Charlotte into her confidence, the matter was deeply discussed, letters were written to her parents, grand-father, and Aunt Mary; after receiving favorable answers, she then wrote to Mr. and Mrs. Willington, and to Lenox. It was quite an undertaking for a school girl, but our Little Doctor was equal to the responsibility.

Of course all answered favorably, and Victoria told Claire of her successful plan for her and Lenox to spend the vacation at Gray Cliff.

Claire was delighted, and sent a happy letter to her parents; also to Senator Kenyon and Aunt Mary thanking them for their kind invitation, and accepting with sweet appreciation. The Friday after it was decided that Claire was to go with Victoria to visit her grandfather, Aunt Charlotte told the two girls of the "interesting assistance" she expected of them both. Miss Dorcey had thought it would give them pleasure, and comfort too, for the summer season, to have some pretty colored dresses made up to wear while away from St. Mary's; so, the night before, she told them she was going to take them to the city on a shopping excursion. They were to go in the big carriage and stay all day.

It was a delightful surprise to them, and they could hardly express their thanks to Aunt Charlotte for her thoughtfulness.

Before half-past eight o'clock on Saturday morning, Miss Dorcey, Little Doctor, and Claire were on their way to the city. They enjoyed their drive almost as much as they did on "Happy Sunday;" and when they got to the large city, and in front of fine stores with show windows as large as a cabin, both jumped out and ran to see what pretty goods were displayed for their benefit.

Victoria caught her auntie's sleeve, saying, "That buff chambra is beautiful, may I have a dress of it?"

"Certainly you shall—you mean the buff and white striped? It is very pretty, also that pink gingham."

Claire was in rapture over a lilac organdie, saying, "I must have that, if it takes my hundred dollars to buy it."

Miss Dorcey laughed heartily, saying, "You can get that one, and ever so many more, for a fourth of your money."

As their admiration for the pretty things in the window had attracted a crowd of small darkies, auntie thought it best to take them inside the store.

Piles upon piles of pretty summer goods were put before the three ladies, and many pieces were cut off for the youthful customers—pink, blue, lilac, green, buff, and white with clusters of flowers.

Miss Dorcey did not forget the dainty white sunbonnets, and pongee parasols for them; also gloves for outings on the river and in the woods.

In the midst of the shopping, Dr. Brentano walked into the store. He took a lively interest in the feminine business much to the amusement of all. He asked for a flaming red calico to be taken down for his inspection, and after examining it closely, he said with the air of a French modiste, "That, trimmed with gilt ribbon and brass buttons, would be stunning."

All agreed with the Doctor, that it would be at least "stunning" and he said, "I will make any one of you a present of it, if you will wear it to church."

All declined the gorgeous offer with thanks and smiles.

A skillful young dress-maker was engaged to come the next Monday to St. Mary's to make up the pretty dresses for the girls.

Claire learned a valuable lesson in shopping, and how to spend her money to advantage. As they drove home she counted over the money left many times, fearing she had not paid for all her beautiful goods lying at their feet in the carriage.

O, what a busy time there was in the sewing rooms in the third story of St. Mary's the next month!

Miss Dorcey had told the girls not to mention the dress-making to their companions, as she feared it would disturb them in their studies; but it was discovered before the first sunset and more than fifty lassies had made secret visits up the last flight of stairs to see for themselves the marvelous lawns, cambrics, organdies, and ginghams, and the pretty embroideries and edgings to trim them with.

As the middle of July drew near, Victoria found it difficult to concentrate her mind on her lessons, and asked to be relieved from study when closing exercises were over. All the pupils had left for home, and Little Doctor and Claire were counting the days until Lenox, Percy, and Doctor Kenyon should arrive.

Percy had a standing invitation to spend his vacation at Gray Cliff, and this year his parents were to meet him there.

Lenox and Percy came to St. Mary's together, arriving the evening before Doctor Kenyon put in an appearance.

Little Doctor sat at her chamber window, dividing her time between watching the clock and the railroad track.

When she saw the puffing engine sending volumes of black smoke up into the clear blue sky, she ran down stairs, and walked out to the carriage road leading to the station, to meet her father. She saw him jump off— surely it was he, for who could be as agile and as fine-looking as her father. She ran as fast as her feet could carry her, holding out her hands to him before he was close enough to take hold of them.

Both were filled with delight to meet once more. After the kiss and embrace, she said, "How is my precious mother and brother?"

"Both well, my darling, and ready to give you sweet welcome when you arrive at your grand-father's."

"And my grand-father and Aunt Mary and Uncle Howard, are they all well?"

"Yes, all in good health, and happy to welcome you and your friends."

"O, it is so like them to open the dear old home to take us all in. I am sure we shall have a lovely time," said Victoria, as she walked at her father's side, with her hand in his.

"Do tell me more about baby Dorcey—is he really like mother, and does he cry much?"

This query amused her father, and he laughingly said, "Yes, he cries more than you did at his age, but we do not expect him to be as good as you were—in my opinion, boys are never as good as girls.

"Yes, he is very much like your mother—her large brown eyes and silky hair."

They had now arrived at the front veranda, where Professor and Mrs. Field, Aunt Charlotte, Percy, Lenox and Claire sat. The meeting was most cordial. The Doctor held the hands of the brother and sister, saying, "Children, I am very glad you are to spend the summer with us. It is just twenty years to-day since your father came to make us a visit at Gray Cliff—you are as welcome as he was.."

He turned to Percy to give him the second greeting— never did man love a youth more than Dr. Kenyon loved the handsome Percy Tyler.

They walked up the broad stairs leading to the chamber in readiness for the Doctor. The Professor had preceded them to the room.

Percy staid with the Doctor, performing all the little acts of service he would do if he had been his own father.

They assembled at the dinner-table, and discussed the past, present, and future, all joining in the pleasant conversation.

CHAPTER XXIV

Six o'clock next morning found the party at the station, all anticipating a joyful trip to Gray Cliff. As the train came in sight around a curve in the road, Reginald Page loomed up, bright and responsive as usual. He took off his straw hat and swung it above his head, then made a low bow with his hand on his heart. Dr. Kenyon and the boys responded cordially, while the girls laughed and recognized the gallant salutation.

He sprang off before the train stopped, and grasping the Doctor's hand said, "Glad to see you, sir. I congratulate you on your new possession—my compliments to Master Kenyon."

He bowed to the girls, shaking a hand of each at the same time with a swing peculiar to himself, then nodded to Percy and Lenox with a triumphant grin which meant "I am even with you for the present at least."

Chloe and the lunchbasket were duly noticed. He always associated Chloe with something good to eat. The basket lid pushed up with over-crowding, showing dainty napkins around cake and pie. This prospective feast was taken in by the hungry youth, who was on the alert for breakfast.

In a few moments all were seated in the coach. Victoria and Claire sat together, Dr. Kenyon and Reginald in front of them, Percy and Lenox just behind them.

The boys had much sport at Rex's expense, but more than once he got the better of them. Percy took a traveling shawl and placing it on the back of the seat,

said, "Rex, let me settle you for a nap, you look sleepy.
I doubt not you sat up all night to join us."

He had indeed, but a shrewd lawyer could not get it
from him if he chose to conceal it. Percy, supposing he
was hungry as usual, asked, "What did you breakfast
on?"

"Fresh air and spring water," was the prompt reply.

"Poor fellow, do you expect to make the journey on
the elements?"

"How could I make it without?" he answered with a
roguish flash of his big black eyes.

"Now we had a more substantial meal, a really fine
breakfast; waffles, coffee, fried chicken, and honey. It is
a pity you were not at St. Mary's to share it with us,"
said Percy with a coaxing smile, wishing to draw Rex
out to ask for something to eat, as he well knew the next
station was many miles off, and cash was always scarce
with him.

Rex settled the question without a word, simply by
looking at the luncheon basket, then at Percy, with a
rolling of his eyes backward in the direction of Little
Doctor.

Percy took the hint, and went to her seat. He whispered a few words to Victoria, who smiled with real interest in the matter, and went to the seat where Chloe
sat, Percy following. They soon prepared breakfast for
Rex, while he chatted to Claire apparently unmindful of
the stir going on for his comfort.

The porter put the table in place. Chloe placed on it
a dainty cloth, hot coffee (made on a small alcohol
stove), cold chicken, boiled eggs, with plenty of fresh
bread and butter. Rex's self-possession and self-assurance were marvelous.

When the breakfast was announced, he thanked Little

Doctor with courtly grace, and took the place prepared for him as a king might do under like circumstances. Percy took a cup of coffee with him to keep him company, enjoying the pleasure of seeing his companion breaking his fast, far more than the fragrant cup of Java.

At twelve o'clock the luncheon was served, and Rex again had appetite and capacity for the lion's share of roast chicken and cherry pie, notwithstanding the bountiful supply of good things he had already received from the big basket.

In the afternoon Dr. Kenyon left his seat to talk to an old friend. Reginald took advantage of the absence of the elder Doctor to consult the younger. "Little Doctor," said he, "can you cure a cancer, I have one on the back of my hand?"

Victoria shook her head with a professional doubt, saying, "Let me see your hand."

He extended a plump dark hand, with a very bad sore on it, much inflamed and swollen. Victoria gave it earnest consideration. She always commanded seriousness and confidence in those she treated, no matter how lightly they approached her.

"That is not cancer, but an old wound you have picked with cruel nails. It must have prompt treatment," said Little Doctor with real concern for her companion.

"Well," said Reginald, "will you take the case?"

"Yes, certainly; but I must give severe treatment— will you trust me?"

"Trust you with my life," was the gallant reply.

A handsome young gentleman dressed in white linen sat opposite. He laid aside the book he had pretended to read, and gave his undivided attention to Little Doctor and her patient. When she asked the boys for some matches, he readily produced a jeweled match-box, and stepping across the aisle, said, "At your service, Miss Kenyon."

Little Doctor thanked him with a suppressed smile, for she had no idea who he was.

This gave him courage to stay near, and with a winsome appeal he asked, "May I look on? I am deeply interested."

Of course Victoria gave the desired permission. She now opened her medical case and took out a small tin box containing mutton suet. She cut off a bit, placing it in a spoon, and held it over some burning matches in the lid of the tin box on the window-sill. When it was boiling hot she took Reginald's hand and carefully dropped a few drops on the sore, saying, "You can do this for yourself for three or four mornings, then it will get well rapidly."

Rex pretended to be completely overcome by the pain, and sank back with closed eyes and quivering lips. He had ability to act, and often gave his boy friends a benefit.

Claire was greatly alarmed. Leaning forward with clasped hands, she watched him with tears in her eyes. The others laughed out, for they knew him of old. Percy ran for water, and sprinkled the upturned face until he revived with a vigorous start, exclaiming, "Percy Tyler, who employed you in this case? You have ruined my collar and cravat."

He wiped his dripping face and neck, then flipped the corner of his handkerchief in Percy's face with mischievous good humor. Taking out his purse (containing a counterfeit ten dollar bill, two dimes, and a poem written by himself), he said, "Little Doctor, what is my indebtedness to you?"

Victoria laughed merrily, saying, "You are the first patient who has asked me for a bill. I practice for love of the profession and the experience."

Lenox had kept up his tender little attentions to Rex, often fanning him with Chloe's turkey-wing fan, borrowed for the occasion; but now Rex could dispense with them, and he waived him away, saying, "You are very officious." Then giving him an arch smile, he continued, "If I were as pretty as you, I would hold a mirror in my hand all the time, and let other people alone."

This taunt took Lenox down. It was not the first time his good looks had been a disadvantage to him. Rex well knew how to reach the tender spot of each of his companions, and was merciless sometimes. Lenox was truly very handsome, with fair hair, a clear fresh complexion, beautiful blue eyes like his sister's, and a mirth provoking expression about his mouth that won him many friends; but ridicule had taken all vanity out of his heart; indeed it had become the burden of his college life. Percy was the only one who had not probed the sensitive wound, and he clung to him like a brother.

Victoria put her case in order, and returned the match-box to the owner with thanks. As she did so, she caught her father's smile. A mute appeal for his approval brought him to her side. Laying his hand caressingly on her head, he said, "Daughter, you did the best thing possible to cauterize that wound; it will soon heal if he lets it alone." He looked at Rex's hand saying, "You must follow directions or you will have trouble with that sore."

The owner of the costly match-box introduced himself to Dr. Kenyon, saying, "I have often heard my parents speak of you and Gray Cliff. We were at your wedding."

The Doctor grasped his hand, answering, "Randolph, I am most happy to meet you. How are all at home? I have not had the honor of seeing your father since he became Governor of Virginia."

"Nor have I, for I have been in Europe for four years. Will you please present me to your daughter?"

Dr. Kenyon turned to the young people and introduced Victoria and her companions. Randolph took Little Doctor's hand, bowing to the rest, calling each one by their names, smiling pleasantly as he did so; then looking at Victoria, he said, "Little Doctor,—(may I, too, call you by this title, it is very tempting and appropriate?)"—she inclined her head with a smile, and he continued, "do please tell me, are you studying your father's profession?"

"I hope to do so, when I finish school," she answered, withdrawing her hand.

"I have often seen wounds dressed on the base-ball grounds, but you could teach our young practitioners something new." He said this with evident admiration for Little Doctor's skill.

Hearing the shrill whistle of the locomotive, he turned to Dr. Kenyon, saying, "I get off at the next station; my parents will be there to meet me, will you see them?"

The Doctor cheerfully assented. Both gentlemen bowed to the young people, and went out. It was pardonable in our girls and boys to take advantage of the coach windows, to see their new acquaintance meet his parents. A splendid carriage and horses stood near the platform. In it sat a lady richly dressed in black lace. Claire's cultivated taste for rich attire soon suggested admiring comments.

"O, just look at that elegant bonnet, pure lace with velvet pansies on it. Ma has one almost like it."

Victoria was much more interested in reading the lady's face, so full of joyous anticipation in seeing her son spring from the coach. The Governor stood at the steps, and father and son embraced affectionately; then Randolph, at a bound, sprang into the carriage to meet his mother. The Governor and Doctor Kenyon greeted each other cordially, holding hands with a tight clasp.

"Come," said the Governor, "Let me see if my wife will remember you."

She did, indeed. Extending her hand in a dainty lavender glove, she said, "Victor Kenyon, I am delighted to see you again. How is Mildred?"

"My dear Madam, I can assure you this is a mutual delight. My wife is well, and at father's for the summer. You are looking well; time has dealt kindly with you."

She laughed, and shaking her fan at him, said, "Victor of old, always ready to say pretty things."

"I would like to introduce my daughter to you, she is here," said the Doctor.

Randolph jumped to the ground, saying, "Doctor, let me have the pleasure of presenting her to my mother."

He went into the coach and brought Victoria, but the Governor detained them. He lifted her from the steps, exclaiming, "My dear child, you are called Victoria for your father, but I predict you will merit the name by gaining victory over self, and others, through the 'Prince of Peace.'"

There was a thrill of prophetic power in his words that deeply impressed Victoria. She bent her head, as if receiving his blessing, thinking he had read in her eyes the fierce battle with self.

"Father," said Randolph, "will you please let mother speak to Miss Kenyon?"

The Governor bowed low, waving his hat in compliance. He had kept his head uncovered in deference to Victoria.

The young man took her hand and led her to the carriage, saying, "Little Doctor, my mother."

The lady smiled sweetly, and extending her hand over the side of the carriage to Victoria, she said "Little Doctor, I am so glad to meet you. Did my son coin this name for you?"

"No Madam, my nurse gave it to me on my first birthday, because I looked like my father."

"Ah, you are like him, indeed, a marvelous resemblance to your handsome father." As she said this, she flashed a merry look at Dr. Kenyon. "I cannot see a trace of your mother's likeness. She was a great favorite with us all. We were at your parent's wedding."

"Yes, I have often heard them mention you and the Governor."

Randolph shyly said, "I too, was at the wedding, and immortalized myself by tumbling down into a well, and had to be hooked out like a shark."

Little Doctor laughed heartily—more at the way this was said, than the incident. For she had a very keen sense of humor, and his face responded to it readily.

The clanging bell and puffing engine warned our friends that they must part. Randolph held a bunch of rare roses in his hand that his mother had brought him. He gave them to Victoria, saying, "These are some of my favorites from my rose garden." Then with a coaxing smile, he added, "Little Doctor, may I come with my parents when they visit your grandfather this summer?"

This request, made in such a boyish way, was so very amusing to Victoria, that she answered him in the same spirit. "Yes, we shall be glad to see you, and you may join our juvenile band in all of our excursions if you like."

"O, that will be glorious; count on my being your body-guard and basket-bearer."

Little Doctor took the lady's hand in parting, and kissed it; then shook hands with Randolph and the Governor. They had barely time to spring on before the train was in motion.

Victoria had evidently made a pleasant impression on the Governor and his family. He leaned back as the horses dashed off in the direction of home, and said, "She is a charming young girl. The same soulful eyes as Victor. What color do you call them?" he asked his wife.

"They are real violet eyes, a rare color, and very expressive. She is an uncommon girl, with such sweet self-possession and grace," answered his wife, looking back at the train.

Randolph was looking after the train too, as it flitted in and out of sight, dashing through the wooded country far away to the east. "Mother, said he, "I wish you had been in the coach to-day to see Little Doctor dress a wound."

"Was there an accident, my son?"

"O no, only a sore on the hand of a companion. She did it with such skill and modesty, I was really fascinated and asked to stand near so that I could see how she did it. I had heard a fellow passenger say she was the daughter of Doctor Kenyon. I recognized the Doctor

as soon as he returned to his seat, and introduced myself. She has a charming personality—is to study her
father's profession, a departure for maiden feet from the
old path; but I must confess I like it. I imagine she has
too much character to be satisfied with social triumphs
and domestic bliss. What age is she?" he added, turning to his mother.

"Well, I ought to know her exact age," said she, fanning herself slowly, "for Victor wrote to your father announcing her birth and name at the time. She is six-
teen years and three months—yes, I am certain that is
her age."

When Victoria joined her companions in the coach,
all were enthusiastic over the roses. She divided them,
giving to each one their choice. Rex said the "Black
Prince" was his favorite, as they harmonized with his
complexion. Claire chose "La France" roses and
fastened them on her shoulder with artistic grace. Percy
took a "Mareschal Neil" from his bunch, and pinned it
just below his collar, saying, "I want it where I can in-
hale its fragrance." Lenox buried his face in his, saying, "I love them all alike, they are so refreshing." Victoria fastened a beautiful white bud in her father's lapel,
saying, "This is mother's favorite." Chloe was not forgotten. She decorated her hat, and placing it on the
seat in front of her, whispered to herself, "Dat hat
sholy look like a flow' pot."

As the sun descended in the western sky, our travelers longed for their journey's end. Doctor Kenyon
went out to learn the time they should arrive at Willow
station. This was a signal for the boys and girls to
gather up their belongings, which consisted of fishing
tackle, guns, game bags, shawls, and satchels; but no
dogs, monkeys, or bird-cages for Chloe to "tote."

Little Doctor beckoned Claire to bring the luncheon basket. She found plenty of provisions still in it, and turning to Rex (who had taken possession of her medical case), she said, "Rex, shall I leave the luncheon basket with you? There is an abundance of food and having it may save you the trouble of getting out for some of your meals."

He thanked her heartily, saying, "You are an angel of the first magnitude, to provide for a small sparrow like me."

Lenox pinched his elbow, saying, with a mischievous grin, "You mean, a sparrow hawk."

One flash of Rex's eyes silenced Lenox, but Percy said to Claire, "Did you see the lightning flash from that sparrow's eyes?" Claire had, and smiling, nodded. Chloe giggled behind the turkey-wing fan, then quoted, "De thunder rolled, de lightnin' flashed, and killed a peeg."

All laughed at Chloe's sauciness but Rex; he recognized his own teaching, and in spirit went back to a certain stormy afternoon in the barn at Beechwood, (he had been hunting and had taken refuge in the barn), with a dusky audience about him, Chloe among them, and he smiled as he recalled the shouts of laughter from them as he quoted the lines above. The young black children remembered this one effort of "Marse Rex," and it became common with them.

Our party arrived at Willow Station late in the afternoon. The Rev. Howard Kenyon was there to meet them with the big family carriage. A young black man held two fine saddle horses, and old Uncle Joe sat on a large wagon ready to take Chloe and the trunks.

Rex looked desolate on the rear platform of the train, as he disappeared from view; but he was not without a

pleasing hope to cheer him; Doctor Kenyon had given
him a pressing invitation to visit them at Gray Cliff on
his return from home, and his head was already busy
planning to spend most of his vacation there.

Victoria, Claire, Dr. Kenyon, and his brother took
their seats in the carriage, and the boys were to go on
horseback. Tasso, the groom, held a spirited young
horse by the bridle for Lenox. As he sprang into the
saddle he handed him a whip, saying, "She won't 'quire
de lash, but city gemmen alers ax fo' a whip." Lenox
acknowledged that he liked a whip, and soon had need
of one, for Madge was not kindly disposed toward the
"city gemmen." Percy mounted a quiet beauty, and
did not have an opportunity to show off his fine horse-
manship before the girls as Lenox did.

The road to the Kenyon home led along the river
bank, cool and shady. The girls laid off their hats and
enjoyed the change. The coach had been so hot and
close all day, and going at such a rapid rate, that they
did not enjoy the beautiful scenery; but now they were
enthusiastic over the rural beauty that met their view on
all sides. The cows standing knee-deep in the river,
with over-hanging trees to shelter them from the afternoon sun, reluctantly started homeward when the small
black children flourished their switches about them; and
the timid rabbits and squirrels flitting in and out of the
papaw bushes, all caused Claire the greatest delight,
for she had not been accustomed to these pretty creatures as our Little Doctor had been all her life.

Lenox proposed to Percy that they should go ahead
of the carriage as outriders, to herald their coming; but,
indeed, it was his great desire to see the place and the
people his father had visited two years before his birth.
As they cantered along, he laughed aloud at his own re-

flections, when Percy looked at him, saying, "What is it, old boy?"

"O, I was just amused at my absurd self. Do you know, I am unable to realize that people and localities existed before my time." He switched his trousers, then looked shyly at Percy for encouragement and appreciation.

"I am with you in the absurdity, for I have doubted these things ever since I was old enough to reason." Both laughed merrily, and took up a popular song, making the woods ring with youthful melody.

When they reached Gray Cliff, a cordial welcome awaited them. Senator Kenyon, Miss Kenyon, and Mrs. Kenyon sat on the front veranda, and met the boys with out-stretched hands and hearty greetings. When the carriage drove up, the girls were much amused to see them looking so completely at home in the group.

The meeting of Victoria with her mother was a most happy one, more so now that they had a new joy to share; there was also the delight of meeting her grandfather and Aunt Mary. Claire held to Mrs. Kenyon's arm, and whispered, "Little Doctor's love for you has taught me how to value my own loving mother."

Mammy came lumbering out with the baby in her arms. "Howdy my blessed chile; see yo' brudder, he is pow'ful sweet." Victoria kissed the old woman's cheek with affection, then cuddling the little one in her arms, she took a good look at the tiny face, and kissed him rapturously, saying, "You precious darling, do you know sister?" He made a futile attempt to seize her nose, but another shower of kisses interrupted the youngster, and he gave a demonstration of the fine lungs he possessed, with a very pink face.

Claire viewed the performance with wonder; and when

Victoria placed him in her arms, she looked frightened lest she should let him fall, because she did not know what part of him she should hold tightest.

Percy saw the dilemma, saying, "Let me show you how to hold a baby." He cuddled him close in his arms, and smiled complacently as he said, "How-do old fellow; how soon can you go hunting and fishing with me?"

Lenox had a genuine love for small people, and insisted on his turn to hold Master Kenyon. He gathered up the long robe, and seated the baby on his shoulder, then danced around the veranda whistling merrily, while the rest looked on with evident surprise and amusement. Lenox and the baby were happy, judging from the smile on both faces

Aunt Mary suggested that our travelers should retire to their rooms to get ready for dinner. Victoria and Claire had rooms adjoining, and Chloe was to serve them both. When they were ready to go down to the drawing-room, Mrs. Kenyon inspected the new dresses and admired the pretty style in which they were made. Victoria had shown much appreciation and discrimination in her attire, ever since she was old enough to enjoy the beauty of colors, and this matter of personal adornment was cultivated in her by her mother, who had exquisite taste in dress.

Accordingly one might notice that Little Doctor wore but two colors. She had always observed this style, and never failed to be admired, even by those dressed otherwise. As Maryland Carroll once said to her, "You always look picturesque. I believe it is because you wear but one color with your white dress. Now that bunch of geranium leaves on your shoulder and at your belt is ever so much more striking than my bouquet of many colors." This habit gave individuality to Victoria's dress, and she recognized the advantage with a passing pleasure.

Percy and Lenox rejoiced to see the girls wearing their hair as they used to do at home; while Chloe was jubilant over the sight of her dear young "Missy" with her locks "in curls once mo'."

Little Doctor's grand-parents, Col. Dorcey and his wife, were at dinner. It had been years since the dear old home had been cheered by such a merry party as dwelt under its hospitable roof at this time, and none enjoyed it more than the Senator and Miss Mary Kenyon.

CHAPTER XXV

Days, weeks, months—yes, three years, had gone by since Victoria entered St. Mary's, and now, on this last day of the dear school life, she stood a woman, ready to go forth and put to beneficial use the education gained in these three well-spent years.

She had graduated with the highest honors—she would not have been satisfied with anything lower, and she had maintained the character which she brought to the school; one of pure, unselfish devotion to the good of others, strengthened and developed by higher culture and more extended contact with the world of school life.

"I came round to say good-bye, my little friend," said the good, genial Doctor Brentano "and to thank you for your very great aid to me in my capacity as physician to St. Mary's. You are no longer the little girl I first met, holding Claire's wounded hand. Indeed, you are a greatly improved edition, physically, of that wise little maid: but, child, you will always be to me my little doctor."

"Dr. Brentano," said Victoria; "you could not flatter me more than to remember me by the dear name by which I was called in my home."

"Why did you never tell me that?" said the Doctor; "here I have been thinking that I had conferred a degree upon you, young lady, and you coolly tell me you had the title from your babyhood—born with it, I dare say."

Victoria laughed merrily: "Yes, Doctor, my nurse gave it to me in the cradle. I always liked to hear you call me 'Little Doctor,' but I did not mention it as it seemed a presumption to claim it in the presence of a real M. D."

"Well, child, I have a little plan of—benevolence, you would call it; and I want your sympathy and interest in it, as it was you who put the idea into my head."

Victoria looked surprised and interested, and waited for him to explain.

"I have been a selfish old fellow, my little doctor; I have had more of this world's goods than I really needed, but it was never brought home to my mind that I could use it for the good of others, until I learned it from the example of the little girl in school who taught me what it meant to live for others.

"I have watched your course, my child, with keen interest, and I found that your unselfish devotion to your companions in school was a greater happiness to you than the usual pleasures of youth; and, though I am late beginning, I wish to share that kind of happiness— for I have found no other in this life."

Victoria had clasped her hands in her lap, and looked at the strong dignified man before her, with something like pained surprise. Tears stood in her eyes, as she said, "You do me great honor, Dr. Brentano. That my little insignificant life could in any way influence the life of one of the world's great intellects is a surprise and pleasure that embarrasses me. But," she said suddenly; "tell me about your plan of benevolence, it interests me greatly."

"My idea is not very clear yet, but I wish to found an institution in New York city for homeless young girls, and place it in charge of the 'Sisters of St. Mary,' the order the Rev. Dr. Warfield has just established; and I want the privilege of naming the institution for my Little Doctor—'The Victoria Home.'"

"I thank you for the compliment you pay me, Dr. Brentano, and in the name of all homeless girls, I thank you for such an institution. I shall always feel a special interest in 'The Victoria Home,'" she said with a grateful smile.

"Another thing," said the Doctor; "your father has told me that you have a similar plan—a home for orphans. It would give me great pleasure to contribute to your enterprise, my little friend."

"That is already provided for, Doctor. My two grandfathers have made it a joint gift. They will also endow the Home; so, you see, my own share in it is simply putting into effect their benevolence; though, I assure you, my dear friend, I appreciate your generosity. We expect to go abroad immediately, and shall spend a year in travel, and when we return, I hope to carry out my pet scheme. I have always had the theory in my mind of a home for children; and, Dr. Brentano, I give you in advance a cordial invitation to be present at its opening."

"Thank you, thank you, my child, you may count on me. And now, good-bye, my little doctor, and don't forget your old friend."

Victoria gave both her hands to him in parting, saying "I will always remember Doctor Brentano."

The last evening at St. Mary's was a sad one to all. Victoria's companions assembled in the drawing-room to show their last little attentions. They had all given her keep-sakes from their little treasures, and all had been carefully packed in the trunks that stood in the hall waiting for Dr. Kenyon's arrival, who was to accompany his daughter to Gray Cliff.

Several attempts had been made to sing Victoria's favorite songs, as they waited the hour of departure, bu all failed—tears were too near the surface, and they finally yielded to their feelings and cried in good fashion; Claire especially, who was also to leave school, was inconsolable. Three years had wrought wonders in the proud, willful girl—now a tall stately woman, self-controlled and gracious in manner, but still impetuous and impulsive.

When the carriage wheels were heard on the gravel' at the door, the weeping girls flocked round Victoria like chattering birds. Professor and Mrs. Field, and dear Aunt Charlotte had taken a more composed farewell.

Dr. Kenyon hurried Victoria away, as the train was nearly due. She waved her hand to the group on the steps, as the carriage turned out of the gate-way, with a tender good-bye to dear St. Mary's.

The Kenyon and Tyler families were to go abroad together and both had agreed to meet at Grey Cliff for a short visit before the steamer should sail.

Percy had graduated, and had been studying law the last year, but his parents concluded that a year abroad was necessary for a finished education; and Percy was charmed to join the Kenyons, that he and Victoria might together visit the wonders of the old world.

A few days after they arrived, our old friend Rex came to Gray Cliff to pay his respects to "Miss Kenyon," as he punctiliously called our Little Doctor.

Time had changed him very little; he was the same bright, witty, self-satisfied Rex as of old; yet there was a depth in the great dark eyes, and a manliness in the still short, square figure that added new dignity to his presence.

Victoria met him with a cordial welcome. She had always a warm friendship for this companion of her childhood, and she was not one to forget her friends. As they met, Rex looked at his old school-mate with the patronizing air of a grandfather, and said "Little Doc—beg your pardon, Miss Kenyon, I am quite satisfied with the result of St. Mary's 'finishing.' What an earthly paradise we should have, if all they send out were as perfect."

Victoria laughingly retorted, "and what a return of the classic age we should have if all university graduates were like our modern Demosthenes!" bowing graciously to Reginald.

It was one of the merriest gatherings that ever assembled under the old home roof; but no family reunion would have been complete without the presence of old Mammy, who had accompanied her mistress from Kentucky. When Victoria arrived at Gray Cliff with her father, Mammy was at the door to meet her "bressed chile."

For the first time Mammy had to reach up her black arms to clasp them around Victoria's neck; "My sakes alive, honey, how yo' is growed," and she took the tall girl in her arms as if she were still the helpless baby she used to nurse, while Little Doctor laid her head on the old shoulder and patted the stout back just as she did when Mammy carried her when she was a tired child.

Mammy very soon noticed her "chile's" dress, and taking a fold of the pretty gray poplin between her fingers—"La's! honey, dis is suttinly like the goods yo' gran'-mamma use 'o wear. 'Irish Poplin' she use 'o call it. I 'member it kase I allers use to hook it up de back fo' her. Has yo' got many putty tings, honey?"

"No Mammy, not many, you know I shall buy new things in Europe, but you shall see all I have—here are

the keys, and when Tasso carries up the trunks, you go and look over them all."

A few days more and our party set sail from New York to spend a year in travel.

CHAPTER XXVI

Fifteen months had gone by since the steamer bore our friends away on the bosom of the great ocean. It was now October, and again Beechwood was a merry scene of preparations for a home-coming.

The negroes, young and old, were rejoicing as if Fourth of July and Christmas had joined hands to make it an occasion of jollification.

The house and grounds were in perfect order, but Mammy went around the house with her feather duster flicking imaginary specks of dust from the polished furniture and mirrors; while Hayden, with his broom, walked up and down the great avenue leading to the gates to brush away a stray autumn leaf that might linger on the smooth gravel.

It was the twenty-fifth of October—the day the travelers were expected. The big family carriage was ready and Ben and Paris were there, just as on that happy day years ago when they were impatient to meet the young master and his bride on their home-coming. One change had taken place—a new, stylish carriage, and a pair of glossy black horses had taken the place of the old handsome chestnuts.

After the carriage started, the servants gathered as of old at the gate. At Gip's side stood a three-year-old girl, who calls George and Gip, "pappy" and "mammy." This is Victoria's name-sake, but known in the quarters as "wee Vic."

She had been impressed with the importance of the

occasion, especially at having on an extra checked bib that covered her completely. She crept up to Mammy, who still had authority in the family—"Granny, is young Missy Vitoye jes like me?"

"What kine o' quession is dat, chile? What make you tink Missy is like yo'? Why, honey, she am white as snow—a bu'ful young lady."

"Den what fo' yo'uns call me Vitoye—will me git white too?"

They all joined in an uproarious laugh at the absurd notion of "wee Vic."

A cloud of dust was now seen, then the sound of horses' feet heralded the arrival of the travelers. Ben pulled up the horses with a grand flourish, and Paris opened the door of the carriage with the importance of a courier.

There were glad, eager eyes meeting each other, and white hands clasped black ones in a common joy. The master's family were home, all safe and well, and the faithful servants stood, an unbroken band. It was a time for rejoicing. Mammy took Dorcey in her arms, saying, "Why, honey, yo' is a big boy, an' jes like you' mudder."

Dorcey thought so too, as he slipped from Mammy's arms and stalked about looking at the servants he had no acquaintance with.

Victoria turned her eyes from one dear object to another. Her home had never seemed so precious as when she came back to it weary with the old world's crowding splendors.

The Tylers had reached home a month before, as the Kenyons had spent some time at Gray Cliff before continuing their journey.

The former had been invited to dine at Beechwood the

evening of the arrival. It was a charmingly familiar little dinner-party that these six people composed. The two families were rejoiced to be reunited; and a little secret between Dr. Kenyon and Percy Tyler seemed to draw the young man instinctively to his host.

While at Gray Cliff the year before, Percy had made a very presumptuous request of the Doctor; though he did not seem to be much surprised at the young man's audacity; indeed, I think the elder people quite expected this request to be made sometime, though no hint of it had ever been given to the two people who were most concerned.

When Percy stammered out his wish that Dr. Kenyon would allow him to address his daughter, he was as timid and frightened as if he had never sat on the Doctor's knee, and played horse on hs foot.

Dr. Kenyon was sympathetic and appreciated the situation: and taking Percy's hands said, "Percy, my boy, I must ask you to wait awhile. Victoria is still very young, and it has been my wish for her to enjoy this year abroad as a child. When we return, you have my permission to ask her what you have asked me; until then, I prefer you both to be simply the friends you have always been."

Percy had respected Dr. Kenyon's wish in the matter and though he was now more than ever desirous of presenting his request, he was not as sure of success. Indeed, the charming little comrade of all his delightful excursions in the Alps, in tourist's dress and staff, was in some unaccountable way changed. Little Doctor had put off the familiar little ways that made her such a fascinating companion, and in her stead a stately young lady appeared, in an elegant dinner dress with sweeping train of shimmering silk; rich, white lace falling over beautiful arms, encircled at the wrists with bands of linked gold; the shapely head crowned with broad braids of golden hair.

Percy had never before seen our Little Doctor in the full-dress of a young lady, and he felt it a barrier between them. With all his culture and knowledge of the world, Percy was very simple in heart. He thought to himself, "It would have been much easier to have spoken to her in the dear little, rough tourist dress, than to approach her in all this young-lady finery."

They had walked out after dinner to see the old garden. Although late in the season, it was still brilliant in color with autumn flowers. Victoria was just regretting that the roses were all gone, when Percy exclaimed, "I see a beautiful La France, but it is so close to the wall, I doubt whether I can reach it."

With some exertion he drew down the branch and plucked the coveted rose. As he gave it to Victoria, she noticed that he pressed his handkerchief to his hand.

"Have you hurt your hand?" she asked.

"It's only a thorn," he said.

"Let me see it, please."

The interested manner was so like Little Doctor that Percy held out his hand in ready obedience. The great thorn had buried itself in his hand.

"Just wait a moment," she said; and, taking up the train of her gown, she hurried to the house, and returned with a small surgical knife. In an instant the thorn was removed, and she held the handkerchief on the wound with a professional-like solicitude.

"Victoria," began Percy, "do you know this is the first time you ever exercised your skill for me; and, Victoria—I would like you to be—Little Doctor to—me always,—darling, will you be my wife?"

Victoria's sweet face rivaled the La France rose that nestled in the lace of her dress, as she quickly released the professional clasp of his hand, and began to gather up her train that lay on the ground.

"Victoria, you have not answered me."

She had recovered something of her composure, and said with that charming arch look in the violet eyes, "Percy, you have not said which it is you want, the 'Little Doctor,' or a wife."

"Both, and all of my Victoria," Percy said, with strong feeling. "You know I have tried to make myself worthy of you, and, if I have failed, you can make me what you will; for you have more influence over me than all the world together."

Little Doctor allowed him to take her hands as he spoke.

"You must ask my parents, Percy."

"Why, my darling, I asked your father a year ago, and he gave me permission to speak to you as soon as we returned from abroad."

Percy held the little hand very close in his own as they slowly walked back to the house.

They found the family still in the drawing-room. Mrs. Kenyon was at the piano, and Mr. Tyler trying to recall something he wished her to play.

Percy laid his hand on Dr. Kenyon's shoulder, and said with something like glad triumph in his tone, "Doctor, I have waited the year, and am rewarded."

The Doctor clasped their hands together saying, "Children, you have my blessing."

Turning to Mrs. Kenyon, Percy said, "You have kept your promise, dear Mrs. Kenyon. Do you remember the first time I saw you, I asked you to find a little wife for me like yourself?"

"Yes, indeed, I can just see the solemn little face with the great gray eyes fixed on me, and the tiny hands folded on my knee, as you asked me to get you a wife like myself. Well, Percy, my dear, I have done better, I have given you one like her father."

Mr. and Mrs. Tyler took Little Doctor in their arms, and welcomed her as their daughter.

That night when Mammy went to say good-night to her "bressed chile," Little Doctor put her arm around the old, withered black neck—"Mammy, your child is very happy."

"Yo' needen tell Mammy no mo', honey; I's spected dat Marse Percy was gwine to ka'ah off my chile. Well, honey, I sho Marse Percy is mighty good boy, as boys go, but none on 'em is fitten to have my bu'ful lamb;" and poor old Mammy covered her face with her apron, and sobbed aloud.

Victoria comforted her with the assurance that Percy was not going to carry her child off; that she was going to stay near home always. Mammy dried her tears when she went to the kitchen to tell the news to her assembled household.

"Sho 'nuff Marse Percy is gwine to maah our little Missy. Hit's all done settled."

Percy was a great favorite with the servants, and they rejoiced that he was to be one of their family; though their chief delight was in the prospect of a wedding in the home.

Ben went to the cellar on the strength of it, and brought up a keg of cider; and Paris, man as he was, attempted some of his old boyish tricks, standing on his head, and the rest.

The morning after the return of the Kenyons to Beechwood was a charming autumn day. Indian summer had cast her pinkish haze over forest, hill, and valley, a pledge of fair weather for days to come.

Percy crossed the meadow to Beechwood. As he neared the veranda, Little Doctor came out and joined him. He took her hand, and they walked along just as they had done since Percy's hand guided the little one in her first attempt to walk.

Percy looked back, "Have your parents gone on?" he asked.

"No, they are coming now, and I also see Mr. and Mrs. Tyler crossing the meadow."

"Why do you not say, 'father and mother?'" said Percy, with a smile.

"O, I shall learn to say that in time."

Parents and children met at the dividing hedge, and walked on to the brow of the ridge that overlooked the creek. It was also in direct line with the main street of the city that lay two or three miles south of it. It was the spot Little Doctor had selected for the erection of her asylum for orphan children. They walked around, viewing it from every point, giving suggestions to each other; but all yielded to Little Doctor's wishes in the matter.

The exact spot was at length decided upon, and in a few days all the available negroes on both plantations were engaged in preparing the foundation for a large, commodious building and chapel.

People passing along the way stopped to inquire what large residence it was to be.

Paris would answer, "Hit no residence, hit de 'sylum what Missy gwine to build fo' de po' chillun."

While the building was in progress, our Little Doctor began a regular course of medical studies with her father. She wished to prepare herself for intelli-

gent work in the home she was establishing. Then she
gathered about herself her old schoolmates and friends
in the city, and interested them in the project on hand.

The old Dramatic Club was reorganized; which
brought together her companions of the public school.
All were now grown, and some married, and all were
delighted to meet again at charming Beechwood.

Reginald Page, who was now established in his profession—the law—paid an early visit to the Kenyons after their return. Victoria was sincerely glad to see her
old-time friend. They talked of their journey, of all she
had seen abroad, and of St. Mary's—and how they
laughed in recalling Reginald's success in out-witting
his companions in the visit to the school!

Before Rex left, he confided to Victoria a bit of private news—he and Claire Willington were engaged to
be married; and his ambition was to secure a good practice, as he laughingly said, "to offset Claire's fortune."

Victoria congratulated him very heartily, and expressed her delight that two such good friends of hers
should be so much to each other.

The two families were again in conference over a site
for another building. This spot was nearer the home
dwelling—just within the limits of Beechwood, and this
time the elder people consulted the younger ones.

The building was to be a handsome stone cottage
for the "children" when they should marry. It was the
joint gift of the parents, Mr. Tyler and Dr. Kenyon.

The Orphanage was ready for occupancy by the first
of June, one year after its commencement, and the
Bishop had been invited to open its doors in due form,
and to consecrate its chapel.

Victoria, as she promised, had sent a cordial invitation for Dr. Brentano and Aunt Charlotte to be

present at the interesting ceremony. Her two grand-parents, Uncle Howard, and Aunt Jane were already guests at Beechwood, and the twenty-first of June was fixed as the date for the opening of the orphanage.

Another ceremony still more interesting to our readers was to follow. The beautiful Gothic cottage was also completed and luxuriously furnished.

George and Gip were already in charge awaiting the new possessors.

The day of the dedication arrived. The Bishop and other clergymen were assembled at Beechwood, when the procession formed and walked over to the Home, where a large congregation was assembled in the little chapel.

As we know, the building itself was the gift of the two grandfathers of Victoria Kenyon; but other members of the family had the privilege of furnishing the chapel.

Dr. Kenyon's gift was a stained glass window in the chapel, to the memory of his mother; Uncle Howard pre-sented a costly organ; Mrs. Kenyon gave the chancel furniture; and Aunt Jane, a graceful marble font. Percy's gift was the furniture for the body of the chapel; and the last and humblest, but by no means despised contribution, was from old Mammy—she gave the door-mats, and her white friends thought as they crossed those mats, perhaps "The last shall be first."

The solemn service of consecration was very impres-sive, and on that same day, two sisters from the Order of St. Mary, of New York, were installed in "The Sheltering Arms," as the Asylum was called, and which had already gathered into its fold fifty homeless little ones.

Victoria herself presided at the organ that day, and

as the congregation withdrew, and the last notes of the organ died away, she bowed her head on the keys before her, and renewed her own dedication to the service of God.

The following day was fixed for the wedding, which was to take place at the orphanage chapel.

As Percy and Victoria were walking out in the evening, they saw a new phaeton standing in front of their future home, and Percy proposed to Little Doctor that they go and see whose vehicle it was. As they came near, they noticed George holding a pair of beautiful white ponies which were attached to the phaeton.

As they approached, George lifted his hat, and handed Victoria a note. It was from Mr. Tyler, and Victoria read:

"My dear child:—Accept this little conveyance for your own personal use in your work among your poor.
Your affectionate father,
PERCY TYLER, Sr."

It was, to Victoria, a complete surprise. She looked inquiringly at Percy who, smilingly assisted her into the luxurious phaeton, and asked if he might, just once, have the pleasure of driving her in her new carriage.

The walk to the cottage had been a part of the arrangement, on Percy's side, in order to find her new phaeton at her own door.

That night, as Victoria was sitting at the window of her own room, old Mammy came in as usual to say good-night to her dear "chile." Gip was busy packing some things in the trunks in the dressing-room. Mammy, noticing Gip's employment, said, "Honey, yo' hav'nt yit showed ole Mammy all vo' weddin' fixin's."

"No, Mammy, I have been so busy since the boxes came, I have not seen some of them myself,—Gip," she called, "bring in all those dresses from the cedar-chest, and everything else that Mammy wants to see. I thought you had shown Mammy the whole trousseau."

Gip spread out the full length of the train of the wedding robe for Mammy to admire, then the lace veil, and long white gloves. These were put away, and a dainty white lace dress was displayed to Mammy's admiring eyes.

These were put away, and a dainty white lace dress, to be worn over pink and blue satin gowns, was displayed to Mammy's admiring eyes.

They were at last all laid away, and Mammy was alone with her dear young mistress.

"Honey, yo' is gwine to lebe old Mammy, Gip's gwine wid yo', an' Mammy won't be fust in de kitchen ober to de new cottage; but you won't forgit yo' ole Mammy, will yo'?"

Victoria knew how sore old Mammy's heart was at the thought that Gip would reign over the servants in the new home. Jealousy was poor Mammy's besetting sin. Victoria did not smile at this childish appeal from her old faithful nurse.

"No, indeed, Mammy dear, I shall never forget you," and she smoothed the old withered cheeks with her soft white palms. "You shall come whenever you please, and no one shall ever be over my dear faithful Mammy."

"Honey, I wants to tell yo', I's no mo' 'fraid o' dat debil's lantern, an' I's done stopped believin' in dat sort o' foolishniss, kase yo's had good luck all yo' life; an' dat ole blazin' tempter, what uster git holt on yo', is clean done gone. I'se been watchin' yo', chile, ev'y since yo' come home, an' I know'd dat de debil is clean gone outer yo'; an' bress de Laud! he'll git in no mo'

Victoria did not smile at the old woman's harangue.

"I am glad, Mammy, that you think I have learned to control my temper, I have tried with all my heart; but, Mammy, I found what you said was true—it is not much use to try if we do not pray to the Lord to help us."

As Mammy was leaving the room, she took a bit of paper from her bosom, and unwrapping it, disclosed a piece of delicate blue ribbon.

"Honey, yo' mus' war dis fo' good luck. I's got Mistis to buy it fo' me. Yo' knows de ole sayin' 'bouten what de bride is to war—

'Sumpin old, an' sumpin new,
'Sumpin borrowed, an' sumpin blue.' "

Victoria took the pale blue ribbon, and assured Mammy that it should be part of the bridal dress.

"Mammy," she said, "I think I can fulfill all the requirements, to please you—my dress is new, and the lace on it is old; and my veil is borrowed, for it belonged to my grandmother, and is now my mother's; and you have supplied the blue."

The wedding morning was gloriously bright—enchanting in nature's fresh new coloring, and murmuring sounds of animated life.

The family had preceded the bridal party to the chapel, already crowded with the friends of the happy young pair.

Mammy and her household were assigned a row of seats to the left of the chancel, which she insisted upon calling "Pious Corner."

Hartley Ward and Reginald Page acted as ushers. The bride's maids were eight beautiful young girls carrying baskets of flowers.

Then came the bride, leaning on her father's arm, and

at the chancel stood the bridegroom, with his best man, Lenox Willington.

The venerable Bishop performed the ceremony, and one of the Sisters of the Sheltering Arms presided at the organ.

Th beautiful service was over, which made our Little Doctor Mrs. Percy Tyler. The phaeton, with its white ponies, waited at the door to carry the happy couple to their own new home, where a reception was held.

The bride and groom stood side by side, graciously receiving their friends until the continual roll of wheels was hushed, and the latest guest had departed. Then our Little Doctor, always her own original self, laid aside her bridal robe, and put on a soft white gown.

She whispered to Gip to bring the tea service, and with those ever helpful hands, she poured out the tea which Percy served to the dear home circle, who still remained with them.

This graceful little act of hospitality relieved the strain on the hearts of the parents at bidding good-bye to their children.

Our Little Doctor, with tears and smiles, said, "No, not 'good-bye' but 'au revoir.'"

Polly's Lion

An Interesting Book for Children

BY MISS LOUISE CARNAHAN

From the Philadelphia Church Record,

Since the appearance of "Helen's Babies," we do not think we have seen a more successful representation of child life than in "Polly's Lion." The story is slight, and so it should be, for, thank heaven, the lives of children are happily unhistorical; but no one will need Miss Carnahan's assurance that "Polly is a real child, and is pretty, lovable and intelligent for her years.' No one but a real child could speak as Polly speaks, and no one but a true lover of childhood could have taken down Polly's speeches with the rare stenographic fidelity of sympathy. We will not say that the scene of the story is laid in California, but that Polly herself was born and still lives in the Golden State, in a household composed of herself, her father, her mother, her brother Robbie and her Auntie Lorraine. Incidentally the reader will find here some interesting information of the fauna and flora of the Pacific Coast, and his eyes will be pleased with several charming illustrations.

From San Francisco Bulletin

"Polly's Lion." Miss Louise Carnahan has placed little people under tribute by adding a pleasant volume to their library, which, in the past decade, has become rich in valuable and entertaining books. "Polly's Lion" is glowing with local coloring as bright and realistic as the petals of the spray of eschscholtzias which ornament the cover of the attractive and well-illustrated story. Fresno County is the center of interest, as it is the home of the Rosebery family whose every-day life has given the thread from which the child narration is woven. All the little incidents, and those minor details so dear to the hearts of little people when listening to stories, have not been forgotten or slighted by the author, and the effect is to produce one of those "really true stories" that children crave. Little bits of city life are introduced into the book, through a visit to

San Francisco, and the thrilling experience from which the volume receives its title is reserved for the grand panoramic scenery of Yosemite Valley, where the Rosebery family are represented as spending the summer season. The author, throughout the book, is without doubt treating of people and incidents dear to her heart, and it is readily to be seen that she has drawn many of her word pictures from life.

Published by Louise Carnahan.

From New York Churchman

Louise Carnahan's story, "Polly's Lion," tells of the doings of a "real" five-year-old girl and three-year-old boy who live in California. In it we learn how Polly and Robbie Rosebery bore a separation from their papa and mamma: how Auntie Lorraine took care of them; about the birthday party; a visit to the country, and many other interesting things, including Polly's exciting adventure with a "really, truly" lion. The story is written in a simple style, with many natural touches, and has a marked unobtrusive moral that commends it for the little folks for whom it is intended. Daintily bound in white cloth, with a spray of California poppies on the cover. Illustrated, 174 pages. Published by the author.

From Oregon Capital Journal

"Polly's Lion," by Louise Carnahan, is a California story for children. The volume is a very richly bound, illuminated and illustrated one. On delicate ivory ground the golden red of the Golden State flower blooms in matchless brilliancy. There is also a colored plate of the same rich-hued bloom. The California children come in for a number of full-page quarto illustrations and very sweet figures they are. The authoress has evidently taken the advice of the great Froebel to parents: "Live with your children." In an ideal literary form she has introduced their actual daily lives and experiences of every sort that can befall active youth under the stimulus of romantic environment and favorable opportunity. It is printed on rich cream paper and has rounded corners, beautiful type and many prettily designed tailpieces at the bottom of the chapters. The price of the volume, which is a perfectly original and exquisite sample of the bookmaker's art, is $1.25. It may well be called the California Child's Book. Published by the author.

From San Francisco Chronicle

A California story. One of the best books for children that has been issued for some time is "Polly's Lion," by Louise Carnahan, a Virginia girl, who, however, has lived long enough in this State to know it well. Her story is founded on fact. It deals with a pretty little girl, Polly Rosebery, who was born in the San Joaquin Valley. The account of her life will be very entertaining for children, as it is told in simple words and pleasing style. The climax is reached in Polly's adventures in the woods, where she is lost and nearly falls a victim to the mountain lion. The book is finely printed and illustrated, and has an attractive cover, with a design of the poppy in natural colors. Published by the author.

From the San Francisco Morning Call

"Polly's Lion," This is a picture of a few days out of the life of two California children, by a Californian, Louise Carnahan. The principal event of the story and that which gives the title to the book is an adventure of little Polly in the Yosemite. She got separated from her party and had to spend the night in a deserted cabin, where she was visited by a California lion. Opportunely however, aid came just as the beast was breaking down the slender barrier between it and the girl. The lion was killed, stuffed, and kept as Polly's peculiar property in their home, somewhere in the San Joaquin Valley.

Polly's Lion," will be read with pleasure by boys and girls, for it is not a goody-goody story but a real picture of real children, who at times are good, at others bad and sometimes only indifferent. It is written in simple English, and, to say the least, as good as numberless stories that have achieved much credit in the East among boys and girls. The "get up" of the book deserves much praise; the material and work are of the best, and the cover with its poppies, our California State flower, is of delicate beauty. Published by the author.

www.ingramcontent.com/pod-product-compliance
Lightning Source LLC
Chambersburg PA
CBHW020849020726
47497CB00005B/1328